Piglet

Piglet

A NOVEL

Lottie Hazell

HENRY HOLT AND COMPANY

NEW YORK

Henry Holt and Company
Publishers since 1866
120 Broadway
New York, New York 10271
www.henryholt.com

Henry Holt® and Ⓗ® are registered trademarks of Macmillan
Publishing Group, LLC.

Library of Congress Cataloging-in-Publication Data

Names: Hazell, Lottie, 1993– author.
Title: Piglet : a novel / Lottie Hazell.
Description: First U.S. edition. | New York : Henry Holt and
    Company, 2024.
Identifiers: LCCN 2023042938 (print) | LCCN 2023042939 (ebook) |
    ISBN 9781250289841 (hardcover) | ISBN 9781250289834 (ebook)
Subjects: LCGFT: Novels.
Classification: LCC PS3608.A9883 P54 2024 (print) |
    LCC PS3608.A9883 (ebook) | DDC 813/.6—dc23/eng/20231005
LC record available at https://lccn.loc.gov/2023042938
LC ebook record available at https://lccn.loc.gov/2023042939

Our books may be purchased in bulk for promotional, educational,
or business use. Please contact your local bookseller or the Macmillan
Corporate and Premium Sales Department at (800) 221-7945, extension
5442, or by e-mail at MacmillanSpecialMarkets@macmillan.com.

First U.S. Edition 2024

Designed by Omar Chapa

Printed in the United States of America

1 3 5 7 9 10 8 6 4 2

This is a work of fiction. All of the characters, organizations, and events
portrayed in this novel either are products of the author's imagination or
are used fictitiously.

For my three.

People eat their dinner, just eat their dinner, and all the while their happiness is taking form, or their lives are falling apart.

—*Anton Chekhov*

It's easier to impress someone than give them pleasure.

—*Nigella Lawson*

Piglet

Part One

98 Days

Piglet was sweating, and the supermarket chill was welcome on her breastbone, her back. Waitrose was full: shiny four-by-fours filling the car park, Saturday-morning shoppers with reusable bags jostling in the aisles.

Oxford was at the end of a heat wave, the novelty of sun-warmed skin worn, and the city was coated in the kind of grime that accumulated in weeks without rain. Outside, Piglet had watched from behind her sunglasses as a man and woman screamed at each other through their open car windows about a parking space.

Even in the cool sanctuary of the supermarket, the mood was irascible. A woman wearing Birkenstocks and ecru-coloured linen pushed past Piglet, reaching for a pecorino.

But guests would be arriving at six, and she didn't have time to seethe among the cheeses. As she shopped, her fiancé, Kit, uld be unpacking their house. Those words—still a novelty, like the stairs, the garden, the mortgage. Piglet stooped to pick up a block of feta and added it to her basket.

It had been her idea—a small housewarming supper for six—and he had been as excited as she was to show off their empty rooms, their white walls, their space. "We can invite Seb and Sophie," he had said. "And Margot and Sasha," she added. He had shrugged.

Texts had gone out, and boxes of saucepans, serving platters, and spices had been located, opened, and unpacked. Margot had replied immediately—"You've just moved in, shall we get pizza?"—but Piglet had insisted: "I'll cook."

She picked up salted butter, thick Greek yoghurt, and cream.

The menu was not modest. Her basket was already heavy with Charlotte potatoes, fresh herbs, and a Duchy chicken.

It was too hot for a roast chicken, but Piglet had once heard Nigella say something about a house only being home once a chicken was in the oven. And anyway, there would be salads: one chopped and scattered with feta and sumac, another leafy with soft herbs. New potatoes, boiled and dotted with a bright salsa verde. Bread and two types of butter: confit garlic, and Parmesan and black pepper. There would be cold wine and open windows, patio doors thrown wide. It would all look and taste exquisite.

There had been roast chickens back in Derby, but her mother's were always anaemic, trussed at the legs and moistened only by a gravy that had started life as a spoonful of granules. For dessert—or afters, as her father would say—there would be an apple pie from the Morrisons bakery or a roulade from the frozen aisle, depending on the season, eaten on the sofa in front of the television. Between bites, Piglet's family—her parents, her sister, herself—would call out the answers to quiz shows, spoons scraping in their bowls. Piglet knew her parents still ate her mother's roast chicken every Sunday. On Saturday it was a takeaway—Chinese, from the shop in town—and on Friday it was fish. No matter the weather, no matter the time of year. These routines, which had once cradled their familial bonds, their Sunday traditions, now made Piglet feel a crawling embarrassment, a creeping pity. She had learned since she left Derby, left her parents, that the only way to serve a dessert from the frozen aisle was ironically.

When she had met Kit's parents, they had served a roast rib of beef. Richard had carved, and the blackened bones, which had stuck into the air, shook as he sliced. When Cecelia apportioned herself a single slice and a heaping of steamed cavolo nero, Piglet had done the same. They had discussed art over dinner—Warhol at the Ashmolean—and Piglet had nodded, beamed, and spoken about *Campbell's Soup Cans* to sympathetic smiles. Kit and Richard ate second helpings with their fingers. Cecelia had sighed, the corners of her lips curling: "Boys."

Piglet's dinner would not be like her mother's or her future in-laws'. There would be jazz music, cigarettes smoked on the patio, and a dessert made from one of the new cookbooks she was editing: an espresso semifreddo with warm caramel sauce and glinting shards of praline. There were easier recipes she could have made—she could have bought dessert, pudding, even—but she did not pass up an opportunity to mention one of her authors by name on the off chance someone might ask for the recipe.

At the checkout, Piglet stood behind a woman with two young boys. They were hanging on the woman's arm, whining about sweets, swinging backwards and forwards, catching glances from the other shoppers before raising their voices, eyeing their mother as she moved groceries from trolley to till with her remaining hand. Piglet tried to catch the cashier's eye: this was Waitrose.

The woman didn't look at her children as she transferred crisps in brightly coloured packaging to the conveyor belt. Cereal, sliced white bread, ice cream. Piglet eyed the shopping, and then the children. She glanced at the cashier again.

By the time Piglet's organic chicken had reached the till, the children were quiet. They had each been handed a fluorescent bag of Nik Naks, torn from their multipack. They grinned at each other, their fingers dusted orange, pulped corn between their teeth. The woman paid, left, and Piglet positioned herself to receive her groceries and compliments on her choice of food. The cashier looked up at her, smiling, inclining her head. "Boys," she said, before she pushed the chicken through the till.

"They're not going to notice if a bit of skin's gone." Kit, his eyes dark with desire, was naked besides his boxers, a pair of yellow rubber gloves. The chicken—a long-legged bird with feathers still clinging to its thighs—had just been removed from the oven, and the kitchen was shimmering with heat. The room was empty, walls white, boxes spilling Tupperware stacked where a table would eventually stand. Kit stood behind Piglet, her skin also bare save an apron strung over her underwear, and she felt the heat of him on her back.

"I thought you were doing the bathrooms," Piglet said as she inspected the bird, her body bending into his.

"They're done," Kit said. "Doesn't take long when they've

never been used." With his arms around her, he began to remove his gloves, pulling a finger at a time until his hands were uncovered and inching towards the chicken, its brown skin crisp. Piglet turned to face him.

"Not for you," she said, leaning closer to his face, gently biting his lip, tasting salt. He smiled, and she felt his lips pull wide, away from her. "I've been saving this for us, though."

Piglet pulled a near-empty round orange Le Creuset pot towards her. She scraped a spoon around its edge and lifted it to Kit's mouth. His eyebrows contracted, his lips.

"Good, isn't it?" Piglet said, smiling as Kit groaned. "Coffee custard for the semifreddo."

Kit took the pot from the stove and cradled it like a child as he folded his legs beneath him, sinking to the floor of their empty kitchen. He slapped the space next to him, and Piglet sat. Kit scraped another half spoonful of custard from the pot and held it to Piglet's lips. She swallowed: a child taking medicine, a communicant receiving the Eucharist.

"Is it too late to uninvite everyone?" he asked.

"You know what? Maybe not."

They sat cross-legged on the floor, the tiles cool beneath their hot flesh, passing the Le Creuset between them, spoon discarded, grinning and sticky-knuckled, custard on their fingertips.

Her hair, dark with water, dripped onto her linen dress, the fabric rippling. The dress had been ironed by Kit and laid on their mattress, which was in the middle of the bedroom, empty besides more boxes piled high and bulging duffle bags bursting with socks, trailing sleeves. The dress, ivory white and peppered with eyelets, spoke to her of summertime, of evenings drinking ouzo in Santorini. She dropped a beach towel from her body and stepped between the folds of fabric. The linen was light against her bare skin and, in the warmth of the early evening, she felt a power in her body: strong and beautiful in her own home.

Downstairs, in the reflection of the patio doors, Piglet tied and retied her apron.

"What do you think?" she called to Kit.

"Perfect," he said, joining her in the distorted image of the door. "And me?"

Piglet turned, appraising him: handsome in his chambray button-down shirt and the fitted sand-coloured trousers they had chosen together. She reached forward, undoing a third button, the hollow of his chest now visible between the folds of his collar. He raised an eyebrow. She turned back to their reflection.

"It's summertime," she said. "And it's our house."

They hovered—straightening tablecloth corners, wiping down sparkling surfaces—until the doorbell rang. They looked at each other, grinning.

"Put the music on," Piglet said. "And the candles."

"Matches?" Kit called behind her.

"I don't know!" she shouted, her voice rising, giddy.

Their guests had arrived all at once: Margot and Sasha with a bottle of vodka tied with a red ribbon, and Seb and Sophie holding a bunch of flowers and a Jo Malone candle. Piglet and Kit greeted them at the door.

"Look at you two," Margot called from the drive, and Piglet could not help but curtsey.

"Come in, come in," Kit said, standing aside. "There are boxes everywhere, but the wine is in the fridge."

"As it should be," Sasha said as she kissed Piglet on both cheeks. "We tried to think of something practical to give you," Sasha said as she pressed the vodka into Piglet's hands.

"So, what's on the menu?" Margot asked, leaning against the counter as Piglet cored a cucumber, its watery seeds heaped in a pile. The others were outside, their conversation rising as their wineglasses emptied. Piglet heard Sophie's whinnying laugh and Seb's voice, loud, tripping over itself as he arrived, jubilant, at a punch line.

"Roast chicken," Piglet said, glancing up and catching Kit's eye, the edge of a smile, before she started to slice the cucumber, "because I couldn't help myself."

"And vegetarians be damned," Margot said.

"Sorry," Piglet said, offering Margot a sliver of cucumber, which she accepted and crunched. "But there's also gorgeous bread and confit garlic butter, salads, and the most incredible espresso semifreddo with caramel for dessert."

"You had me at bread." Margot turned to the sink, moving slowly, refilling her glass with water. She had started to cradle her stomach with each movement even though the bump was still imperceptible beneath her loose linen shirt, long-point collar high at her throat. "It's all I want to eat."

For a moment, Piglet did not know what to say, and she

felt the air around her, huge with uncertainty. Like her friend's body, things were already different, even if they did not appear to be so.

"Me too," she said, dicing the cucumber into perfect cubes.

———————

Piglet kept her guests outside until the table—an improvised stack of cardboard boxes, pushed together, covered with tablecloths—was laid. Ice cracked in a carafe as Margot filled it with water, and Piglet arranged dishes of food. She placed the chicken in the centre, testing the cardboard below with her hands before she set the bird down. On either side of the chicken, she placed a bowl of salad, a neighbouring tureen of potatoes alongside. Next to these, at each end of the table, she positioned platters of sliced sourdough and small bowls of whipped butter. Wooden tongs, arranged symmetrically, bookended her dinner. It looked how she had imagined it would.

Margot reached for a slice of bread, and Piglet waved her hands. Margot rolled her eyes and sat, ready to eat.

"Food's ready," Margot called out to the patio. Piglet stared at her. "What?" Margot said. "I'm hungry."

"Look at this!" Seb said, his cheeks pink with wine and 8:00 p.m. sun. Piglet smiled, gesturing for her guests to sit.

"Wow," Sophie gasped, hovering behind a chair. "God, where do you get off cooking like this when you've only just moved in?"

"She's terrible, isn't she?" Margot said, a piece of bread in hand. "Sit, Sophie, so I can eat this bread without being told off."

"Do sit," Piglet said. "Anywhere is fine." She watched her

friends find their places around her, leaning forward to inspect the dishes with shining eyes.

"Please," Piglet was saying, gesturing to the food, when Kit lifted a hand.

"Before we start, everyone, I wanted to say a few words."

Piglet sat back, folding her hands into her lap as she looked up at Kit, watched him push his chair back and stand. Margot lifted her tumbler, bread briefly discarded, tapping her fork against the glass.

"Thank you, Marg," Kit said, smiling, and she inclined her head. "A little toast," he said, holding his glass. Piglet watched the honey liquid swirl, glimpsing the edges of his distorted smile through the wine. She leaned forward to see him better, her eyes locking on his.

"To my good fortune, really," he continued, looking at Piglet. Sasha laughed, and Margot swatted at her. "Yes, I know," Kit said, turning in Sasha's direction, "as if I deserve any more good fortune. But here I am in our new home with dear friends and the most astonishing woman, who I have, somehow, convinced to marry me." Kit turned his gaze back to Piglet and held his glass high.

Piglet lowered her head, aware of every eye on her, and smiled to herself. When she had been growing up in Derby, this life, this man, had been beyond her imagination.

"Anyway, I wanted to say, with wine, that I am thankful for it all." He lifted his glass higher and raised his eyebrows, encouraging their seated guests to do the same. "So, to the cause of every good thing I have in my life: to my future wife. To Piglet."

Piglet listened as her friends said her name, clinking their glasses with one another, laughing.

"Kit, that was adorable," Margot said, her water glass drained, "but you two are disgusting."

"We are." Kit nodded, sitting down.

"Why can't you do toasts like that?" Sophie muttered to Seb as salads were lifted from their bowls with wooden spoons, grains of bulghur wheat breadcrumbing across the tablecloth. Piglet did not look at them and instead leaned forward, pinching a piece of chicken from its platter with hungry fingers, and stretched across the table, placing it into Kit's mouth.

"Best food I've ever had," he said, meat between his teeth.

The food really was the best they'd ever had—Sophie kept saying so, although Sophie was the kind of person who ate boiled chicken breasts by choice. When they had met, and Piglet had described her job as an assistant editor at Fork House, Seb had said stridently how Sophie loved to cook too, and how they batch-cooked a chilli made with turkey mince every Sunday.

———————

"I still can't call you that," Sophie said, placing her cutlery together before leaning across the makeshift table, boxes shifting, placing her hand over Piglet's.

They had finished eating—mostly: Seb was still slathering crusts of bread with the last of the butter, mopping up the juices from the chicken platter—and the conversation had turned to Piglet's culinary skills. She had been receiving the praise with grace, she thought, the corners of her lips upturned, her eyes cast down, while she let the compliments fill and invigorate her like an after-dinner espresso.

"Everyone calls her that," Sasha said from the other end of the boxes, and Piglet noticed her eyes had started to become small with drink.

"I don't call her Piglet," Margot said, leaning over her wife.

"Margot is literally the only one who uses my real name. When she says it, I feel like I'm in trouble. Everyone calls me Piglet. You can thank my parents for that."

"Don't you get along with your parents?" Sophie leaned closer, taking Piglet's hand and squeezing it, her lacquered nails shining.

"Let's have pudding." Piglet withdrew her hand from Sophie's and stood up to remove the semifreddo from the freezer.

Later, Kit would say how nice it was to have couple friends who made an effort. When Sophie sank her spoon into the semifreddo, she smiled across the half-empty bowls and said sweetly, "You should go on *Bake Off*." Margot caught Piglet's eye, and she had to look away; Sophie did not realise this was not a compliment. Piglet said thank you, anyway.

"You'd win, hands down." Seb grinned before turning to Sophie. "She's making her own wedding cake, some French thing—remember I told you?" Piglet smiled as she watched Seb lean forward to cut another slice of ice cream, his muscular arms straining beneath a Ralph Lauren shirt.

"A croquembouche," Piglet confirmed.

"That's it." Seb nodded, sucking a finger that had trailed in melted espresso cream. "How cool is that?"

"That's so cute," Sophie said, wrinkling her nose. "I wish I had the time to do so much baking."

Piglet shrugged.

"Although when I eat food like this—delicious, by the

way—I can literally feel myself sweating out the butter," Sophie
continued.

"There's no butter in ice cream," Piglet said.

───────

It had reached the point in the evening when the plates were
empty and the atmosphere was souring like Piglet's tongue, dry
from wine. The drink and conversation were no longer pleasurable and instead, they made her head throb. She closed her eyes
as Kit's voice rose, untired by company, the alcohol, or the hour.

"What do you think then, Sash? Does the house get your
seal of approval?" Piglet heard the chair creak as Kit leaned back.
She could picture him: head cocked to the side, his legs splayed
apart. She could imagine Sasha across from him: eyebrows
raised, lips sealed.

Early in their relationship, Piglet introduced Kit to Margot at
one of Sasha's open mic nights. They had drunk red wine, eaten
nothing, and Kit and Sasha had argued loudly, disagreeing about
the viability of universal basic income. Sasha had dedicated her
last poem, "I Have This One Tory Friend," to Kit. Piglet and
Margot had spent the following days planning how to broker a
peace—a roast at a neutral location, they had decided, absolutely
no alcohol—before Kit revealed that he and Sasha had already
arranged to meet the following week: a public lecture at the LSE
on economics for the common good. In the subsequent years
they had learned to argue in a way they both appeared to enjoy.

Piglet opened her eyes to find Margot staring at her. She
lifted two fingers to her mouth, an invisible cigarette between
her lips. Piglet nodded.

"It's a gorgeous house, Kit," Sasha said.

"Fresh air," Piglet excused as she stood. Kit reached for her, brushing her waist, but his eyes remained fixed on Sasha. His voice rose, excited.

"You're tempted, then?" Kit said, goading. "What about property is theft?"

Across the table Margot stood too, her hands at her stomach, creating a curvature at her middle. Sasha lifted her fingers to her wife while shooting back, "Let's not do this tonight; I'd hate to school you in your new home."

Piglet stooped to pick up a lighter and packet of Marlboro Gold, their foiled box obscured by an image of an artery, flayed like a skirt steak, oozing yoghurty plaque. She pushed the back door open and held it for Margot, who eased out of the kitchen after her.

The garden was a copy of the neighbours' on either side, and of all other newbuild houses: a yellow strip of paving slabs and tufty green turf. Piglet leaned back, sliding down the glass until she was sitting on the patio. Margot joined her.

"Is tonight the night?" Piglet jerked her head in the direction of Kit and Sasha.

"That they finally kill each other?" Margot tilted her head from side to side as if weighing possibilities. "No," she concluded, holding out her hand for the lighter, "it would disturb poor Sophie."

Piglet laughed.

"Where did you find her, anyway?" Margot asked.

"She and Seb got engaged at Christmas."

"Tacky." Margot flicked the lighter, and it flared. Piglet lifted a finger to her lips, shushing, before nodding. She pulled a cigarette from the packet.

"Yes. She calls us the WTBs—wives to be—which I find depressing." She leaned over, and Margot held the lighter until the cigarette glowed.

"That sounds like a genital condition." Margot shivered before rolling her head back and inhaling deeply. "God, that smells so good."

"What will Sasha think of you inhaling secondhand smoke?"

"I think until she does the childbearing and the—you know—birthing, I get to win all the arguments."

"Oh, handy."

"Yeah."

Smoke spiralled above them into the clear, dark sky, and Piglet felt the buzz of nicotine ease the pain in her head. She breathed deeply. "You can see the stars," she observed. Margot nodded.

"Pleased with your dinner, then?"

"I think so. Although I'm ready for them to get out of my house now." Piglet leaned back, the crown of her head knocking on the glass door.

"My house," Margot echoed.

"I know," Piglet said, looking up.

"When did you get so old? A homeowner and a WTB."

"Graduating to a W on October thirtieth," Piglet confirmed. "In ninety-eight days exactly."

"Counting down to events in days makes you sound like a serial killer."

Piglet laughed, smoke billowing from her mouth in clouds.

"You're a grown-up," Margot said.

"You're pregnant!"

"Fourteen-year-olds get pregnant. You're engaged and you own a house."

The cigarette had burned down to a stub. Piglet flicked it across the patio, and it glowed in the dark.

"OK, I am getting old." Piglet winced. "I want to go and pick that up and put it in the bin."

It was one in the morning before Piglet and Kit waved off their guests, standing in the doorway at the front of their house. Margot lifted her hand as she reversed her rusting Ford Focus out of the driveway, and Sasha, next to her, raised a long middle finger to Kit, who blew a kiss in return. Seb called his thanks out of the window of a taxi as Sophie looked down, her face illuminated, her eyes scrolling.

"What will the neighbours think of us and our loud friends?" Kit peered either side of the house.

"I don't think we have any neighbours yet," Piglet said. There were no lights on in the identical box houses that stood on either side of them. The driveways were empty.

"So"—Kit wrapped his arms around her, pulling her back inside and closing the door—"we can make as much noise as we like."

In their bedroom, cast in moonlight, windows bare without blinds, they took stock.

"A success, then?" Piglet asked as Kit threw his clothes over a cardboard box.

"A triumph," Kit confirmed, lowering himself onto the mattress. "Seb wants the recipe for dessert."

"Does he?" Piglet looked up. "What did he say?"

"He said it was the best thing he'd ever eaten. I told him that it was a recipe from a cookbook you're editing and, if he promised not to share it with anyone, I'd ask you to email it to him."

Piglet nodded, slipping the straps of her dress from her shoulders. She paused, smiling to herself.

"And I'm the most astonishing woman?" she asked as the dress fell from her body, blooming on the floor around her.

"The most astonishing woman," Kit confirmed, reclined on their mattress, his eyes on her. "Of course."

She smiled, warm despite her nakedness, alert despite the hour, and fell on him, ravenous.

He would tell her thirteen days before their wedding, and she would feel his words lodge like a shard of bone between her ribs.

20 Days

Piglet lay in the dark, listening to the mammal noises of Kit's breathing. It was before 7:00 a.m., and their bedroom was still shrouded in the quiet shadow of an October Sunday morning. When they had first moved in—before the blinds had gone up—the sun had woken them before their bodies could: stomachs rumbling, bladders full. Now: darkness. Now: Kit's gap-lipped breath, dry-tongued and heavy. She wouldn't see sunlight at this hour until spring next year, and by then, she'd be married. For a moment she closed her eyes, turned to her fiancé, and considered sleep, before slipping from their bed. She wanted to be in her kitchen.

She had spent the night waiting to wake, her body on standby, and had opened her eyes thinking about Margot and her promise to stock her freezer. This gesture was all she had to offer in their third-trimester conversations. When Margot relayed anecdotes from her NHS prenatal classes, where the advice was free but the parking was ten pounds, Piglet responded with menu ideas. She had bought fifty foil trays.

Piglet closed the door behind her—if she was quiet, Kit would sleep for another hour—and turned on the cooker hood light. At the kitchen table she cleared a space among the debris of their life, adjusted an ornamental wooden calendar—twenty-one days, twenty days—and pulled a cookbook towards her. She sat for a moment, savouring the half light of the kitchen and the image of her body within it, preparing to labour while everyone else was asleep, before turning to a recipe for vegetarian shepherd's pie, wondering how Margot would recount her efforts to the faceless pregnant women with whom she sipped frothy, decaffeinated cappuccinos.

She had been standing over her Le Creuset, watching carrots, celery, and onions slacken, their crisp edges becoming soft and nibbled with brown, when the kitchen spotlights flared.

"Dark in here," Kit said as Piglet flinched. He moved towards her, kissing the hollow between her cheekbone and forehead, and she felt the urge to pull away, turn off the lights, and huddle over the stove, her back to him.

"I thought you were asleep," she said, not looking at him, not able to communicate how his presence shattered the image of her industriousness, her private productivity.

"Onions," he replied, waving his hand towards the stairs. Piglet frowned, covered the pot with its round, orange lid, and crouched to retrieve a bag of potatoes.

"For Margot?" Kit asked, oblivious to her mood, filling a moka pot with coffee and water and placing it on the hob next to Piglet's softening vegetables. She made a noise of assent from the cupboard and considered whether to crawl inside.

"Have your parents seen Margot since she's been pregnant?" he asked, crossing the kitchen to lean on the countertop next to her. His fingers trailed at his side, stroking her shoulder as she continued to hunch. She felt his fingers flatten to a palm on her back as he crouched beside her. "Can I help, by the way?" he asked, and she looked at him, his puffy blue eyes wrinkled with a smile. She had woken him, she knew, and she had the urge to place her lips on his eyelids. She withdrew, her hands full with potatoes. She shook her head.

"Mum has—when we were dress shopping—but she wasn't weird," she said, inferring the motivation for his question. She took each potato and peeled, her hands speckling with starch as it dried on her skin.

"No"—he contemplated—"no, I can't imagine she would be." Kit watched her knife as it started to cleave. He shifted his position. "I can imagine my dad might say something, though."

Piglet looked up.

Richard tended to say very little. His conversational libido surged on weekends, when the rugby was on, or the cricket. It was the only distasteful thing about the Summertown house: the television on, always on, the volume too loud. When Piglet was there, she always knew the score of Saracens versus Wasps, Harlequins versus Worcester: the television would tell her, or Richard would.

"He won't try to be offensive, but I can imagine him asking Margot about the father on the top table." Steam bubbled and hissed at the lip of the Le Creuset.

"Asking is fine," Piglet said as she put the potatoes on to boil.

"Well—" Kit paused. "I think he'll have opinions."

Fathers, in Piglet's experience, seemed to feel at a permanent liberty to express their opinions as if they were facts. Both her father and Richard had no embarrassment in voicing their beliefs without self-consciousness, while her mother and Cecelia were expert at ignoring their husband's venting and any offence it caused.

"Well, can you make sure he doesn't share them with Margot?" Piglet asked.

"He's harmless." Kit shrugged, Kit shirked. The coffee pot on the stove started to whistle, steam starting to stream from the spout, condensation beading on the splashback. "You know what he's like." He made to pick up the pot as Piglet went to lift the lid of the Le Creuset. They clashed.

"Can you get out of my way?" she snapped. He looked at her, his stare steady, expression calm. She didn't move. Kit picked up the coffee pot and placed it on a coaster.

"Well," he said quietly.

He leaned forward, reaching for a cupboard of mugs in front of her. "Excuse me," he said. She didn't move. She imagined opening the door, smashing it into his face. "Excuse me," he repeated, louder, and she stepped aside.

Kit sloped upstairs, coffee in hand, and Piglet felt the adrenaline of their disagreement thump through her veins: useless. She looked at the mug he'd left for her, steam rising from the black liquid. She did not know how to drink this coffee: how to fight and accept care, how to hate and how to love. The sun was up now. She flicked off the lamp on the cooker hood, she crossed the kitchen to turn off the spotlights.

Beneath the lid of the Le Creuset, the sofrito was yielding.

Onions, carrots, celery, and garlic smelled like a school night: the beginnings of cooking for a crowd. She thought about Margot eating the food she was making, tired eyes touched by a smile, as Sasha held a formless baby. Margot would have a crowd of her own soon. In just over two months, there would be far fewer boozy dinner parties and a lot more posseting, more picnics eaten in the park, Piglet averting her eyes from Margot's exposed, dark nipple. She was annoyed at Kit. She might be annoyed at Margot.

It would not be the first time she had felt the creep of belligerence as her friend's life morphed into a shape different to her own. When Sasha had been introduced, brought along to one of their Friday dinners as if she had been invited, they had teased Margot over tofu, swapping stories, competing through hard grins. After the plates were empty, and they turned to leave, hands entwined, Margot mouthing "thank you" over Sasha's shoulder, Piglet felt bereft: the beam of her friend's attention turning from her.

She rinsed a kilo of lentils and added them to the pot along with a tin of tomatoes, spices, and chilli flakes. The pan hissed: water making contact with oil and hot iron. She boiled the kettle, and as she dissolved Marmite and a stock cube in a jug of hot water, she made herself a cup of mint tea. She countered her self-reproach with rationale: she hadn't wanted caffeine anyway. She poured in the stock, and the lentils bloomed to the surface. She poured away the coffee and wondered if she and Kit would ever be ready for a baby.

Margot had never been embarrassed of her desire for a child. Before Sasha, when their late-night, wine-soaked conversations turned deep—and after they'd covered the climate crisis, violence against women, and institutional racism—their talk would turn to the future. "I've always wanted a baby," Margot would say, a dreamy smile drifting onto her face as if they were high. That surety: Margot had always had it.

Piglet slid a knife into the potatoes jostling with each other in the deep pot on the back burner. She drained them, and the windows of the kitchen were briefly opaque.

Piglet hadn't been worried then. They were barely in their twenties. They still had time. She thought she still had time.

She heard the lentils—the angry, thumping hiss of something catching on cast iron. In their stew of tomatoes, stock, and sofrito, the lentils were beginning to bounce. Bubbles of heat shoved their way to the surface. She turned the flame down.

They had been everything to one another—there had even been bracelets, exchanged ironically—but then there was Sasha, and not long after, Piglet met Kit. They were still close—of course they were close—but Margot's family was growing in a direction away from Piglet, as she had planned it, as she had always known, and there was something hurtful about this choice: Margot striving ahead, as she always did, sure of herself, making a unit of her own rather than waiting for Piglet, leaving her behind.

She returned the potatoes to their empty pan and sloshed in milk; two, three pats of butter; and salt and white pepper. She breathed in as the fog in the kitchen dissipated. She held a masher in her hand and listened to the stew bubble: rhythmic. It would all come together. Everything would come together.

"Why do people keep making me things with lentils?" Margot exclaimed when Piglet handed over the pies. "Give me pasta. Give me cheese." When Piglet had arrived at Margot and Sasha's cottage—the façade overgrown with ivy, the porch covered in fallen leaves from a red maple, paint peeling from the blue front door—Margot had called from the doorway: "I hope they're brownies."

"Who else is making you food with lentils?" Piglet smiled as she placed the silver trays into Margot's fridge, moving aside jars of pickles, plates of leftovers, and an overripe plantain.

"You," Margot said, holding up a finger, "and Sasha," she continued, lifting a second.

"So, me and your wife?"

"Ungrateful, isn't she?" Sasha said, as she walked into their kitchen. "Hi, P."

"Sash, I just made you a cup of tea." Margot pointed to three steaming mugs on the table before her. "How could I be ungrateful?"

"I think you're confusing gratefulness with common politeness," Sasha said, lifting one of the mugs to her lips.

Piglet followed Margot through a narrow hallway with uneven walls to the living room at the back of the house. This room, which always surprised Piglet with its brightness, was a contrast to the rest of the dark, low-vaulted cottage. Bifold doors stretched across the back wall, and skylights had been installed in the sloping ceiling. "Sorry it's a mess," Margot said as she picked through piles of washing, books, and unopened boxes containing a breast pump, a changing table, a cot. Margot gestured for Piglet to sit down as she lowered herself into an armchair. A birthing ball had been squashed beside a brown, button-backed leather sofa.

"You're not going to sit on this?" Piglet asked, indicating the ball. Margot shook her head as she adjusted her position, her hand at her bump. Piglet pulled the ball towards her, rolling it from one hand to the other.

She looked at her friend, perched on the edge of the armchair, and she couldn't help her eyes wandering to Margot's belly. It protruded from her now, balloon-like, almost cartoonish. Each time Piglet saw her, Margot's body had changed. After the first month of her pregnancy being visible, Piglet had forced herself to stop asking questions. Margot would answer, but Piglet had always felt little-girlish, naïve, in her marvelling.

"I know," Margot said, following Piglet's eyes. "I am a behemoth."

"You're not," Piglet said. Margot laughed.

"It's OK. I'm harbouring a human, I don't mind being huge," Margot said.

Piglet slapped the birthing ball, trying to make it bounce.

"Imagine what you're going to look like in a month," she said.

"A Weeble, I expect. Although I anticipate nothing but falling down." Margot lowered her head, stroking her swollen stomach, smiling as if she were remembering some private joke. As Piglet waited for Margot to return to her, she lowered herself onto the birthing ball. She felt her pelvis tilt, her knees bend.

Margot looked up and laughed at Piglet rolling her hips.

"Suits you," she said, winking. Piglet snorted. "Anyway,

how are you? And actually you. I'll be charging one pound for every mention of the wedding."

———————————————

"She's so big now." Piglet leaned forward, picking up a tumbler of sparkling water from a coaster on their low coffee table before turning to look at Kit. "House is a mess, though." She sipped, running her fingers along the soft velvet of their pale-pink sofa.

They had transformed their house in the few months they had lived there. The living room was now clean and carefully furnished. A gallery of photographs hung above the sofa; a tall monstera stood by the door; a drinks trolley glinted in the glare of the television.

"They're not organised people, though, are they?" Kit said, his mouth full of bean sprouts and green mango. He didn't look up from the television. "Not like us."

Piglet had been thinking about the wedding when she stopped at the new Thai place in the town centre to pick up boxes of pad pak and summer rolls for dinner. Her thoughts had been a fusion of images—she and Kit laughing, embracing, the picture of joy; their guests' admiration, their jealousy; and, as always, her body, her dress, the photographs that would sit on her parents' mantelpiece. In the restaurant she had scoured the menu, looking for vegetable dishes and words she could pronounce. Kit had cheered when she opened the door holding the paper takeaway bags, and she hoped he had inferred her apology, delivered between sheets of translucent rice paper.

"I don't know how they're going to cope when the baby

comes," Kit said, leaning forward to pick up two rolls fat with sliced cucumber, bean sprouts, and vermicelli noodles, ribbons of fresh herbs encased like veins beneath skin. He handed one to Piglet, the rice paper sticking to his damp fingertips.

"Neither do I," she said, snaking one hand into his lap as they settled back into the sofa, licking their lips.

There were some things that you could not tell your friends. She knew that truths, once spoken, had the power to strip her of the life she had so carefully built, so smugly shared.

16 Days

Piglet was lit blue in their living room, 5:00 a.m. darkness fractured by the glare of the television. She had not turned on the lights and instead fumbled for the remote where she knew it would be on the coffee table. She stood in a sports bra and trainers, the house still about her. Overhead, Kit slept.

She rolled out a yoga mat on a vast, geometrically patterned rug—a gift from Richard and Cecelia after a trip to Marrakech—and started to squat in synchrony with a woman wearing a coordinating crop top and shorts. For twenty minutes, the room shook minutely around her, drinks trolley clinking as she sprinted, jumped, and lunged. When she felt the echo of her own flesh, reverberating as she moved, she intensified her efforts until her legs burned, her chest heaved, and sweat poured into her eyes.

Kit was still in bed when she stepped into the shower. She

held herself there, beneath the first deluge cold of water, and watched her skin pimple and tighten. As she dried herself and slathered herself in a buttery cream, she inspected her limbs, pinkened with exertion. In the low morning light, the contours of her body looked smooth.

"Coffee for the road." Kit stood at the front door in his dressing gown, holding a reusable glass cup. "And I've put a banana in your bag."

"I'm not hungry." Piglet smiled at him.

"You look great." He smiled back and leaned over to kiss her. She rolled her eyes.

"Sixteen days," she said.

"Eat the banana."

Piglet dropped the fruit in a bin at Oxford train station, which had been decorated for Halloween: paper pumpkins hung from the ceiling, the announcements board draped in spiderwebs. Grey-faced commuters hunched over coffee cups shuffled on their platforms, inhaling vapours.

The station was on their side of the city, and Piglet could walk to her train in the morning. It was one of the reasons they'd chosen the house. Kit's parents—who had provided a large part of their deposit after their engagement—had protested.

"It's the other side of the A34." Which, to Cecelia, meant beyond the city centre's warmly coloured turrets and domes, edging dangerously towards industrial estates and affordable housing.

"You know your mother doesn't like to drive through the town centre."

"We're ten minutes from Summertown," Kit had said. "And anywhere in Oxford is better than London, right?"

Anywhere in Oxford was also better than Derby. Cecelia and Richard's deposit had come with the condition that they purchase outside of the M25—the motorway that encircled the capital—and Piglet refused to consider anywhere farther north than Milton Keynes. Somewhere nearer Kit's family had appealed. She imagined shopping trips with Cecelia; golf mornings for Kit and Richard; Christmases spent at the house in Summertown: the porch decorated with evergreens, a goose in the oven.

"Won't your parents be upset if we don't look near them?"

"They know I'm not coming back. And anyway, Margot's already down here. They'll understand."

Piglet hoped her parents did not understand her desire to be away from them, from their redbrick terraced house. Since meeting Kit, she had hardly been back. When she took him to meet her parents on an Easter weekend, it was not only her old bedroom—now inhabited by her sister, Franny, and her boyfriend, Darren—that felt small. It was the house, the town, the minds of the neighbours, the minds of her parents. Their easy ways—their yellow custard in a Pyrex jug on the small dining table, draped in doilies—embarrassed her. She found herself muttering apologies to Kit, making unkind asides about her parents' conversation when he did not respond, and, when he laid his hand over hers and told her, "Enough," her insides had withered: paper burning, curling into ash. In the space where she was both at once her parents' daughter and Kit's fiancée, she did not know how to be.

Over Easter lunch—garlicky lamb, new potatoes, peas, and mint sauce served from the jar—she had found herself telling her mother to talk properly when she described Franny as mardy.

She had meant to joke, trying to balance the dichotomy of her life—herself with her family, herself with Kit—but her voice was loud, the edges of her syllables sharp with steel, and the conversation at the table faltered. In the quiet, Piglet's neck prickled, and her mother excused herself to get the simnel cake even though they were still eating. Her father said, "Well now," and Piglet cut her lamb into smaller and smaller pieces.

"They're nice," Kit had said as they travelled home after one-armed hugs and half-hearted requests to come again. When Piglet only nodded, he added, "Decent people."

When Piglet had called to tell her parents that they were buying the Oxford house, her mother had gasped.

Piglet had not told her parents that she had been forced to beg for a pay rise from her manager, Sandra, on the advice of their mortgage broker; instead, she had packaged this episode as a promotion. Her father had been thrilled.

"We're proud of you, Piglet," he said. "I know that doesn't mean much from your old dad back in Derby, but we are so proud."

"He tells everyone down the pub about you," her mother called, her voice distant.

"A big job in London, a fiancé, and now this. A house, Pinky. A three-bed! You're a star."

"We couldn't have done it without Richard and Cecelia," Piglet said, hoping to underline her gratitude, but she thought she heard her father's breath catch.

"You've found a good one, Duck, a good one. But you are a star. Don't forget about us as you go around shining."

The walls of the Fork House building were lined with cook-books, with more stacked on swivelling office chairs and spilling from cardboard boxes that littered the floor. When Piglet arrived at a bank of desks, Toni—a senior editor who wore only black and worked on literary cookbooks with very few photographs—was already there, leaning back in her chair, a pen held in her mouth like a cigarette.

"OK, so you're getting married," Toni said, looking at her computer screen, pen jerking between her teeth, as Piglet set down her bag.

"I've told you before, Toni, it's too late to propose," Piglet said, unfastening her jacket. Toni looked up.

"What? No." She shook her head and removed the pen from her mouth, pointing at the screen. "I love the way this woman writes, but her book is about catering your own wedding. Would you buy it?"

"No," Piglet said.

"I thought you were doing your own wedding cake?"

"Yes. A croquembouche, remember?"

"Exactly. So, you'd buy it?"

"Still no. I'm not catering the whole wedding, Toni. I'm not insane." Toni waved her hand.

"Olivia," Toni said, turning to an intern who had been neatly unpacking a pencil case of highlighters, "weigh in for us here." Olivia's ears reddened as she stammered.

"I'm—I'm not sure it would be—"

"Philistines, the pair of you," Toni exclaimed, winking at Olivia before hunching back over her computer, eyes scanning the screen. Piglet laughed as she sat down, watching the elevator doors.

As Toni started to reel off how many Tupperware boxes one would need—approximately—to transfer canapés from home to venue, Sandra walked through the elevator doors and into her glass-fronted office.

"That's less than twenty containers," Toni was saying to Olivia as Piglet stood. "And you could reuse them, so it's eco-friendly too. You could do the jacket in green."

When Piglet knocked, Sandra glanced up, looking at her through huge, red-framed glasses.

"Sorry, Sandra," Piglet said, poking her head around the doorframe. She was holding a pitch: a proposal for one hundred potato recipes from a blogger who had found her email, addressed her as "Dear Fork House." With her father's words still playing in her mind—"You're a star"—she had convinced herself to present the book as if she had scouted it herself, as if she had been promoted.

"Come, come," Sandra beckoned, before running her hands through her short, blond hair. Piglet slipped into the office and closed the door behind her.

"I was wondering if I could talk to you about a book idea from—"

"One second." Sandra lifted a finger, not looking at Piglet. She pulled a bowl from a bottom desk drawer and stood up to retrieve an open box of Dorset Cereals muesli. As she poured out a torrent of oats and dried fruit, she looked at Piglet, impatient. "So?"

"Sorry," said Piglet. "I wanted to talk to you about a book idea. It's one hundred recipes that use potatoes, and the submission is beautifully put together. The author—she's a blogger—writes—"

"Let me stop you there," Sandra interjected, holding up her bowl. "I need to get milk and get ready for a meeting."

"Oh, of course."

"Shall we talk about this tomorrow?"

"Friday?" Piglet asked. Sandra, who was in her mid-forties, had two girls of around ten and didn't work in the office on Mondays or Fridays because she was a parent and needed to be with them. Piglet wasn't sure what they did on Tuesdays, Wednesdays, and Thursdays.

"Oh, of course not," Sandra said, rolling her eyes. "Lunch today, then. There's a great new bagel shop that's just opened up and I can't stop thinking about their Reuben."

"Great." Piglet smiled as her stomach contracted.

"Meet me in the foyer at twelve thirty. Bring your pitch."

The bagel shop was small and only had high tables where groups stood clutching their foil-wrapped bread. Piglet slouched as she and Sandra waited in line. She eyed the piles of bagels behind the counter as Sandra made queue small talk.

"How's the wedding planning going?" she called up to Piglet over the clamour of the shop. Piglet bent down to reply. She always felt bigger than should be allowed, but next to Sandra's petite frame she felt especially huge. Her size seemed to invite men who didn't know her to ask if she played basketball. This question would come arbitrarily: on the tube, at the checkout of a grocery store, in the doctor's surgery. Surely, these men must think, this woman has good reason for being so large.

"It's all pretty much done," Piglet replied, her voice raised, a hand covering her mouth.

"What?" Sandra asked, looking up at her. Piglet lowered her hand.

"It's mostly done. It's just over two weeks away now, so"—Piglet waved her hand—"final touches." Sandra nodded. Piglet straightened.

At the counter, Piglet adjusted the straps of her bag, shifting for her purse, signalling her readiness to pay. Sandra turned, noticing her movement, and shook her head, handing over a black credit card. "This is a working lunch," she said, holding her hand out for the receipt. Piglet followed Sandra's fingers tucking the card away, silver numbers shining, folding the thin piece of paper. "We'll expense it."

Piglet marvelled: she had not known about these rules, that this was allowed. She took the bagels, fat with filling and sliced in half. Piglet could see the layers of pink pastrami, packed so tightly they were almost pressed to a paste.

"So, tell me about this book idea," Sandra said as she took a bite. Piglet inhaled, tearing her eyes away from the sliced gherkins, the shiny Swiss cheese.

Sandra had finished eating by the time Piglet had finished her pitch.

"I have to say," Sandra said, brushing her hands together, "I like the sound of it." Piglet held her breath as Sandra removed a sesame seed from beneath one of her nails, flicking it to the floor. "But I don't want you to send it up the chain." Piglet dropped her eyes to her hands, counting the layers of pink, wet beef.

"We are growing the team, and I need to hire a new editor for Fork House," Sandra continued. "Someone to take on the high and the low. Stuff like this." She gestured towards Piglet, who was gripping the bagel in her hand so tightly that the pastrami began to bulge. "I want you to put yourself forward for the job."

Piglet looked up.

"Really?"

"Yes." Sandra smiled, her thin lips stretching. "I like your taste. And you're a hard worker. You're not afraid to ask for what you want, and I appreciate that. If you get the job, I want you to take this forward as its primary editor."

"Are you sure?"

"I'm not making any promises." Sandra stopped smiling, looking Piglet in the eyes. "The job will be advertised." Piglet nodded, thinking about how she'd tell her parents. She imagined her father's voice, purring, proud, her mother's intake of breath.

There were some things that you could not tell your family.
She knew that truths, once spoken, had the power to return
her to them.

14 Days

For seven Saturdays in a row, Piglet and Cecelia had spent an hour a week in a high-ceilinged room with a man who spoke in the third person—"Ryan thinks you can do better," "Ryan wants you to push really hard now," "Ryan likes that"—and whose trapezius muscles were so large they bulged like melons.

Cecelia had presented the offer of eight weeks of personal training classes in July as if it was a Christmas present. They had been at the house in Summertown—a barbecue in the garden, Richard wielding tongs—when Cecelia had handed over a thick, navy-blue envelope.

"Just a little something for us to enjoy as we get closer to the wedding—now that we're neighbours."

Piglet, light with Pimm's, had hugged Cecelia before opening the card. Their jewellery clinked as Piglet inhaled a mouthful of Cecelia's blond hair, bitter with perfume.

"Thank you, Cece."

Cecelia waved her hand as Piglet eased open the envelope.

"Exercise classes," Piglet exclaimed, looking down at the thick card in her hand, calligraphed like a wedding invitation. She adjusted her stance, dropping a hip, breathing in.

"What's that?" Kit had asked, walking over with a burger in a floury white roll in one hand. Piglet offered the card to him.

"Weekly personal training sessions at the club for my daughter-in-law-to-be and I in the lead-up to the wedding," Cecelia had said, laying a hand on Piglet's arm. Kit took a bite of the burger.

"You two don't need personal training sessions," he said through a mouthful of beef, flour dusting his cheeks. His mother rolled her eyes and laid her arm on Piglet's as if sharing a private exasperation.

"Food's ready, by the way," Kit had said, gesturing the hand holding his burger over his shoulder towards Richard, who was engulfed in smoke, eyes narrowed.

Piglet had not moved.

Over two months, she and Cecelia had stretched, lifted weights, and flexed their muscles in unison. They had pointed their toes as they extended one leg and then the other.

Piglet would look at Cecelia: her long limbs, her blond hair, her shaped eyebrows. She pictured her own mother there, the rolls of her body round in spandex. In her imagination, she wore a sweatband, her hair pushed back. She would be panting, her cheeks flushed with exertion. Cecelia's skin was always bronzed, and she did not seem to sweat.

"Good, girls," Ryan would call, watching their legs like a cat following a twitching piece of string. "You can tell you two are mother and daughter." Neither Piglet nor Cecelia ever corrected him.

Now, for their final session, Piglet arrived to find Cecelia and Ryan already in motion. Cecelia was on her back, her eyes closed, one leg lifted in the air. Ryan straddled her other leg, a hand at her hip, another on the ankle hovering above her face.

"Sorry," Piglet ventured. Cecelia opened her eyes.

"Hello, darling. We were just killing some time."

In the sauna, afterwards, Piglet watched Cecelia. She sat on the wooden bench opposite with her head thrown back. She wore a black one-piece, and as her chest rose, the fine wrinkles of her skin evened. The soft flesh of her thighs hung loose, but apart. Piglet looked down at her own legs and saw thighs packed as tightly as sausages, bulging beneath her. She noted Cecelia's toenails: varnished a dark, shiny red. Her collarbone: prominent beneath a fine gold chain. Her pubic line: smooth.

"Kitty's a good boy," Cecelia said, her head still tilted back.

"I know," Piglet said. "I feel so lucky to have found him." Cecelia was quiet.

"Marriage is . . ." Cecelia trailed off, head back.

"A blessing?" Piglet offered, unsure of where Cecelia was going with her train of thought.

"A commitment," Cecelia said, lifting her head.

"Of course," Piglet said, meeting her eyes. "I know."

"You don't," Cecelia said, lowering her head again, "but you'll make a good wife." Piglet ladled more water over the sauna's grey-white coals and, as they hissed, she glowed.

They showered, emerging with their cheeks flushed and hair wet. Piglet shuffled a towel across her body while Cecelia stripped to nakedness without inhibition. The first time she had done this, she laughed at Piglet's expression. "Oh, darling, wait until you come to the house in France." Piglet had protested her embarrassment as she stole glances at Cecelia's nipples, the hollow curve of her stomach, the twist of hair between her legs.

"Not long to go now, darling," Cecelia said outside the club as they kissed good-bye, bumping her cheekbone against Piglet's. "A fortnight will fly by."

Margot was blotting chamomile tea from her nose. They were in the Summertown Gail's, as they had been every Saturday lunchtime for the past seven weeks. When Piglet told her about Cecelia's exercise plan, Margot had wrinkled her nose. "I assume Kit hasn't been offered the same gift?" When Piglet shook her head, Margot laughed. "How about," she said, "once you're done working out, you come and meet me for lunch?" Piglet would text when she left the club, and Margot would meet her at the bakery, an order of fat-bottomed cinnamon buns waiting on the table she'd secured.

"Do you think Cecelia realises she sounds like she's reading from a Francis Ford Coppola script?" Margot adopted an Italian accent, lifting her hand, her wrist rotating. "You'll make a good wife for my son, sweet Cannoli."

Piglet leaned forward, waving at Margot, sugar on her fingertips, tears of laughter starting to roll down her face.

"Stop," she gasped, as the eyes of their neighbours slid sideways.

"Come now, Gabagool," Margot said, her wrist still raised, eyes almost closed with glee. She gestured wildly, nudging the woman at the next table. The woman's coffee slopped, crema spilling over porcelain. "Sorry," Margot said, dropping her wrist, her accent. Her eyes met Piglet's, and she grinned.

"That's *The Sopranos*, anyway," Piglet said, the hysteria subsiding. She wiped her eyes.

"It's still ridiculous," Margot said, tearing the end of her sugar-flecked cinnamon roll in two. "Posh people, hey?"

Piglet tilted her head from side to side.

"I still can't get over the fact she gets naked in front of you," Margot said, throwing the bread into her open mouth. "Imagine if your mum did that!"

"It's chic!" Piglet protested. "They're always naked at the house in France."

"Of course they are!" Margot shouted, mouth full, flinging her arms from her body. The woman whose coffee had spilled shifted her chair away. They looked at each other across the table and started to laugh again.

"Come on," Piglet said. "Let's go before we get kicked out."

"Hold on," Margot said, one hand at her back, the other on the table. "Sasha asked me to bring home some babka."

At the bakery door, Piglet ran her hands over her body as she watched her friend queue. Her limbs ached from her morning with Cecelia, but she enjoyed tensing her legs, noticing her muscles become taut. Her fingers caught on her jutting pelvis as Margot turned to wave, and, while looking at her friend, she felt svelte, her bones sharp beneath her skin. She still had her body, she thought, before shaking her head, chiding herself. Margot turned, facing forward until she reached the cashier. She laughed with the teenage boy on the till, and when he offered Margot her change, she indicated the tip jar.

They had been walking to their cars, arms linked, a brown paper bag clutched between them, when Margot stopped.

"Actually, do you mind if we just dip in here?" They had broken apart, Margot's one hand already on the door of the JoJo Maman Bébé, the other resting on top of her bump. Piglet followed her friend, trying to keep up, still clutching the paper bag of babka.

Margot's energy had shifted, the laughter—uncontainable, infectious—gone.

This was how it had been when she had first told Piglet about her pregnancy. Piglet and Kit had been invited for lunch—a rarity; Piglet usually cooked—and the mood had turned from easy, relaxed with full-bellied laughter, to reverential. Over Sasha's variation on a groundnut stew—soft sweet potatoes sunken in a nutty gravy instead of chicken—Piglet and Kit had been told the news. Piglet had put her wineglass down, sobered, as Margot shared their story, her fingers entwined with Sasha's. In the moments after Margot spoke the words, "Thirteen weeks today, actually," looking down at her belly as though she were in love, Piglet noticed the creamy residue of peanut butter on her palette, the tack of it on her tongue, and registered that she had not said a word. Then Kit clapped his hands together and moved to hug them, his action reminding her how to be. The rest of their lunch had been oddly formal: carefully enunciated syllables, small talk about spice blends, knives and forks held with elevated wrists. Margot had kept glancing in her direction, but Piglet did not know how to look at her, her friend, who seemed to belong to her less and less: someone else's wife, someone else's mother.

Now, in the baby shop, Margot reviewed the racks of body-suits with serenity, speaking in a low voice. She held her protruding stomach as she walked, her back arched. Piglet, in an attempt to recapture the pleasure of the bakery, picked up a sleepsuit and held it to her front.

"Hey, what do you think?" she called to Margot. "Would suit me, right?"

Piglet watched Margot's eyes narrow, her head shake. She watched as her friend did not laugh and, instead, turned away from her. Margot spoke with a sales assistant, a discussion in which information was exchanged in units of weeks, months, trimesters, and Piglet wandered, trying to find her way. She picked up a romper. This could be from her: it was embroidered with fruit.

"I thought I'd buy this for the baby," she said.

"Well, if you do, could you hang on to it for a year or so? It's for toddlers," Margot said, pulling at the label: eighteen to twenty-four months.

"Ah," said Piglet, pressing her lips together. "Babies have so many rules." There was a pause, and the silence seemed to gestate, the space growing between their bodies. Was this really happening to them? A gulf growing between them, stretching wider as Margot's belly swelled. Piglet felt repelled, the balls of her feet pushing into the ground, ready to move. "I've actually got to get going. My family's coming tomorrow, and I've planned to cook enough food for about twenty people."

"Oh?" asked Margot, her eyes wide, a hand outstretched, inviting Piglet closer, inviting Piglet back. "Tell me what's on the menu." Piglet did not move.

"Lamb—not up your street."

It would be the first time her family had made the trip to the Oxford house, and she and Kit had decided to eat at home. Everyone is more comfortable at home, they had agreed. The last time they had taken her parents for dinner was when they had lived in London, before she and Kit had vacated the capital in favour of Oxford and Cecelia and Richard's conditional house deposit. Piglet's parents had come to visit for the day, and they had all seen *Les Misérables*: a redeemed Christmas present for her mother. Once they left the theatre, the talk had turned to food, and her parents began to repeat themselves, reciting "Our treat" and "Well, you paid for the tickets" as they peered into restaurant windows.

Piglet had suggested a favourite dim sum restaurant in Chinatown. She had been giddy, leading her parents in their anoraks through central London from the Sondheim Theatre, and had forgotten that her father objected to chopsticks on principle: "They just don't make sense. Why would you not use a knife and fork?"

"There are no prices on this menu," he had murmured as they stood outside.

"I don't like all that MSG, myself," her mother had said. "It's not clean."

When they turned a corner onto Leicester Square, her father's face had lit up.

"Now there's somewhere we all know," he said, pointing to a Pizza Hut.

"Oh no, Dad," Piglet had said, grimacing.

"Too good for pizza now, are you?" he said, his chest thrown forward, square in his raincoat. Kit had placed a hand on her father's shoulder.

"How about a steak?" he said, her father deflating at his touch. "There's a great place in Covent Garden. Just two minutes away."

"Well, you can't go wrong with a steak, can you, Pig?" Her father let himself be guided by Kit as she and her mother fell in behind them.

They sat at a long table, spouses on one side and strangers on the other. Piglet's father spent the meal leaning in to her mother to avoid touching the shoulder of the man next to him, but he had eaten enthusiastically: "Look at the size of these chips, Linda." Her mother had complimented the olives.

But when Kit and Piglet plumped for a carafe of rioja—the sixth wine on the list, her father had noted—they had ordered the house red, and when the bill came, their steak-greased lips had tightened.

"One hundred and eighty-two pounds for four steaks?" her father asked under his breath as he ripped open his Velcro wallet and began to count out twenty-pound notes. Her mother tutted quietly, and Piglet felt the eyes of the neighbouring diners.

A waiter whisked away the notes, and her father had waited in his anorak, ready to leave, for the change. Piglet had felt as if she might melt into the floor: fat rendering into liquid.

So, they would eat at home. A visit to Oxford for her parents, Franny, and Darren would take in only the sights of Piglet's front garden and a glimpse of the Thames on the A34. But she and Kit had agreed—it was better this way. "We can go out in town with my parents," Kit had said. Piglet nodded. At home, they could serve expensive cuts of meat and wine from the top shelf of Waitrose without her parents worrying.

"OK, well, I'll see you next week for your dress fitting?"

Margot said from among the booties, the breast pumps, her fingers still reaching.

"Yeah." Piglet nodded, lifting her hand to Margot and, for some reason, the sales assistant.

"Love you," Margot said, moving forward, wrapping her arms around Piglet, and Piglet felt Margot's bump between them, hard against her body.

With his help, she had made a feast of her life. Sit, she encouraged their loved ones. Look at what I have made.

13 Days

The little table was laid for six.

Piglet had been careful with the crockery. White bone china would have made her parents eat with their elbows held high, afraid to cut their lamb. Instead, she had laid the table with mismatched tableware: assorted Wedgwood bowls nestled among speckled Denby dinner plates. The cutlery was antique, its ornate brassy handles engraved with flowers. Between hessian place mats were stubby candles burned down to slouching puddles and stout crystal tumblers filled with branches of eucalyptus. Kit had laughed when Piglet had told him how expensive it had been to curate such a shambolic setting, but she had smiled, picturing her parents: "You did all this, Pig?"

She had put Norah Jones's *Come Away with Me* on the music system in the kitchen. It was a record she knew her parents had on CD, and the unobtrusive sound that had always signalled the arrival of guests in Derby, and the beginning of best behaviour, drifted through the house.

Her outfit had been modelled on her mother: clothes obscured beneath an apron, a woman hosting in her own home. Although her mother wouldn't have spent the money she had on the loose-fitting Anthropologie dress. She tightened the apron, smoothing it over her front. They would be arriving soon to witness her handiwork, her house, her husband-to-be.

"T minus fifteen minutes," Kit said as he walked into the kitchen smelling of the shower and fresh aftershave.

Piglet was shelling chickpeas that had been soaking overnight. The process had taken nearly half an hour, and her fingers were now puckered with wetness, but Toni had told her that it was sacrilege to make hummus any other way. She would be serving a spread of Middle Eastern dishes: food you could eat with your hands. She imagined her parents—eyes wide—as they followed her example, scooping baba ghanoush into their mouths with blackened flatbreads. She looked over her shoulder.

"You look nice," she said. He was wearing a yellow cashmere jumper, a high white shirt collar at his neck. He walked behind her, kissing her ear.

"Can I help?" he asked, and Piglet smiled, imagining what they must look like.

"No."

She tipped the shelled chickpeas into a food processor and added four tablespoons of tahini, the same again of the good olive oil, two cloves of garlic, lemon juice, and a teaspoon each of ground coriander and cumin before pinching in large crystals of Maldon salt. Kit took a seat at the set table.

"Then let me tell you about the trip I've booked for us," he said. Piglet spun around, her jaw dropping in delighted surprise.

"What have you done?" she asked in playful reprimand.

"A little minimoon for us," Kit said, grinning.

"I thought we were going to wait until next year?"

"I thought not, darling one."

"Tell me, then," Piglet said, leaning forward.

"Well," Kit started, "Seb and I were talking, and he was telling me how he and Sophie were going to their chalet in France on the first weekend of November."

"Right," Piglet said, standing up straight.

"And I was thinking what a treat it would be to do a little skiing with my new wife. Eat cheese in the hot tub. Drink vin chaud on the slopes."

"With Seb and Sophie?" she asked. "The weekend after the wedding?"

"Yeah." Kit nodded. Piglet turned around to the chickpeas. "His parents' chalet is quite high up in Alpe d'Huez so normally gets snow from the end of October. And if there's no powder"—he shrugged—"we'll have only paid for flights. What do you—"

Piglet turned on the food processor, and the rest of Kit's question was swallowed by the sound of blending chickpeas, tahini, and olive oil.

"What do you think?" Kit repeated once Piglet had stopped blending.

"I think it will be our first weekend as a married couple," Piglet said, her back still turned to him.

"The perfect first weekend as a married couple," Kit nodded. "I've told Seb—"

She turned on the food processor again. The chickpeas pulverised to a paste.

"Piglet," he said, voice raised.

"Sorry," she said. "It needed to be smoother." Kit exhaled. He had started to talk again—something about flights, business class to celebrate—when the doorbell rang, its chime musical and polite. She jumped.

"They're early," she said.

"Darling," Kit said, standing up, "they're going to love everything."

In truth, she didn't know if her family would love her food: repeating the word "sumac," smacking their lips like the spice had been a lemon, an acidic taste left on their tongues. They would prefer pie, or lasagne, or casserole. Crumble, treacle tart, or bread-and-butter pudding.

She turned back to the kitchen, her hands fluttering over the hob as Kit opened the door. Piglet could hear her sister's voice in the hallway.

"You live on a building site," Franny observed before saying, "Hi, Kit."

"Lots of houses going up. It's a sought-after area," Kit said politely before his tone changed. "Daz, my man, good to see you." Piglet heard the clasping of hands. "Come through. She's in the back, cooking up a storm."

"Piglet!" Franny cried before embracing Piglet from behind. Piglet had been squeezing another lemon—the flavour profile of the hummus was too flat with tahini—and her hands were filled with spent pith. She turned to hug her sister with arms extended away from them both and felt Franny's small body against hers.

"Hi, Darren," Piglet said over her sister's shoulder. Darren, who was short and well built, with hair shorn closely to his scalp, nodded hello. "Where're Mum and Dad?" Franny pulled back, and Piglet looked at her sister's slight frame, shrouded in a magenta puffer jacket. Franny waved over her shoulder.

"They're coming," she said.

"Looking into your neighbour's houses, I think," Darren said.

"In the meantime, can I tempt either of you with a drink?" Kit asked.

"Please!" Franny said. "I'm gasping."

"What can I get you?" Kit asked, moving his hips and hands from side to side. Piglet had never seen him like this with guests: clownish in his accommodating. "We've got everything," he said. "Wine, beer, something sparkling, something stronger, something soft."

"Something soft!" Franny laughed. "You're going to be marrying my sister in a fortnight and still so much to learn. Wine, please. Whatever's open."

"Coming up." Kit clicked and pointed his fingers at Franny. Piglet blushed into the hummus. "And what about you, Darren?" Kit asked, starting again with the hips and the hands.

"A beer?" Darren asked, and Piglet noted the absence of any please or thank you. Earlier in the week she had bought beer with Darren in mind. When they lived in London, she had once offered him an Aperol spritz, and he had laughed in her face before leaving their flat to pick up a six-pack from a Tesco Metro. When she had stood in front of the rows of shiny silver tins in Waitrose, she had purposefully passed over the Carlsberg and the Coors and purchased brown bottles of Westmalle, a golden beer she had read was one of the best blond ales you could buy on this side of the Channel.

Piglet looked up from a ball of labneh she had been coaxing from its muslin when Kit handed Darren the bottle. He inspected the label before taking a small sip.

"Nice, isn't it?" Piglet said. Darren nodded, swallowing. "That's a proper beer."

"Oh, that sounds like them," Kit said, peering back into the hall.

Piglet heard her father's voice from the hallway: "Looks big even with furniture in, doesn't it?"

"Hi, Dad," Piglet called from the kitchen. "We're through here." She turned to Kit, who was swigging beer with Darren, and hissed: "Can you go and say hello, please?" Franny's eyes slid between them, her hands clutched around a glass of wine.

"It's alright," Kit whispered as he walked past, laying a hand on her arm.

A second round of cheek-kissing started in the hallway. As Piglet listened to shoes being removed—"We've brought our slippers"—she poured a glass of wine and took a gulp. Red liquid spilled over the corners of her lips, and she wiped her face with the back of her hand. Darren, who was sitting at the table, smirked.

"It wasn't a bad drive," her father was saying over his shoulder to Kit. "Straight down the M1 and then a couple of A roads. Door-to-door in less than two hours." He entered the kitchen. "And would you look at this." He held out his arms, beckoning to Piglet.

"Hi, Dad," Piglet said, her voice muffled against his shoulder.

"Look at you, Duck," he said, holding her at arm's length. Piglet's mother peered over his shoulder.

"Look at you," she echoed, shuffling forward for her own hug. "And this is for you and Kit." Her mother held out a bottle of wine. "It's from all of us," she said.

Piglet took the bottle, eyes lingering on the cartoonish label as she laid a hand on her mother's arm. "Thank you. We love Shiraz," she said. Piglet's mother nodded, and for a moment her parents stood there, coats on, in the kitchen.

Kit clapped his hands together.

"John, Linda, what can I get you to drink? And let me take your coats."

Glasses in hand, her family drifted away from the kitchen and the set table and towards the living room. "Make yourselves comfortable," Kit said before ducking back into the kitchen. "Are you OK?" he whispered. Piglet was rolling out rounds of dough, lowering them into a frying pan that shimmered with heat. She nodded, not looking up from her rolling pin. "Have you got a drink?" he asked, and she pointed towards her wine-glass, half-empty, half-full. She paused her rolling as he kissed her from behind before stepping back into the living room. "So, how are we all?" he asked, as Piglet flipped a flatbread, one side now blistered black.

Between breads, Piglet ducked into the living room, catching snatches of conversation. She worried for Kit as he rattled through icebreakers. Work: her father's, Franny's, Darren's, his. Holidays: none planned. "Alpe d'Huez, you say? France, is it?" Sport: Kit asking if her father was a rugby man, the conversation faltering when Kit was asked which football team he supported.

"Well, we're Rams, of course," Darren was saying, gesturing between himself and her father, as Piglet entered the living room. "But we don't agree when it comes to the Premier

League." Piglet watched Kit nod attentively as her father called across the room.

"I'm sorry, son, but Leicester are shocking. I can't forgive it, even if they're our neighbours." Kit looked up, smiling at Piglet.

"How are we getting on?" he asked. Piglet laid a hand on his shoulder.

"Ten minutes. Lamb's warming through."

"Don't you think, Kit?" her father said, as if Piglet had not entered the room, as if she had not spoken.

"Please," Franny said, closing her eyes. "I get enough football talk at home. Can we have a tour, instead?"

"Kit started it!" her father said, laughing with Darren. Kit quickly joined in.

"Come on then, Banana," Piglet said to Franny. "Although I am quite precious about the carpets still, so shoes off."

Franny kicked off a pair of sagging shearling boots. Her parents, already slippered, stood. Darren removed his trainers and became even shorter, his denim jeans too long, covering his greying socks. For a moment, it felt formal, or funereal, the six of them standing there with their shoes off.

Piglet shepherded her family from room to room, fielding questions about bathroom tiles and paint colours. Kit trailed behind the group, nodding when Piglet asked him about the details of their home insurance, their broadband provider. "That's right, darling," he said, and her mother giggled.

"You'd pay half the price for this house in Derby," Franny said, looking out of the window in the back bedroom. Behind her, Piglet pulled a face.

"Well, we're not in Derby, are we, Franny?" she said, shepherding the group back towards the stairs. As her parents, Kit, and Darren traipsed down, discussing their choice of carpet, Franny grabbed Piglet's wrist.

"Can we stay up here?"

"Lunch." Piglet gestured downstairs, starting to laugh.

"I have something I need to tell you," Franny whispered. Her eyes were wide, her grip tight on Piglet's arm. Piglet's gaze dropped to her sister's stomach, her temperature rising, and Franny shook her head. "Nothing like that."

Piglet led Franny into Kit's office and closed the door behind them. Franny sank into the corner armchair, and Piglet crouched in front of her, searching her sister's fine-boned face. Franny had always been the slighter of them both. When they were younger, Piglet had thought Franny, two years her junior, would eventually match her size, but where Piglet's body had filled, Franny's had not. As teenagers, they would stand together in front of the bathroom mirror in their underwear, noting the faults of their bodies. Piglet would look at her sister—shorter, smaller—and feel ashamed at the sight of her own skin.

"It's Darren," Franny said, her head down, hands in her lap.

"What is it, Fran? What has he done?" Piglet leaned forward as Franny picked at the skin of her thumb.

"It's his company," Franny said, and Piglet exhaled: breathing away the thought of her sister's boyfriend wrapped around a stranger in a dark, anonymous nightclub. Darren ran his own business: something to do with fitting furniture in chain coffeehouses all over the Midlands. He had been self-employed from the age of seventeen, and when he had met Kit and the talk turned to university, Darren had recited the revenue he had made at ages eighteen, nineteen, and twenty.

"What happened?" Piglet asked, squeezing her sister's knee.

"It's gone." Franny sighed. "It's all gone."

"How can that be?"

"Something about suppliers, contracts changing. I don't know."

"What does it mean?" Piglet asked.

"There's no business left. No money." Franny looked up, eyes shining.

They had been saving, Piglet knew. They had moved in with her parents, and when Piglet had confided in Franny that she could never have done the same, Franny had told her that she hadn't had to.

"I told Mum, but Darren doesn't want Dad to know," Franny said, sniffing, and Piglet nodded. "I just wanted to tell you before the wedding. I know we were supposed to be getting you the new blender, but I don't think we can right now," Franny said, looking around the room.

"Franny, that's fine," Piglet said. Franny shook her head.

"I know Kit's family will probably be doing these big gifts and I know his parents are paying for everything. I didn't want to let you down."

"Banana," Piglet said, "when would you ever?" Franny jerked her shoulders. "Can we do anything to help?" she asked, feeling the implication of Kit—his inherited stability—hang in the air between them.

"Not unless you own a few hundred coffee shops." Franny

got to her feet, shaking out her blond hair. "Don't mention this to Darren, will you?" she asked, looking at Piglet.

"Of course not," Piglet nodded.

⸻

"I turned the lamb down," Kit said as Piglet and Franny walked down the stairs. "I think it's ready to go." They exchanged a look as Franny sat back down on the velvet sofa, her hand twisting into Darren's lap.

"Yes." Piglet nodded. "I'll start serving up now."

She divided a large bowl of couscous, studded with shards of pistachio and pomegranate seeds, between two roughly shaped earthenware platters. She transferred the lamb stew from the Le Creuset to an oven-warmed tagine pot and scattered over toasted, flaked almonds. The hummus, baba ghanoush, and labneh had been spooned into terra-cotta ramekins, and she finished each dish with a flourish of grassy, yellow-green extra virgin olive oil and a flurry of fresh herbs. A green salad, trailing tendrils of coriander, parsley, and mint, stood set for service. The scorched flatbreads were stuffed into hammered copper serving bowls. Kit moved around her, ferrying full dishes to the table, removing candles and jars of greenery to make room for her feast.

"Thank you," she said to Kit, her hand on his arm. He kissed her, and Piglet felt the eyes of her father, her mother, her sister.

"Where shall we sit?" her mother asked, as they hovered with their wineglasses.

"Wherever you like." Piglet waved her hands.

As they took their seats, Franny and Darren struggling to

coordinate themselves on the bench, they surveyed the food. Piglet named her dishes, pointing to each in turn, and her family nodded. "Do dig in, by the way," she said. "We don't stand on ceremony here," and the symphony of spoon lifting and "'Scuse fingers" began.

"What a feast," Kit groaned, leaning back from half-empty dishes of couscous and stew. "I think we could have fed another six people." Piglet dipped a scrap of bread into the last of the labneh.

"I think I got a little carried away," she said, smiling at the end-of-meal mess. "But I like everyone to feel like they can eat as much as they want." She put the bread in her mouth and chewed.

"You're a feeder." Her mother nodded, placing her cutlery together on her plate, gravy-covered apricots pushed to one side.

"The stew will keep, but can anyone finish the dips?" Piglet asked, offering up the near-empty bowls of hummus and baba ghanoush.

"See," her mother said as her father laughed.

"Typical Pig," he said, shaking his head. He addressed Kit across the table: "I assume you've noticed how she can't leave a table until every bite has been hoovered up."

Kit looked from Piglet to her father.

"Well, who would want to waste any of this?" he said, placing a hand on Piglet's knee beneath the table.

"You've always been the same," her father said, turning to Piglet. "Even when you were a little girl." He looked at her, smiling, from the other side of the table.

"That's how she got her nickname," her mother piped up. Kit's fingers tightened on Piglet's knee.

"That's right." Her parents nodded at each other before retelling the story of their daughter who ate. Darren picked up a spoon and the bowl of baba ghanoush as her father recited their family lore, her mother correcting, interjecting.

"And then there was the time with Franny's birthday cake." Her mother laid her hand on her chest, shaking her head.

"Franny's thirteenth, so Piglet's fourteen or fifteen at this point," her father said, buoyed by the beginning of this familiar story.

"And as it's a special birthday—a teenager—we buy Franny her favourite." Her mother took over.

"A chocolate cake," her father confirmed.

"That's right," her mother nodded. "Then on the evening of Franny's birthday party—we had a big party planned with the family—we go to get the cake from the fridge." Her mother looked at her father.

"And what do we find?" he said on cue.

"Nothing more than a slice left!" she exclaimed. "I mean, Piglet quite often finished off Franny's food."

"You always have loved your food." Her father nodded.

"And Franny's always been a little stick of a thing," her mother said. Franny raised her wineglass, her eyebrows.

"But this was something else."

"Something else."

"Anyway," her father resumed, "we didn't have far to look, did we, Pig?" Piglet smile-grimaced.

"I'm not sure you were so concerned about food going to waste then." Her mother laughed.

"More concerned about food going in your face!" her father shouted.

Piglet was aware of Darren's wide smile between swigs of beer.

"We had to put Franny's candles in a quiche," her mother said.

"I'd forgotten about the quiche." Her father was laughing. "Do you remember that, Piglet?" He sighed. "Do you?"

Piglet remembered it differently.

Sometime after Franny's twelfth birthday, the room she and her sister shared had begun to smell sweetly of rot. The scent caught in Piglet's nose as she lay in the top bunk, staring at luminescent stars and planets stuck to the stippled ceiling, their blue tack cores opaque. When she asked Franny if she could smell the same, she had been met with silence. In the morning light, Piglet had held her nose in the air, inhaling, trying to track down the scent, and Franny had shouted. "Stop being a freak!" she had screamed. Her mother stomped up the stairs: "I don't care who started it, I'm finishing it," she had said. Franny had opened the windows.

Piglet had found the stash of food a few days later. She and Franny had been rearranging their room—something to entertain themselves with while their parents were at work—when the decaying heap had been found in the bottom of a desk drawer. Amid the chaos—their bunk bed in the middle of the room, mouldering suppers among their stationery—Franny had told her. She confided what she had been doing in crumbs: scraps of information that had scared Piglet. When Piglet had told her she should at least tell Mum, Franny had cried. When Piglet had told her she couldn't keep doing this, Franny had begun to shake, her breathing jagged. So, Piglet had bargained: "Promise me you'll eat at least a quarter at teatime, and I'll take care of the rest."

She checked their room for food, she watched Franny's
ribs when she changed, she thought she was doing the right
thing.

When the cake had been brought into the house, nearly a
year later, Franny had curled into a ball in Piglet's bunk. "I can't
have people watch me eating it. I can't, I can't." Franny had
screwed up her eyes, pressing the heels of her hands to her face,
rocking among Piglet's pyjamas, her old stuffed animals. She had
started to shake her head, slowly at first, but then violently. Piglet had moved to her, using her body to still her sister's. Franny
twisted beside her but made no effort to escape.

"It's OK, Banana," Piglet said, stroking her back. "We'll
work something out together." Franny's breath juddered. "It's
OK." Franny's body went limp, and Piglet hugged her tight.

She thought she was doing the right thing.

"Did she tell you she's being promoted?" Kit asked, leaning
over the table, his voice loud, as her parents' laughter subsided.
Piglet's stomach twisted.

"Already?" her father asked, his eyes wide. "I thought—"

"Yes, already," Kit said, nodding. "They would have been
fools not to." He spread his hands wide. "All of these are recipes
from your books, aren't they?"

Piglet nodded, and her father looked between her and her
fiancé.

"Well, Pig, you should have said." He lifted his glass as Piglet turned away, looking at the table.

"She's too modest," Kit said. "But she's brilliant. Everyone
at her work knows it."

Her family left after they had finished slices of love cake and a conversation about wedding-eve sleeping arrangements. They would all be staying in less than a fortnight, arriving the day before Piglet and Kit were due to be married. Her parents would be in the spare bed, and Franny and Darren on a sofa bed in the living room, while Piglet would be upstairs, Kit at his parents'.

"We're looking forward to seeing them again." Her mother nodded as she pulled on her coat. "A proper chance to say thank you." Her father averted his eyes, car keys jangling in one hand. When they reversed out of the driveway, Franny blowing kisses from the backseat, Piglet and Kit waved from their doorway.

"Why did you tell them I'd been promoted?" Piglet asked, after she closed the door.

"I'm sorry." Kit sighed. "Just the way they were going on."

"That's very sweet of you, but you know I haven't got the job yet."

"I know," he said. "But you will." He moved to hug her.

"Thank you," she said, her voice muffled against his chest.

They cleaned the kitchen together: her transferring leftovers to plastic containers and him washing the wineglasses at the sink. Once they had finished, they would migrate to the living room, wrap themselves in blankets, and find something to watch on the television. Maybe he'd eat the last of the cake. Piglet paused in the middle of searching for a Tupperware lid. She walked over to Kit at the sink, wrapping her arms around his waist. He twisted his body, his wet hands still among the suds of the wineglasses. They kissed, their bodies curved towards one another.

"I am lucky to have found you," she said, resting her head on his shoulder.

"To have found each other," he corrected, turning back to the sink.

"No," she said, pulling at his torso, turning him around until his hands left the glasses and trailed a stream of bubbles down his arms. "You'd be fine without me."

"Not true," he contradicted.

"But you'd still be you. You'd be with someone else, but you'd still be who you are now, living your life. You'd still be happy." She paused. "I don't know where I'd be if I wasn't with you. Maybe back in Derby, maybe living with my family."

"Top and tailing with Darren," Kit smirked.

"I'm serious," she said.

"After the wedding, we don't have to see them until Christmas if you don't want to," Kit said. Piglet nodded and held him tight.

"Thank you. After the wedding, you'll be my family," she said, and she felt Kit's head nodding above her.

I have to tell you something, he said. Leaning over her in bed like that, his face looked slack, full of blood.

His eyes were creasing and his lips were curling. Tears, she realised, her mind slow, fear unfurling in the bowl of her pelvis.

He reached out, his hand touching her thigh. His fingers crept at her, and she felt her eyes swivel in her head, looking down at his clutching extremities. She heard him talking, saw him grasping, and noticed how her flesh puckered beneath his fingers.

In between the creases of their sheets, he told her what he had done.

She lay broken. Her body, naked, looked as if it had been spilled.

Do you still want to get married? he asked, and she could not bring herself to shrug.

I have to get up soon, she said. There was work in the morning, a wedding in thirteen—twelve—days. He nodded, he lay down next to her, mirroring her curled body, two question marks in their premarital bed.

12 Days

Her face was not her own. In their en suite, blackness at the frosted window, she inspected her reflection. Puffed eyes; red, blotted cheekbones; a bulbous nose. She tugged at her swollen lips. She bared her teeth in the mirror.

She could sense him, in the next room, awake in the dark.

In the shower she tested her tolerance. How hot could she run the water before she stepped out from the steaming stream, instincts kicking in? When she came to towel herself dry, her skin glowed like a cooked lobster. She had not eaten lobster until she had met him.

She applied makeup in the bathroom, her mouth gaping, leaning over to wipe the fogged mirror. She smeared foundation, painted little flicking stripes over her eyelids, and rubbed red into her lips. She leaned back: assessing. You wouldn't know by looking at her.

"I've made you breakfast," he said at the bottom of the stairs, "and coffee." He was holding a bowl of porridge and her usual mug, face haggard, dressing gown loose. Piglet looked at the bowl and was not moved by the banana neatly chopped, the honey carefully swirled. She found she didn't have a single word to say to him. He stood there as she pulled on her trainers, the coffee cooling. She picked up her bag and rolled her tongue up to the roof of her mouth as she unlocked the door.

"I love you," he said.

She closed the door behind her.

Their neighbours had decorated for Halloween. Only the eighteenth of October, and the houses on their road were covered in spiders, littered with pumpkins. When had it started? When had it happened? She hadn't noticed anything last year, the year before, the year before that.

She walked quickly and felt her flesh ripple in the stark, quiet cold. She noticed, as she pulled her coat more tightly around her, how the exposed hair on her wrists arched, long and dark. At the train station, she was shocked to find everything as it should be: commuters, coffee cups, the 7:20 on time.

The sun was up by the time she reached Paddington. She found the daylight relentless and had the urge to burrow, to be underground. At the Praed Street traffic lights, where she usually turned left to walk through Hyde Park and on to the office, she turned right, in the direction of the gaping mouth of the Bakerloo line.

Down, down, down, she went with the other Monday commuters, the other unhappy jostlers shuttled in from outside of the city. She turned right, southbound, and was funnelled farther underground. Three tubes passed before the tide of people pushed her to the front, presenting her body like a stone washed up on a shore. In the carriage, people pressed against her.

Edgware Road, Marylebone, Baker Street. A woman boarded at Regent's Park holding a baguette. She stood between a grey suit and a blue and, as the train juddered forward, the woman sunk her teeth into the bread. Piglet looked at her watch: eight thirty. She shook her head, adjusting her position to watch the woman. It was a bánh mì, she realised, stuffed with sausage, coriander, shredded carrot, pickled cucumber. Mayonnaise and sriracha oozed onto the woman's fingers. As she watched, a glob of sauce fell from the sandwich to land on one of Grey Suit's shiny, black shoes. He shuffled, tutting, adjusting his Air-Pods. The woman raised a finger, nodded an apology, but kept chewing, kept eating. Piglet watched. Oxford Circus, Piccadilly Circus, Charing Cross. The woman still hadn't finished the sandwich when they pulled into Embankment and the intersection with the Circle and District lines. Piglet thought about staying, about following her, about slipping into her life.

The Fork House office was already busy when she stepped out of the lift: employees circling a table.

"Over here." Olivia the intern waved madly at her. "Look," she squealed, pointing at a bunch of roses and a cookie the size of a cartwheel, shaped like a heart. Twelve days, the icing read.

"Does he have a brother?" Olivia giggled.

"No," Piglet said, picking up the roses.

When Toni arrived, she had to peer around the flowers to say good morning.

"From the boy?" she asked, removing her leather jacket.

"Yes," Piglet said.

"He knows what he's doing, doesn't he?" Toni said as she sat down at her computer.

"Yes," Piglet said again.

By the time Piglet left her desk for lunch, she had five messages from him. Are you OK? Can we talk? I love you. Can I call you? Can you call me? She had opened each of them as they arrived to leave her read receipt. Her phone was in her bag as she walked down the stairs, out of the office. She looked at her watch—she would wait for thirty minutes to pass before she replied. She crossed the road from the Fork House building on to the embankment. She walked in the opposite direction of the Thames's current and felt she had to fight against the tide of the river, of the people—everyone in her way. She pushed past tourists stopping to take photographs of Waterloo Bridge, the Houses of Parliament, Big Ben shrouded in scaffolding. A man dropped his phone as she shoved past, and he ran after her shouting about cracked screens, stupid bitches. She turned to stare; he stopped. At Westminster Abbey, she pulled out her phone and told Kit that she was on her lunch break and out of the office. The screen lit up in Victoria Tower Gardens: it vibrated with his name, his face smiling up at her. She stopped walking, leaning on the wall overlooking the river. She slid her finger across the screen, tracing his smile, and lifted the phone to her ear. She counted: one, two, three, four.

"Hi." His voice was small.

Five, six, seven, eight, nine.

"Are you there?" he asked. She considered, she looked down.

"Yes," she said. The riverbank was litter strewn, lined with pieces of broken glass, bricks worn away into misshapen red rocks.

"Did you get my gift?"

"Yes," she said again. The water was dirty, foaming as it lapped at the shore.

"Do you want to talk?" he asked.

"You called me," she said. She heard his breathing.

"I feel so sick," he said. "I haven't been able to concentrate. I haven't been able to take any calls this morning. I've barely even been able to eat." He paused, leaving a space for her that she did not fill. "I can't stop thinking about what I've done to you. To us." He paused again, and Piglet refused his offer to soften. "We're getting married in two weeks." His voice cracked as she mentally corrected him: twelve days. She held the phone away from her ear, up to the sky, and could hear him sobbing. She thought about the wedding, the guests. She thought about Margot in her maid of honour dress, altered to accommodate her pregnant belly. She imagined telling her: Margot swearing, indignant; Sasha shaking her head. She brought the phone back to her ear. She heard his ragged breathing.

"Are you there?" he asked.

She pictured Franny. This time she was sitting in the office armchair, Franny at her feet. Her sister's eyes would widen—shock and relief. She would throw her arms around her. If it's too good to be true, it probably is, she would say. Nobody is perfect, Piglet.

"Yes," she said, her voice level.

Her parents would nod. The tilt of their heads confirming that yes, this daughter didn't know what she was doing after all, and she was so, so far from home.

Sophie would pout, shake her head, and tell her she should still come to Alpe d'Huez. Although, she'd add, head cocked, I'll have to double-check with Seb. Sandra might soften—a shame—beckoning Piglet in, averting her eyes, embarrassed. She imagined Cecelia in the sauna: Marriage is a commitment.

"I don't know what to say," she said.

"Say anything," he whined. She tilted her head back, and water glazed her eyes as she balanced tears. What could she say? What sentence would pierce him while leaving her intact? She had built her life so carefully around him. To say something, to do something, to feel something, would be to self-destruct.

"Be angry with me," he pleaded, and she could hear the crumple in his face, the stoop in his body.

"No," she replied. "I'm not going to punish you."

"Please," he said, his voice rising.

"No," she said and hung up the call.

She went back to her desk. She read emails and felt the weight of her body: a stone in her office chair. Olivia had questions, and she answered. Toni had jokes, and she laughed. Kit had apologies and apologies and apologies, and she read them.

Her running clothes had been packed for today—twelve days, maybe—and she contemplated them as the office clock ticked towards five. In the Fork House bathrooms, she changed, folding her skirt into her bag. She buckled the rucksack across her chest as a publicist came out of a cubicle. She looked at Piglet, smiling. "Rather you than me," she said.

Piglet felt no shame sitting, wet and red, on the five forty-five: she was in leggings, trainers; she had moved her body more than any of these commuters. As the train pulled out of the station, heading west, she thought about the evening ahead. She would go to Waitrose, as usual for a Monday. After the weekend, they were always out of milk. After this weekend, she wanted to be out of the house. Normally, she would arrive home with armfuls of shopping to find Kit reclined on the sofa, or in his office, tapping at his keyboard, the day still not over. She would unload, and they would reacquaint: how was your day, what's for dinner, I missed you. What would he be doing today, she wondered? Would he help her with the bags? Would he put away the groceries she had bought to generate another week of their eating together?

The walk from Oxford train station to their house was cold. The sweat on her running clothes had dried, streaking to salt. In the night air, her bones ached; the exposed back of her neck pimpled. She stood for a moment when she reached their front door: he would be inside. She pulled her keys from inside her rucksack and turned from the door to the car. On the driveway, she revved the engine until it made a ripping sound. She saw a shadow in the door's window. She pressed the accelerator.

When she returned, shopping rustling in the backseat, the house was dark. He had wanted her to demand he stay in a hotel, sleep on Seb's sofa. She hadn't, but he might have done so anyway—fled after he heard her on the drive, desperate for a doghouse. Her white fist, weighed down by reusable bags, gripped her keys as she turned them in the door.

The heat of the house hit her. Her glasses fogged, and she was blind, struggling with the bulk of the groceries. She kicked the door closed, hands still tight. Her lenses began to clear, and

from the doorway she could see the dim living room. At the
sound of the door, her struggling in the hall, a body shot up
from the sofa. He had been lying there in the dark. She hauled
the shopping bags past him, through to the kitchen. She turned
on the light, and it was too bright, bouncing off the walls, windows, and one dirty breakfast bowl in the sink, a spoonful of
porridge remaining. His, she knew; he always had one mouthful
too much.

He hovered in the dark, hands gripping the sofa like a life-
boat. Light from the kitchen spilled onto his face: tear-streaked,
shining. "I thought you'd left me," he said.

"Monday is shopping night," she replied.

"Yeah, but I thought you left me. I was so scared," he rasped,
face folding.

Two pints of milk, two tubs of Greek yoghurt, Parmesan,
and smoked mackerel for the fridge.

"Well, I haven't," she said. "I went shopping."

Whole wheat spaghetti, two tins of chickpeas, two tins of
tomatoes, and red lentils for the cupboard.

"Are you OK?" he asked.

Garlic, sweet potatoes, and red onions for the bottom
drawer.

"Darling, please talk to me," he begged.

Bananas, apples, and Comice pears for the fruit bowl.

"Darling, please. I can't have you not talking to me."

A bar of 85 percent Green and Black's and Kettle Chips for
the top cupboard.

"Darling."

"Can you put the bags back in the car, please?" she asked,
not looking at him.

"Yes," he replied, head lowered in penance.

She did not want to cook for him, but she did want to eat.

The cold had made her crave pasta: hot and steaming and slick. She would make carbonara, with lots of garlic and more egg yolks than were necessary. There was butter in the fridge and leftover bacon from the weekend. How many years had it been since she had stood there, apron on, him pouring wine for her family?

She considered making only enough for herself, but the thought of him bringing this up in a future argument—how many would there be?—made her weigh two hundred grams of dried spaghetti.

"Where do we go from here?" she asked.

He presented himself with contrition, body meek, shuffling towards her, and the decision, she knew, would be hers to make.

She set the bowls down at the table, which he had laid with shiny cutlery, an apologetic solitary pepper mill. "Thank you, darling, this looks delicious," he said. She said nothing; he wasn't welcome.

They ate in silence before she turned on the radio, inviting the blather of a DJ into their kitchen so she could stop listening to his breathing, his regretful snuffling.

Her bowl was clean within five minutes, and she stood to rinse it and load the dishwasher. He remained at the table. "Sorry, I'm not hungry," he said. "I just don't feel like I can eat. Maybe I can have it for lunch tomorrow?"

"Fine," she said.

"I'm going to get a shower."

"Fine," she said again.

His carbonara was barely touched. The cream of eggs and

starched water had pooled beneath the whole wheat spaghetti: nutty, brown, virtuous. Little puddles of fat were exuding from the bacon. The grated Parmesan lay flat.

She heard the shower turn on overhead, and she reached for his bowl. She stood at the sink, her running clothes stiff with dried sweat, picked up his fork, and ate until the bowl was clean.

She was proud, in a way, that she could still smile as the delicious life she had been savouring turned maggoty in her mouth.

9 Days

In the following days he would text her. Are you OK? Are you OK? Are you OK? Piglet would pick up her phone immediately, open the message, but not reply. She would put a timer on for one hour. Yes. Yes. Yes, she'd reply. She was fine. She was managing.

She had been arriving first in the office. This way, she had time to rehearse speaking, practise smiling, before her colleagues started to file in, Toni nodding, rolling her eyes at the weather, the Northern Line, the bus. She had time, if she wanted, to let tears silently slip down her face, drip onto her pile of submissions, little circles of salt water wrinkling the paper.

They had learned to stop talking about it. Life had gone on, and it was both fine and terrible. She often thought back to Sunday night, his face looming over her in their bed: I have to tell you something. It had felt so huge at the time, so tectonically altering, she thought that they might have to take a break from life, a few days of annual leave to assess the scale of the damage. But they hadn't. She woke up. She went to work. She smiled at people all day before coming home, cooking dinner, and returning to bed with him. When she woke in the night, she tried to unravel what had happened, what was happening. She wondered—if they were to carry on as they had before—what was less important. She wondered—if they were to continue as if nothing had ever happened—if it was his betrayal, or herself, that meant so little, that it could be so easily brushed aside.

Piglet heard the Fork House lift doors open. She snorted mucus and began to wipe her face with the back of her hand. Sandra emerged, her blond hair obscured beneath a slouching grey beanie. She was smiling, walking towards her, two fingers extended from a coffee cup in greeting. Then she saw Piglet's face.

"What's going on here?" she asked, and Piglet wiped her face again.

"Oh, nothing," Piglet said, looking up, smiling. "Sorry."

Sandra looked at her, frowning.

"Come to my office." She beckoned, turning around, pulling the beanie off her head, ruffling her hair. Piglet stood. Sandra held her glass door open, and Piglet stepped in, stooping, her shoulders sloping. Sandra pulled off her coat, hanging it on the back of her chair, and threw the grey beanie onto her desk. "Sit." She gestured to another chair. "Do you want a cup of tea?"

Piglet's stomach contracted. How excruciating it would be for Sandra to make her a cup of tea: for Piglet to sit in her office while she boiled the kettle, brewed the tea, and discarded the sodden bag. Piglet imagined her handing it over—"There you go, love"—and shook her head.

"I've already got one, thank you," Piglet lied. Sandra made for the office door, gesturing her thumb towards Piglet's desk.

"Let me get it for you, then," she said, and Piglet half stood from her chair.

"No," she said, too loudly. "I've already finished it."

"OK," Sandra said, stepping deliberately back into the office, taking a seat in her high-backed chair. "Do you want to tell me what's going on?"

Piglet didn't want to; she shook her head, but as she did so she felt pressure—hot, prickling, insistent—gather behind her eyes. Sandra watched as the tears fell, and Piglet lowered her head, resigned to her body's betrayal. Nothing was said.

"I've put pressure on you, I know,"

Sandra said, breaking the silence. "Applying for the editor job, on top of everything else you're doing. I know the wedding is fast approaching too."

The wedding, Piglet thought. The job.

"It's OK," she sniffed, her head still lowered.

"I know the timing is not great for you. Weddings are"— Sandra waved her hand above her, frowning—"hectic," she concluded. Piglet nodded, eyes fixed on her hands clasped in her lap. "When I got married the second time," Sandra continued, "I only invited a few people and I still took a whole week off beforehand." She smiled, tilting her head to one side. "One of the many life lessons that comes with remarrying, I suppose." She sighed.

Piglet looked up. Beyond shallow how-was-your-weekend small talk, Sandra had never spoken to her about her life outside the office.

"But it would be a shame," Sandra said, meeting her eyes,

"if you missed out on the editor job." Piglet nodded, her glasses steaming, flecked with tears. She pulled them off, and Sandra leaned forward and placed a cool hand over Piglet's. Piglet stayed still: an animal caught off guard.

"I tell you what," Sandra said, stroking a soft thumb over Piglet's knuckles. "Get some work done this morning and then get out of the office this afternoon. Find a quiet spot and put together a cover letter and polish your CV. Send it to me when you're done." Piglet took a breath, her chest rising. "OK?" Sandra asked, pulling back. "We can't call you to interview unless you apply."

"Thank you, Sandra," she said, wiping her glasses on the corner of her sleeve.

"Of course." Sandra was using her feet to roll her chair back towards her desk. She looked up at Piglet as she stood to leave. "I wish I looked like you after I'd been crying." She smiled. "Nobody will be able to tell."

Piglet left her desk at twelve. The minute hand aligned with the hour in the middle of the office clock as she turned off her computer, zipped up her bag. Between emails, and questions from marketing about cover copy, she had been thinking about her family, about Margot. Her father, whistling at the prospect of thirty thousand pounds. Franny and Darren, saving. Her mother, when she had received her pay rise, saying, "You're a career girl now. You're going to have it all."

Piglet had been replying to Margot's voice notes with text messages, unable to record herself, to bring a brightness to her voice.

"OK, I'm about to send you a photo," Margot's latest note had said. "Can you guess if this image shows A, a doner kebab; B, a mature tree trunk; or C, my left ankle?"

Piglet replied with a string of pita emojis, and Margot had immediately quipped: "If I could reach, I would genuinely shave a bit off to check." Piglet heard Margot audibly shifting on a leather sofa, her breathing heavy. "Sasha," Margot started calling out, "Sash! Come and see if my leg's turned into a shawarma. Bring garlic mayo!" The note ended with Sasha's laughter, her incredulity.

Piglet sent a row of little salivating yellow faces. How could she say anything else?

She had planned to find a quiet place across the river, somewhere she could order a coffee and eat her packed lunch: a satsuma and a sandwich prepared by Kit. Perhaps the café in the National Theatre, its seats likely sparsely occupied on a Thursday afternoon before any matinee. She would cross Blackfriars Bridge and walk along the river past the OXO Tower, Observation Point, and she would sit to update her CV.

The leaves on the sycamores that lined the Southbank Boardwalk were yellowed, falling. The trees' bark was dappled green and cream: an impressionist's camouflage. Tourists were weaving between the trees, kicking leaves, stopping to pose, taking pictures of nothing—the better views were down the river. She had intended to stop, but Piglet was walking past the National Theatre, its stories of concrete austere and angular against the midday sky. There was a crowd gathering beyond Waterloo Bridge.

Street food, she saw. Silky pasta, doughy pizza, steaming pho, obnoxiously tall burgers. Benches had been nestled behind the Royal Festival Hall, and they were filled with people eating personal feasts from paper plates: vast thalis; racks of sticky, black ribs; half lobsters with melting garlic butter and bread. Rows of diners craning to read menus wound between food trucks; queues intermingled, new arrivals negotiating for space. Piglet looked around, the National behind her. She had left the office early, she reasoned; she had time before finding a place to work. She edged forward, walking among the tables. The benches were full, some having to stand, juggling their fried chicken with their phones. There were young men who talked too loudly, laughed with their mouths full, and wore round, tortoiseshell glasses; glamourous women in their fifties and sixties, lunching and drinking; and au pairs with charges no older than twelve who ate salt beef bagels, cacio e pepe, and laksa. As she walked, smelling the air, stepping over littered napkins, Piglet imagined what life might have been like, how different it could have been, if she had been eating food like that at their age. She stopped.

In a yellow van, four men moved around each other, one pushing banana leaves heaving with curries, rice, and breads towards a group of waiting people. Another leaned out of the truck, offering his ear to shouted orders. She couldn't see the face of the third man, his back turned to the open hatch, the expectant diners. He stirred something at one end of the van while calling over his shoulder to the final man, who was positioned by a cash register, his arms moving like a conductor's. Piglet moved closer and watched as the man stationed by the register produced a shining, palm-sized piece of dough. He dipped it under the van's counter—for more oil, she supposed—before flattening the round, pale ball and then wiping it, as if he were scrubbing a window, palm flat, moving in circular motions. He pulled his hands down, the disc of dough lengthening, before pinching it between two fingers and swinging it towards the counter like a matador's cape. The dough stretched to a membrane as the man continued to slap it onto the counter, and in seconds it was vast: the hide of an animal stretched over shining stainless steel. In one fluid motion he folded the dough in half, one way and then the other. With loose wrists, bored, he threw the dough—now gathered, layered, almost back to its original size—to one side.

"Yep?" the man leaning out of the truck called, looking at her. Piglet shrunk back.

"Oh, no. No, not for me," she said, her cheeks becoming hot. The man shrugged and looked over her head.

"Yep?" he called to the person behind her, and a man, top two shirt buttons undone, leaned over her to make his order.

Piglet took a step back and looked from the yellow roti van to the benches: still packed. She imagined asking one of these groups if they could move up, if they could make space for her, and her palms began to sweat.

Back on the boardwalk, she shook her head. What was wrong with her? Could she not even ask for a seat now? Not bring herself to partake, to indulge in her own pleasure? She was walking back to the theatre, rationalising, thinking that she might order a cake alongside her coffee—a small slice of something: ginger, carrot, lemon drizzle—when she saw the Golden Monkey. Garlands of artificial marigolds had been strung around the restaurant's doors, and tourists were stopping to take photos with them, sticking out tiny triangle tongues. She thought of the yellow van, the curries served in broad, green banana leaves, the man stretching his dough so thinly it had the transparency of an eyelid. She thought of Kit: eyes closed, mouth open, mucus streaming down his face.

"Table for one, please," she said at the concierge stand, which had been adorned with red flowers: hibiscus with long, plasticky pistils. She peered around the maître d' to the other diners: half-empty bottles of wine, freckle-glazed crockery. She could write a cover letter in here.

She followed a short waiter through rows of tables and felt important, being led somewhere, shown to her seat. She would be a food critic, she thought, or an editor—in fact—scouting for talent. She would eye the waiters and the chefs in the open kitchen. She would ask the staff which dishes they'd recommend, what the chef was excited about, and she would review the menu thoughtfully before ordering lavishly. They would watch her with curiosity, this woman eating alone who had ordered enough for two, three, four. They would whisper among themselves—their eyes on her open laptop, her table laden with dishes. Maybe she's from the *Standard*, the *Guardian*? She must have the best service, the best food. Her mouth watered.

The waiter stopped at a small table in the corner of the restaurant, and Piglet paused. He was extending his arm, directing her body into the space he had allocated for her. She considered, bending to sit, before straightening, shaking her head.

"Would you mind if I sat in the window?" she asked, and the waiter inclined his head, leading her to a table in the front, laid for four. From her seat, she could see the sycamore trees, the people walking past. As she unfolded her napkin, placing it into her lap, a family strolled past, a little boy making eye contact with her as he shot forward on a scooter.

"Can I get you a drink, madam?" the waiter asked once she

had sat down. Piglet noted his address and straightened in her seat.

"Yes." She nodded, picking up a wine menu printed on thick, textured paper. "In fact"—she closed the menu—"I'll start with sparkling water and order wine once I've decided what I'm going to sample." The waiter nodded and left the table. She was sure his eyebrows had risen at the word "sample."

Lunch menus made of the same weighty paper had been laid on her table where place mats should have been. The list of dishes was short and the descriptions sparse: "Paneer, Spinach, Yoghurt, 10.5." She pulled her laptop from her bag and placed it, open, in the space next to her, a knife and fork framing the keyboard. Her phone vibrated, and she read Kit's name. She opened the message without reading it and turned the phone screen-down.

"Your water." The waiter had returned, placing a slender tumbler of fizzing water in front of her before stepping back. "Have you had a chance to look at the menu?" he asked.

"I have." Piglet nodded, not looking up at him, perusing. "But I would appreciate your recommendations."

He gave them. She ordered every dish on the menu.

Her limbs felt light with adrenaline. The waiter's eyes had widened when she had started listing dishes, reading from the top of the menu to the bottom. He hadn't questioned her, but nodded, repeating her order back to her in a murmur.

"And to drink?"

"Yes," Piglet said, reaching for the list of wines again. "With this selection, I think a dry white, don't you?"

"We have a very good sauvignon blanc, madam," he said,

bouncing slightly on his toes. Piglet wrinkled her nose, and the waiter stilled.

"I think not. I'll have the Riesling." She pointed at the menu.

"A glass or a bottle?" he asked, lips curling.

The scant menu had done the food a disservice. As the dishes arrived, ferried from the kitchen by a team of waiters, she surveyed the food. She swallowed at the sight. It was a lot. There were katoris filled with daal, as thick and silky as rice pudding but yellowed with turmeric, finished with cream; a dark, oily, goat curry, chunks of meat blackened by a tandoor; neatly cubed paneer swathed in spinach; prawns, pink and black and glistening, scattered with coriander, sitting spikily in their dish; grilled chicken thighs, reddened with spice, scattered with chilli. Among the plates were little bowls of rice and folded naan, roti, and feather-layered paratha. How much should she eat? How much could she eat? She had nowhere to be, and why would the restaurant eject her? She would be spending hundreds. She could arrive home late. What would he say?

"How is it?" The waiter was back. Piglet's mouth was full. She nodded, she covered her lips with one hand and held up a finger with the other. He waited for Piglet to swallow, to speak, glancing at the amount of food she'd eaten.

"What's the head chef's name?" she asked, pulling her laptop—so far untouched—towards her.

When the waiter turned, she pushed the laptop aside and, with her hands freed, began to shred paratha. She dipped between dishes, loading pieces of bread, sauces intermingled. She pinched rice between her fingers—the way she had seen done on television, in films—and plunged from one curry to another. She tipped her head back and dropped the rice into her mouth, not wanting to spill a grain on herself. She had dispensed with her cutlery, grease on her fingertips, goat meat beneath her nails.

She was being watched, she realised, by the waitstaff, who looked at her with sideways eyes as they passed her table. She imagined their expressions should she take the food to her face, rub it into her skin like a mask.

She visited the bathroom before replying to Kit. Over the sink, she wiped her mouth, applied lip balm, and dabbed at her eyes. In the mirror she turned to the side, stroking her belly: bulging, swollen with food. She allowed herself to hold it as Margot had at the weekend. She smiled down at her own stomach, that secret joke now hers. What would Margot say if she told her? How would it feel to have Margot know the truth? She turned back to her belly. She imagined what Kit would say if she told him she was pregnant. How sorry would he be then? They could have a child, she thought, imagining his declarations of love, his public adoration. It was something to stay together for, something to move things along. She thought of her parents, their wedding photos: her mother in a white meringue dress, puffed sleeves, rounded midriff to match. She faced herself in the mirror, examining the bump, painful with food and exertion. It was less appealing from the front: her body now wide and shapeless, belly button gaping, the fertile curve gone.

At the table, she opened Kit's message, his usual. "I'm fine," she replied. She raised her hand to call for the bill and, for a moment, with that flourish of the fingertips, she felt like him. The waiter reacted immediately.

"Everything to your liking?" he asked, his hands clasped together.

"Yes," she said, remembering Sandra's cold hand on hers, how she had tucked the receipt away in the bagel shop. This had been research, she told herself, a working lunch. She would expense it. She entered her PIN number and felt the waiter's eyes on her: this could have fed four. It did feed four, she'd say, if she was ever asked.

Piglet felt uncomfortable on the train from Paddington to Oxford, one seat not enough to accommodate her burgeoning body. She sweated in her jacket, shuffled, and readjusted. The feeling of lightness in her limbs, the thrill at asking for what she had wanted, had gone, replaced by a heavy self-consciousness. Her seatmates shifted.

Between Maidenhead and Reading, her phone began to vibrate. She lifted it from her bag, expecting to see Kit's face. Instead: Franny's. How had it been just four days since her sister had sat in their house, Kit pouring her wine, her eyes on them as they had kissed: the picture of perfection. Anxiety pressed at her chest, her guts becoming watery. Surely her sister wouldn't sense what had happened? She was miles away, so far away, and likely calling about her dress, something their mother had said, or Darren.

"Hi, Banana," Piglet said, turning away from her neighbouring commuters, smiling at her reflection in the train's window. "Are you OK?"

"Hi, Pink." Franny's voice was bright, quick. "Mum's just texted me and asked me what the plan is for Saturday. I don't know the plan, so . . ." She trailed off, and Piglet exhaled.

"Of course," she said, smiling, watching her shiny teeth move in the glass as houses flashed past. "The dress fitting is at eleven. You can either meet Margot and I there or come to mine first and we can all go in one car. Up to you."

"I'm not sure how Mum will feel about driving into Oxford," Franny said. "We'll come to you first."

"Half ten, then?" Piglet said.

"I'm going to have to get up at, like, seven," Franny groaned. "If you get married again, can there be less early mornings? Or can they at least be nearer home?" Piglet said nothing. The train rattled, and the silence reverberated between them. "Joking!" Franny said.

"I'll see you on Saturday, then," Piglet said, starting to lift the phone away from her ear.

"There actually is one more thing, Pig," Franny said, her voice lowered.

"Yeah?"

"The thing I told you at the weekend," Franny started. "The thing about Darren."

"Yeah?"

"Well, I need to ask a favour," Franny whispered. Piglet imagined her in their parents' house, their old bedroom door closed.

"What is it?" Piglet asked, anticipating her sister's request.

"This is weird to say, so I'm just going to get it over with," Franny started in a rush. "Would it be odd—I mean, would it be OK"—she lowered her voice even further—"if we borrowed some money?"

Piglet closed her eyes. She thought of Kit, of telling him, their shared expression, their raised eyebrows.

"We'll pay it back, obviously, and it's not much. There's just some bills, you know, and my salary isn't much even when we're not paying proper rent." Franny was gabbling now, still speaking in a whisper, her voice hissing.

"How much do you need?"

"No more than a couple of grand. That will keep us ticking over for a few months, and Darren is sure he's going to have sorted something by then." Franny's words were flying, the edges of each syllable blurring, merging.

"I'll have to talk to Kit," Piglet said.

"Darren will have something sorted in the next couple of weeks; I know he will."

"Let me talk to Kit," Piglet said. "I'll let you know."

She stayed twisted in her seat as she ended the call. She thought about her fellow commuters hearing her ask, "How much do you need?" She thought about the waiter in the Golden Monkey calling her madam. She thought about Cecelia, head tilted back in the sauna at the club: Marriage is a commitment. Franny wouldn't have asked their parents. Even if they had the money, there was no way her mother would lend such an amount without her father's approval. No, she had turned to Piglet. No one in her family would have predicted this for the little girl who ate everything—now, somehow, superior: the host; the dispenser of food, of finance.

When she opened the door, her feet aching and her stomach bloated, she hadn't expected to find Kit in an apron, holding a wooden spoon. She nearly laughed at Kit bent over the stove, the flowered pinafore tied neatly over his shirt, the wooden spoon held to his lips.

"I didn't know when you would be home," he said by way

of greeting, "so I've made us dinner." He stood back to reveal her Le Creuset bubbling with a butternut squash soup, silky and orange. "I think I've done it all right," he said, dipping the spoon into the pot and holding it out to Piglet. She hesitated. The apron had been tied in a double bow at his front. Would she ever tell Margot? Would he say yes to Franny borrowing the money? She leaned forward to taste the soup. Kit held the spoon to her mouth, his free hand beneath her lips, ready for something to spill. "I know it's not as good as yours," he said. Piglet stepped back.

"What time will it be ready?" she asked.

They slipped back into their skins, shrugging on the familiar feeling of self-satisfaction. I have never questioned whether we should be together, she said, and they nodded as one, finding comfort in their lie.

7 Days

On that long night, there had not been time. After he had told her, peeling back his flesh like a gill—showing her what she had not seen—there had not been a moment to think. Between his bouts of confession, she had been preoccupied. As his truth ripped at her, she had held together the tatters of her body, picking up her shredded personhood from the bed around her like fallen confetti. But now, with hours passing—days—there was time. She began to imagine how it would be to tell people, how it would be to not tell people.

Saturday: a week until the wedding. Margot sitting before her. She, Piglet, conscious of the hollowness in her gut that made her want to fill the space between them.

"So, now we start the day with affirmations," Margot was saying from Piglet's pink velvet sofa, on form and performing, a cup of peppermint tea steaming on the coffee table before her, "and then we tell the bébé to stay inside at least until after the wedding, and then I do about half an hour to forty-five minutes of low-level hyperventilating." Margot looked sideways at Piglet, smirking. "OK, it's more like an hour—sometimes two."

Piglet had asked Margot how she was feeling, knowing that the question would be returned to her, and wondered, as her friend spoke, how she might answer when it was.

"And where do you find these affirmations that make you hyperventilate?" Piglet asked, reminding herself to partake in their conversation.

"They're on the fridge," Margot said. "Printed and laminated by Sasha." She smiled as she sipped her tea. "But they don't make me nervous—besides their mild culty nature and the possibility they'll transform me into someone who wears a 'Mama' T-shirt. This does." She pointed at her bulging belly beneath a pair of wide-legged brown Lucy & Yak dungarees.

Piglet nodded, half listening, her mind instead on an imagined interaction. "I just can't believe it," she pictured Margot saying. "Not Kit. No. How is that even possible?"

In the present, Margot was still speaking, expounding on the size of the baby—her eyes gleefully wide, her hands splayed around her stomach—and Piglet, momentarily, felt a flare of impatience. Ask me how I am, she thought, ask me how I am feeling.

"When we passed honeydew melon a couple of weeks ago, I just deleted the app." Margot closed her eyes, her hands making a dismissive gesture. "I mean, I just don't want to know. By that point it's not helpful, is it?" Margot opened her eyes and looked at Piglet, her hands extended before her, imploring. Piglet adopted a sombre demeanour.

"Terrifying," she said, her face deadpan.

"Terrifying!" Margot confirmed, and at the height of her exclamation her voice broke, her eyes suddenly glassy, filling with tears.

Piglet had not been paying attention.

She moved her body alongside Margot, her stomach a stone in her guilt, in her private self-absorption.

"Oh, Marg, I'm sorry. Not terrifying! That's a stupid, unhelpful thing to say." She cast around the room before turning back to her friend's rounded shoulders. "Terrifying isn't one of the affirmations, is it?" She gently shook Margot's wrist, trying to prompt a laugh.

"That's not even the worst bit," Margot said, shoulders starting to shake. "Although it is fucking terrible—why is birth the way that it is? Why is evolution misogynistic?"

"Margot." Piglet moved closer, rubbing her friend's back. "What is it?"

"I can't say," Margot moaned, and for a moment Piglet's heart stopped. Had they been sitting, side by side, a secret apiece, concealed by their smiles and their stories from their happy, happy lives?

"Margot," Piglet said, leaning back to better see her friend's face. "Look at me."

"Sometimes I don't know if I want it," Margot whispered, her head cast down, her voice hushed. Piglet exhaled, disappointed, relieved, realizing that Margot's crisis was one of her own confidence. Margot continued. "Not the baby itself—you know that—or maybe the baby—I don't know—but at least our lives, you know? As they are. As they were. Wine! Dinner here. Late-night open mics. Just me and Sasha on a Sunday." Margot was gabbling, and Piglet placed a hand on her leg.

Piglet caught her breath before she responded, struck abruptly by the balm of comforting another: this sheltered, irresistible position from which she could dispense advice, secure in her objectivity, invulnerable in neutrality.

She could not resist leaning closer, fingers squeezing her friend's knee.

"Stuff's changing," Piglet said, her spine curved to see Margot's face, to make eye contact.

"Stuff is changing!" Margot whined, sniffing.

"And these past years of our lives, your life, have been good, Marg," Piglet said, the words coming easily now. "We haven't skimped on the wine or the dinners. But you've been wishing for this—planning for it—ever since I've known you."

"Yeah," Margot said reluctantly. "I suppose."

Piglet nodded, composed.

"And while you and Sasha won't be alone on a Sunday anymore, I hear people are still allowed to have dinner and even drink wine."

"You promise?" Margot said, looking up, eyelashes dewed.

"I'll make it my personal mission to ensure you have a good supply of both, and someone to enjoy it with." Piglet moved closer, kissing her friend's cheek. She felt Margot's head drop to rest on her own. Piglet pulled her closer. "You're going to be great, you know? You're going to be so perfect for that little melon child."

"Thank you," Margot said, her voice muffled. Piglet

responded with another kiss to Margot's cheek before starting to suck the tears from her face like a vacuum.

"Get off, you gremlin!" Margot yelled, pushing her away, laughing.

"An affirmation?" Piglet asked, leaning back to check for Margot's smile.

"Right!" Margot said, clapping her hands together. "Enough of my drama. Today is about you, my love, and the wonderful silly dress you'll wear only once." She wiped the remaining tears from her face with decisive fingers. "Now, tell me how you're feeling?"

Piglet felt the apples of her cheeks lift and knew, in a way, that Margot had started to put her back together: the cracks of herself papered over, her heart, newly knotted with scar tissue, closed to confession.

Piglet held her breath. Her mother, sister, and Margot were in her car, exchanging looks, exchanging news. Margot's head was turned in the front seat, two hands on her bump; her mother and sister leaned forward in the back, their seat belts straining. Piglet had been sure that these women, when all in the same place, would know—their combined intuition dissolving her resolve, dismantling her façade. As she drove, she felt like an animal, camouflaged, hiding in plain sight.

Piglet looked in the rearview mirror at her mother, who had dressed for the occasion of her final gown fitting: a cream blazer with coordinating trousers, a string of pearls at her throat. Franny was clothed equally as consciously, as if she were auditioning for the part of sister of the bride: a floral pinafore, coral on her lips and cheeks, her blond hair falling around her face in soft waves. Margot had shrieked at them both on sight. "Look at you two!" she had exclaimed, clicking her fingers. "Serving bridal-shop realness. Sorry I didn't dress up," she said, thumbs at her dungaree straps, "but sweatpants are all that fit me right now." Piglet, feeling increasingly inadequate and unfeminine in her Donegal jumper and neutral linen jumpsuit, snorted, shaking her head.

"I was on the phone to Aunty Irene last night," her mother called from the backseat, and Piglet glanced up. "We were just talking," her mother continued, and Piglet sensed the imminence of a favour, "and I do think she's worried about the journey next week. She's eighty-seven." Piglet nodded, her eyes back on the road. "I said that I'd talk to you about staying over." Piglet stole another look at her mother, who was looking out of the window, biting her lip.

"Why didn't she say?" Piglet asked. "The rooms at the Ardington are all taken now."

"They were a little rich for her blood," her mother said, eyes flicking as she watched cars pass.

"I couldn't ask Kit's parents to pay for everyone, Mum."

"No," her mother said, turning away from the window, meeting Piglet's eyes in the mirror. "I actually thought your house might work." She paused. "I mean, you won't be using it, will you? You and Kit will be in your special suite." Piglet tilted her head to one side, and her mother said: "She's family, Pig." Piglet turned back to the road, her fingers white on the steering wheel.

Cecelia had suggested the Allegra Joy Bridal Boutique after Piglet confided the search was not going well in Derby. Her parents had insisted, when they met Richard and Cecelia after the engagement, that they would like to buy the wedding dress. When Kit's parents had shaken their heads, told them not to worry, Cecelia extending a manicured hand, her father had raised his voice: "Please." The boutique, on the edge of the city, was somewhere Cecelia and Piglet had scouted together—slim flutes of champagne, cream carpets, only trying a few of the dresses together—before Piglet had told her mother: she wanted to look at some shops in Oxford.

"There aren't any prices on these," her mother had hissed the first time they had visited the boutique together, smiling and nodding at the shiny-haired sales assistant whose eyes lingered on their fingers. Sometimes, when she was on the phone to her parents, they would still say, "Three thousand pounds," as if, at the sound of their eldest daughter's voice, they were unable to contain their reverberating shock, its echoing through time.

The boutique had been decorated for autumn: garlanded in scarlet maple leaves and green ivy. The foliage hung above a glass window filled with angular-shouldered mannequins, cream gowns hanging from their smooth, fiberglass frames. Franny looped her arm into Piglet's as they walked, laying her head against Piglet's shoulder. She wondered if they were both thinking about their phone conversation: "No more than a couple of grand." The door of the boutique did not move when Piglet pushed, and she knocked, stood back, a red flush creeping up her neck as Margot and her mother congregated behind them.

Allegra Joy appeared: caramel-skinned and long-limbed, honey-coloured hair pulled back in a white ribbon. She held up one slim finger as she reached above her head to turn a series of locks.

"Here she is." Allegra Joy smiled at Piglet. "Come in, ladies, come." She ushered them into the shop, closing the door, locking it behind them. "Just so we're not disturbed while we do your fitting." She turned around to face them, clasping her hands together, wrinkling her nose like a rabbit. "I'm hoping champagne isn't a silly question?"

"Not for me, Allegra," Margot said, pointing at her stomach, performing a comedy eye roll.

"Allegra Joy," Allegra Joy corrected, smiling, before she disappeared through a door concealed behind a shelf of veils. Margot snorted.

Margot lowered herself onto a plush velvet sofa in the middle of the silk-and-chiffon room and said, "Where do you think she gets so many off-white pieces of furniture?" Piglet stifled a laugh, and Margot continued: "I mean, is there an outlet, or . . . ?" Her mother sat in an armchair opposite, watching Franny flick through a row of dresses.

"Your turn next," she said as Franny walked over to a mirror, a hanger slung over her head, a gown bouncing at her front.

Allegra Joy returned with an open bottle of champagne, languid in a silver ice bucket, and four glasses. She poured, handing a flute to each of them, holding one out to Margot, saying: "They do on the continent."

"Are you ready for me to go and get her?" Allegra Joy asked, and Piglet nodded.

She returned, her arms full with a body bag filled with organza and lace. Franny, holding her glass and Margot's, started to cry.

"Wait until you see it on." Allegra Joy smiled, her teeth gleaming. Piglet followed her to a changing room at the back of the shop, shrouded in cream velvet curtains. They walked into the space together, and Piglet felt very close to Allegra Joy's body as she drew the drapes around them. Piglet could smell her perfume, sweet on her skin. "If you just pop off your clothes," Allegra Joy said. Piglet pulled off her jumper, her jumpsuit, folding her torso, balancing on one leg. Next to this almost-stranger, this composed woman, she noticed her body: its pallor, its size.

"Here she is." Allegra Joy unzipped the bag and pulled out a tangle of organza clinging to an embroidered corset: lace flowers glinting with sequinned stamens. "She is such a beauty." Piglet nodded as she eyed the corset. "OK, let's get her on." Allegra Joy moved around Piglet, lifting her limbs, touching her skin, folding pieces of her away. "Right, now, team effort." She grunted and nearly lifted Piglet off her feet as she pulled the corset up, tight around her back. Piglet tried to look at Allegra Joy in the mirror, this delicate woman's willowy limbs wielding her weight. Allegra Joy strained, and Piglet tried to make her body smaller, drawing in her shoulder blades, arching her back.

"Now, this is the final fitting," Allegra Joy said, turning Piglet towards her, "so we could make some adjustments if we wanted to." She smoothed her ribboned ponytail. "I've had to clip a few buttons on the corset at the back," she said, her eyes darting across the dress, brandishing a silver buttonhook in one hand. "But if I were you"—she spun Piglet so she was facing her reflection in the mirror—"I would do a little fast a few days before the wedding and keep your measurements as they are. I would hate the bodice to bag—it is so beautiful." Allegra Joy plumped the skirt, flicked lint from Piglet's shoulder. Piglet looked into the mirror and saw someone—herself?—a tall woman with broad shoulders wearing a dress that was designed to make her look smaller than she was. Allegra Joy peered out from behind her: elfin.

"Ready to make your mum cry?" she asked, drawing the curtains. "Pull those shoulders back."

Piglet processed back to the middle of the room, shoulder blades tucked like a bird's. Margot whooped from the sofa, and Piglet laughed. Her mother gasped.

"There will be hair and makeup on the day." Piglet gestured at her face, her dress rustling behind her.

"So beautiful." Franny's voice broke as she poured herself another two glasses of champagne. She sat, flutes of streaming, sunlight-coloured liquid in hand, mascara streaking down her face.

"A perfect bride, Pinky," her mother said, fumbling for her purse. "I want to send your dad a video clip. Give us a twirl," she instructed as she held up her phone.

Piglet rotated. Allegra Joy stepped back.

"It's not buttoned properly," Piglet's mother said, standing, her phone forgotten, hands outstretched. Allegra Joy moved forward.

"We can adjust," Allegra Joy said, nodding, "or we can do a little pre-wedding fast. Most brides do." She smiled, waving a hand.

"Pig," Piglet's mother said, and Allegra Joy flinched. "Let me just"—she reached for her daughter, and Allegra Joy stepped forward.

"The beading is very delicate," she said, spreading her arms in front of the dress.

"Don't, Mum," Piglet said, trying to turn.

"I can do it," her mother insisted, her hands at her daughter's back.

"Please, Mum," Piglet said, and she realised she was crying.

"Makeup on the dress!" Allegra Joy cried.

"Stop, Mum," Franny called from the sofa, her voice thick.

"I can make her fit." Her mother grappled with Piglet's back, pushing at exposed pockets of flesh.

"The beading!"

"Leave her alone, Mum!" Franny had begun to sob on the sofa, her champagne spilling. Margot was trying to stand, her eyes on Piglet.

"Linda, it's fine. Don't—"

"Mum, I said no!" Piglet tore her body from her mother's hands. Margot gasped. Had Piglet shouted as she had freed herself? Had she screamed? She stumbled on the hem of her dress, organza catching between her toes. She fell; she heard ripping.

Her mother stepped back.

The cream carpet was soft beneath her fingers.

"I'll do the fast, Mum," she said from her knees. Her mother wasn't looking at her, her eyes fixed on the mannequins in the shop window: elbows sharp, cheekbones gaunt. Piglet could hear Margot from the sofa, still inhaling sharply, panting, sucking in air.

Allegra Joy crouched beside Piglet, hands fluttering over the dress. The seconds dragged as she smoothed the soft fabric and Piglet's body beneath it. "No harm done, ladies," she concluded.

Piglet looked up from the floor to see Margot's eyes wide. She had thought they had been sharing one of their looks—one of their glances that confirmed they were the only sane ones in the world—but Margot's forehead was creasing, her lips were trembling, she was gasping, still, and Piglet realised she had misunderstood. Piglet looked down to Margot's hands clutched at her middle, her fingers taut. "I'm sorry," Margot mouthed before she dropped her head, her eyes shutting in pain.

Piglet was on her feet, searching for her car keys. The other three women were looking from Piglet to Margot, their skulls rotating on their spines.

"What's happening?" Allegra Joy asked, leaning forward to inspect the sofa beneath Margot. "Your waters haven't broken, have they?"

"It's not supposed to happen now," Margot was whimpering. "It's too early."

"Where are my keys?" Piglet said. "Where are my fucking keys?" She was shouting. Margot was breathing through her mouth, lips round, nostrils flaring.

"Language, Pig." Her mother glanced at Allegra Joy, who was touching the sofa, the fabric pale beneath Margot.

"Don't touch me!" Margot said, her voice rising as Allegra Joy's fingers continued to run over the velvet, searching for soiling. Franny held up Piglet's bag, keys jangling inside.

"Here," she said. "They're here."

"OK, Marg, let's go." Piglet walked over to her, the netted train whispering. Margot looked up, her head shaking, eyes wide.

"The dress." Allegra Joy looked up, a hand pinching Piglet's forearm.

Piglet looked down at herself, her body encased in embroidered lace. Margot started to hum with anxiety, trying to lift herself from the sofa. Piglet flailed, trying to unbutton the corset.

"No, no." Allegra Joy snatched at Piglet's grasping hands. "In the dressing room. I can be quick."

Piglet looked at Margot: Franny now with her, lifting her from beneath the armpits.

"Go!" Franny gestured to the dressing room. "I'll get her in the car."

"My midwife, Franny," Margot was saying, "we need to call my midwife."

Allegra Joy roughly drew a single curtain and directed Piglet's body behind. Her hands flew to Piglet's back, now damp, and her fingers worked on the buttons, the silver hook discarded. Piglet felt her body free itself. She looked up to see Margot, visible in the mirror past the half-drawn curtains, hunched over, steadying herself on a glass cabinet of gleaming tiaras. Piglet began to tear at the train beneath her, and Allegra Joy slapped her hands away. She lifted her stinging fingers into the air and tried to dip her hip, tuck her bones away, let the dress fall from her body and onto the floor.

Piglet watched Margot: leaning on her mother, being guided out the door. She saw her car outside the shop: Franny in the driver's seat, a phone cradled at her ear. "We're nearly there," Allegra Joy panted. Piglet's eyes shifted back to her body: almost naked. The skin across her torso was blotchy, her limbs sticks, pale. Her mother had left the shop door open, and two women— one older, one younger—had walked inside. She watched them: their fingers trailing gowns and one another's shoulders. As the older woman wrapped her hand around the younger's waist, they caught sight of Piglet, half-naked, unconcealed at the back of the shop. They broke apart, they averted their eyes, they walked back out the door.

"OK, you can put your clothes on." Allegra Joy drew back, gathering the fallen dress to her chest. Piglet scrambled for her jumpsuit. She yanked it over her feet, the left leg catching at her toes. She didn't stop when she heard the sound of ripping cotton. Allegra Joy winced.

"I'll have to pick up the dress another time," Piglet said, her jumper balled under her arm, and Allegra Joy nodded, her mouth puckered as if by a lemon.

Piglet ran from the changing room, past the half-drunk champagne, and through the open door. Outside, Franny and her mother were lowering Margot into the passenger seat of Piglet's car. She flung open the driver's-side door and hurled herself inside.

"OK, Marg?" she said, feeling the blood pounding behind her eyes. She reached her hand out to Margot's body, guiding her into place. Allegra Joy watched from the glass door as she locked the boutique, sliding bolts back into place. Margot reached for her seat belt, eyes closed, and shook her head. Piglet pushed the gearstick into first.

"The hospital?" Piglet asked, her eyes darting, thinking that she had never been to the John Radcliffe. When she was younger and she had cut her forehead open, or when Franny had spilled baked beans, boiling on the hob, into her lap, they had been rushed to the Royal Derby Hospital. She watched her hands twitch on the steering wheel. She would not know what she was looking for.

"No," her mother said, shaking her head in the backseat. "Not yet."

Piglet turned to Margot.

"My midwife wants me to go home," Margot said. "My bag's there. It's close enough to the Women's Centre."

"But you're in labour, aren't you?" Piglet asked, and Margot leaned her head back, tears seeping from beneath her eyelids.

"They'll want her to labour at home," her mother said, extending a hand and placing it on Margot's shoulder, "until the contractions are more regular. Until it's time." Piglet watched her mother's fingertips massage her friend's shoulder. She watched Margot reach up to cover her mother's hand with her own.

"Three in ten, right?" Franny said to nods from Margot and her mother. Piglet stared at her sister in the rearview mirror.

"Please," Margot said, her eyes still closed, "can we go?"

Piglet felt the magnitude of her inadequacy as she negotiated her way through the town centre: bursts of speed interrupted with slamming brakes, the four women jerking forward. Margot kept her eyes closed, her hands on her stomach.

"Can someone try Sasha?" Margot asked as they waited at the St. Clement's Street traffic light. Piglet handed her phone to Franny.

"Here," she said. "Passcode's thirty-ten."

"The wedding." Franny smiled as she swiped.

"I'm sorry about the dress," Margot said, rolling her head back, tears starting to fall again. Piglet turned in her seat, placing a hand on Margot's leg.

"It doesn't matter." She squeezed Margot's thigh. "The dress is fine. Although we might need to make some alterations to yours now." Piglet smiled. Margot laughed through tears.

"I think we might have to rethink my maid of honour

commitments," Margot said. Piglet did not reply. She noticed her hand loosen on Margot's leg.

"It's green, Pig," her mother prompted. Piglet looked up, placing both hands on the steering wheel, and the car lurched forward.

"No answer," Franny said, jutting her chin forward, Piglet's phone held to her ear.

"She's at a workshop today," Margot moaned. "We thought there was still time."

"Don't worry, love," Piglet's mother said, her hand on Margot again. "Don't worry."

———

Piglet's mother opened Margot's blue front door, turning the key that had been handed to her in the lock, and stepped back to let Margot inside. They moved through the house together, and Piglet thought she heard them talking quietly as they entered the living room. Margot had lowered herself onto her birthing ball, her head resting against the back of the sofa. Piglet smiled, the sight of her friend prompting the beginnings of laughter, and opened her mouth to make a joke.

"Another one is coming," Margot said, looking past Piglet and towards her mother, who had been drawing curtains, bringing the room to a low light.

"I make that fourteen minutes, then," her mother said, hurrying to the sofa, one curtain left undrawn, her wrist held in front of her. "Let's breathe through it together, shall we? I took Lamaze classes before I had Piglet. I'll follow your rhythm."

Piglet watched her mother—in her cream pantsuit and pearls—hold her best friend's hand as they inhaled together, nostrils flaring, before releasing their breath, in unison, through pursed lips, and realised this was not something she and Margot could share. She considered, as she watched them breathe, that she and her mother had never really spoken about her life before Piglet, before Franny. She watched her mother and her best friend and was unsure if she recognised either person.

"Phone!" cried Franny. "Phone's ringing!" She held up Piglet's mobile, screen lit with Sasha's name. Margot let out a sob.

On loudspeaker, in the darkened living room, Sasha's voice was clear.

"I'm nearly home," she said. "Tell bébé to wait. I'm coming, my brilliant girl, I'm coming."

"I'll get us a taxi, Mum," Franny said after Sasha hung up.

Margot looked up.

"I'll still be here," Piglet offered, her voice raised, and her mother nodded.

"Piglet's here," her mother confirmed, "and Sasha is on her way."

"What happens now?" Piglet asked, her words sounding more petulant than she intended, as the door closed behind Franny and her mother.

"I'm not comfortable," Margot said. "I want to get changed." She started to heave herself up from the birthing ball, and Piglet hurried to help her, her friend's skin feeling hot beneath the brown fabric stretched over her stomach.

"There's a nightdress in my birthing bag." Margot pointed. Piglet pulled out a floral, floor-length dress—pink—and held it up in front of her.

"Nice muumuu." She smiled, looking at Margot for a reaction.

"It's my birthing gown," Margot said, her face straight. "You're going to have to help me."

Piglet faltered.

"Help me," Margot asked again, and Piglet moved forward.

She knelt, easing off Margot's heavy boots as she stood on one foot, gripping Piglet's shoulder. She carefully removed Margot's dungarees, untying them at the shoulder, and crouched to pull them over Margot's body, Piglet's ear grazing her warm stomach, her belly button visible beneath fabric stretched tight. Despite the proximity of their bodies, Piglet again felt the yawn of distance from her friend, their different choices, their diverging paths, manifested so clearly in their physiques. She pulled Margot's top over her head before shrouding her in the gown, buttoning it at her back. Margot gripped Piglet's shoulder, her face creasing.

"Fucker," she said through gritted teeth.

In the absence of Piglet's mother, Margot's breathing sounded sharper.

Time passed, Margot's contractions quickened, and Sasha did not arrive. At the sound of distant traffic, a neighbour's movement, Margot's head jerked towards the door. She had started to make low, flat noises when pain seized her body, and Piglet felt like an imposter, rubbing her back, telling her to breathe as she had seen in films: in, two, three, four, out, two, three, four.

"Sasha would be telling me to walk," Margot said from the sofa, her face crumpled, her full lips turning down. "She would be telling me that our ancestors didn't sit down.

They walked into the woods and laboured until the baby came."

"But they didn't have lovely leather sofas, did they?" Piglet said, stroking an arm, trying to joke. Margot let out a sob, her throat expanding, and Piglet felt useless.

"This isn't how it's supposed to be," Margot cried, shaking her head from side to side, tears mingling with sweat. "Sasha should be here," she said, her voice getting louder. "I can't do this without her."

"What can I do to help?" Piglet said. "How can I help you?" She was leaning forward, trying to reach Margot, trying to hold them both together as she felt herself, and her friend, starting to slip.

Margot rolled her head to look at Piglet, her lips pouted. "Distract me," she said.

Piglet looked at her friend: her face sheening with sweat, her chest rising beneath her flowered dress. She felt her skin prickle as an image flashed into her mind, the same one that she had been seeing for the past six days: Kit. Kit hanging over her in bed, his eyes bulging, his face red with the blood pooling in his cheeks. I have to tell you something.

"I wanted to tell you," she lied. She was saying the words that she had pushed down, down, down to her stomach. She was letting them surface, bile-covered, and hang in the air. Margot's eyes widened as she spoke: nobody knew; two years, maybe three; he's sorry, he says he's sorry, he promises he's sorry. The truth had spilled from her like vomit.

"Why are you telling me this now?" Margot asked, her eyebrows creased.

"You wanted me to distract you," Piglet said, half smiling.

"I'm about to give birth," Margot said, her voice louder, and Piglet imagined the sinews around her own heart tightening until the organ was contracted into a fist.

"I know," Piglet said.

"No," Margot shook her head. She had stopped crying. Piglet tilted her head, tracing a finger along the back of Margot's sofa. "What were we doing this morning?" she asked. "Drinking champagne, your dress, acting like everything's fine?"

"We're going ahead with the wedding," Piglet said, circling her finger around a button sunk deep into the brown leather.

"Oh, come on," Margot said, and Piglet felt the chill of exposure. Her flesh rippled with goose bumps as if a wind had whipped past her, high on a cliff, moving her body, leaving her teetering on the edge.

"It's what I want," Piglet said, her eyes fixed on the button, her teeth gritting.

"You deserve more than this!" Margot shouted. "This is not OK."

"I think I get to decide if it's OK." At once she was obstinate, and she felt her jaw clench.

"No, you don't," Margot said, her voice raised. "Not if you make decisions like this."

Piglet lifted her shoulders. Margot's body folded with pain. The front door opened.

Sasha's eyes were wild, her braids in motion. She looked around the room—Piglet, the discarded clothes, the open hospital bag—and her eyes landed on her wife: Margot, hunched on the sofa, pain racking her body. Sasha ran forward.

"Are you OK? I'm sorry. How long between? Are you having one now? I'm sorry. Have you been walking? Oh, darling,

I'm sorry." Sasha was out of breath, her hands on Margot's forehead, in her hair. Behind her, Piglet stepped back.

"No," Margot said, her hand reaching past Sasha, grasping at Piglet's arm. "Don't go." Her eyes were shining. Piglet held Margot's hand. When will I see you again? she thought. When will you look at me without that expression, those eyes?

"Sasha's here now," Piglet said, extricating herself from Margot's grip. She rubbed Sasha's arm. "You're going to be brilliant." Sasha barely looked at her, lifting her hand in farewell, turning her body so she faced Margot, away from Piglet.

"What did the midwife say?" Piglet heard Sasha ask as she turned around, walked away.

"You're late," Kit called from the kitchen.

"Margot went into labour," Piglet said, and Kit ran into the hallway, his mouth hanging open. "And she knows," she said, closing the door behind her.

Lost, she wondered what she was doing, and what, if anything, had ever given her a sense of satisfaction?

6 Days

Sasha's text had arrived at 11:58 the night before. Piglet opened it in the dimness of the morning light. She squinted, her face lit with blue. It was a photo of a tiny baby with mottled skin, a sloping forehead, and puffy, closed eyes. She wore a knitted pink hat, and Piglet could almost hear Margot: "An hour old and already gendered." Beneath the photo there was a message from Sasha: "Meet Layla. Born at 8:18 p.m. on the 23 October. Thank you for taking care of my girls. Look after yourself."

"Look after yourself"? Piglet wrinkled her nose. Margot had told her, she thought. She did not know which words to use in reply so tapped out a string of hearts and little yellow faces with varying expressions of delight. She turned onto her side and saw Kit's back, broad, constellational with freckles. They had argued. Their first argument where they had both been allowed to participate since he had told her. She turned back over, kicking at the sheets. He remained still.

Before Margot, they had been starting to talk, the dark bookends of their days filled with bargaining. He had promised to be truthful, she had promised to believe him. It had been decided without saying that the wedding would go ahead: She hadn't left, hadn't packed up a bag, hadn't taken the car. He had stopped lowering his eyes when she entered a room. Her staying, her infallible presence, had seemed to heal his sense of wrongdoing. Their conversations evolved: If only you had . . . if only we had . . .

But he had been indignant at her inviting a witness into their fractured coupledom, a betrayal that seemed to parallel his. He had started to spit when he spoke, tongue catching on sharp syllables, and she had been disoriented: unable to access their shared moral code, which, since his confession, had become tarnished, soiled, and no longer available to her. Since he had confessed, much had become unavailable, and her life—their life—was like walking a familiar path after an earthquake, a bridge of rotted wood: questioning every step. As they fought, she tried to make sense of the feeling that they had not lived a truthful life. Margot knowing had felt like a secret in the hours that Piglet had known and he had not, and she struggled to understand how he could have deceived her for so long. How had it not eaten him? She imagined his insides, empty: darkness where there had once been a heart, lungs.

He appeared in the kitchen after she had turned the radio on, volume up, dedicated love songs blaring. She slammed a saucepan down onto the hob, threw in oats, flakes falling. He sat at the table, his spine straight. She jerked open the fridge, glass bottles jangling.

He would normally make coffee, reaching around her for the moka pot and grounds. Now, he sat as she ripped the lid off the milk, poured it into the saucepan, spilling it on the hob. She could feel the thump of impending conflict in her chest as their conspiracy to carry on as normal, their commitment, began to crumble.

"Do you want any help with breakfast?" he asked. She let out a short exhalation.

"Go on, then," she said, stepping back, gesturing towards the hob as if it were a shrine. She slammed the fridge door closed as she took his place at the table. She had wanted to scream, but, even now, they prided themselves on their ability to argue without alerting the neighbours. What self-control, they would congratulate themselves once the scores had been settled. What composure.

He crossed the empty space between the fridge and the dishwasher. He stood by the stove, looking at the porridge oats: wet and milky in the saucepan. His hands hovered over the hob, beginning to ring. She was sure he would choke.

He reopened the fridge. He poured another stream of milk into the pan. He pulled open the cupboards to find honey and nuts. He was doing it—he was making them breakfast.

She did not look at him as he worked. Instead, she picked up the blocks of their wooden calendar, turning them over: reversing time, fast-forwarding it. She couldn't turn her head; she couldn't be seen to look. Her eyeballs strained in their sockets. She glimpsed the edges of him: stirring, chopping, doing it all wrong.

She could hear the hob—too high, the quiet roar of the flame causing the porridge to drumroll.

She could hear him chop walnuts, the give of their soft, oily flesh, their papery skins. His knife cleaved downwards in isolated, awkward strokes—nothing like the light patter of hers. The nuts would be rough, the pieces too large.

She could hear the porridge gasping on the stove. She would have turned the flame down, she would have loosened it with water. But she wasn't cooking—he was. She was doing whatever it was that he usually did.

He beat the porridge with a plastic spatula—the one she reserved for cooking with onions. They would be able to taste another night's dinner on their breakfast, the allium echo of a meal from the past.

He placed two bowls next to the pan with a clink. He doled out the porridge, the dull thud of the spatula on the bottom of the pan, the side of the bowls. He dumped the nuts on top and squirted over a shot of honey. He walked towards her; he set down the bowls. "There you go."

She couldn't look at him, her eyes fixed on the breakfast he had made, the breakfast for which he had pushed her out of her kitchen. The porridge was sticky and thick, nothing like the ambrosial oats she usually made: smooth and silky. The nuts were poorly chopped, unartfully scattered. She shook her head, she dipped her spoon. She forced her mouth open. Close and chew, she thought, her jaw moving mechanically. Swallow this: you are getting married in less than a week. She moved the oats around her mouth, towards her throat. As she swallowed, she thought of cold sick, and suddenly her neck was hot, her tongue writhing beneath her hard palate, pushing against her teeth.

She shoved the bowl aside.

"I don't want to eat this." She threw the spoon down onto the table. Kit nodded as if he had been expecting this, moving his head from side to side.

"I hope you're not going to be like this at my parents' today," he said, lifting his spoon to his mouth. Where her voice had been loud, his was quiet.

"I don't want this porridge. It's too thick," she cried, hating herself, sounding like a child.

"Well, excuse me, Goldilocks." He laughed, looking at her. "I was just trying to help."

"You're not helping if you do it wrong," Piglet said, and Kit put his spoon down.

"You don't get to talk to me like that after I've done you a favour."

"I can talk to you however I like," she said, and her throat was ripping open. She imagined a new self crawling out, lifting itself from her cracked rib cage. "After what you've done, for the rest of our lives, I can talk to you how I want." Kit blinked, and she continued. "And what favour have you done for me? Making me a terrible bowl of porridge? Making me go for a terrible lunch with your parents? Making me . . ." She trailed off, her anger ahead of her speech.

"I'm not making you do anything," he said, his voice level.

Piglet's limbs felt weightless with fight. If he was not making her live this life, who was? She could feel her pulse in her fingertips as she picked up her bowl. She felt his eyes on her as she lifted it over her head, brought it down, smashing it onto the tiled floor. Shards of ceramic and congealed oats sprayed across the kitchen. Kit drew his feet up onto his chair. They both looked at the floor, and in the quiet she felt the rawness of her throat, the pounding of her head.

She walked upstairs.

"Very mature," he called after her.

Her hands shook as she curled her hair, painted on her eyebrows. She pulled on one dress, looked at herself, removed it, and then tried another. She thought about her wedding gown, pinching at her flesh, not fitting; about clothes discarded to the floor of her childhood bedroom, her teenage flesh throbbing. She thought about Margot shouting from her brown leather sofa: You deserve more than this. Sasha: Look after yourself. She imagined them at the wedding, Margot still in her floral birthing gown, shaking their heads, the baby screaming as she walked down the aisle.

At the front door, she pulled on her jacket in silence. From the hallway she could see him, still sitting there, the shattered bowl at his feet. She left their house without saying a word, slamming the door behind her. I'm not making you do anything.

She strode towards Summertown, to Kit's parents on the north side of Oxford. As she walked, she imagined more retorts hurled to hurt, more plates smashed, and the porridge, turning cold and thicker still, spilled across the kitchen floor. She had intended to walk there, go straight to Richard and Cecelia's house and tell them about their son. She imagined Cecelia opening the door, her hair in rollers, face bare of makeup. She imagined them on the bar stools in the kitchen: Cecelia taking her hand, Richard pacing, shaking his head. "We'll sort this all out," Cecelia would say, Richard nodding. "Sweet girl, we'll sort this all out."

Her phone buzzed: Margot. "I survived. They should be

letting us out today. Will you call later?" The image of her future
in-laws vanished, replaced by one of Margot, half listening, trying to learn how to keep her new baby alive, nodding, exhausted
as Piglet wallowed. The baby would scream, and Piglet would
have to raise her voice to compete. She would not call: Margot
could not help her, not now. She slowed her pace.

She was walking through the city centre: quiet on a Sunday
morning, only parents with strollers and couples of wandering, elderly women on the streets. She passed the theatre, doors
locked; the bookshop, closed. She turned left along Magdalen
Street. Some of the restaurants were open: the sound of steam,
frothing coffee, the smell of maple syrup, bacon. She looked
at her watch. She didn't want to be too early: Cecelia sighing,
raising one not-yet-pencilled eyebrow to Richard.

She stopped in the doorway of a diner serving brunch.
As she stood, she watched a woman sitting alone. She looked
tall—not as tall as Piglet, but her legs were long, boots grazing
her knees beneath the marble countertop of her table. Her
hair was piled on top of her head, and misshapen gold hoops
hung from her ears. Her face looked fresh: cheekbones dewed,
eyebrows combed, lips stained red. She wore a leather jacket,
and Piglet could glimpse the tendril of a tattoo sneaking over
her shoulder. When the woman's food arrived—waffles piled
high with fried chicken, a tumbler filled with ice and slices
of citrus, a cinnamon roll on the side—her cheeks lifted and
glowed.

"Can I get you a seat?" A waitress, suddenly in front of Piglet,
was holding a leather-bound menu. The tattooed woman had
been reading as she ate, wiping her fingers between turning
pages. Piglet had not read the book, a hardback that had won

the Booker. She shook her head. She looked at her watch; she looked at her phone: nothing.

Their car was already on the drive by the time Piglet arrived at Cecelia and Richard's. She pushed open the iron gate and walked between their cars, Richard's—a shining silver Porsche—and the run-around, Cecelia's car: a green Mini Countryman. She ducked, walking under a trellis trailing late-flowering roses, and stood inside the red-tiled porch, the backs of her thighs starting to sweat at the thought of Kit: surly, unaffectionate in front of his parents. Her stomach twisted, and she swallowed, focusing on a row of clean Wellington boots beside two neatly pruned bay trees. Piglet inhaled their medicinal scent, steadying herself. She picked up the gold door knocker, shaped like a lion's head, and rapped twice.

Cecelia opened the door, a red striped apron tied around her waist. She smiled, and Piglet felt her muscles unclench.

"Darling." Cecelia leaned forward to kiss her. "Did you walk?" She leaned back, lifting a hand to her face, inspecting the moisture Piglet had left on her powdered cheek.

"Yes," Piglet said, smiling broadly. Cecelia nodded.

"Everything go well with the florist?" Piglet's mouth hung open. "Kitty said you needed to check something with the flowers?" Cecelia prompted, and Piglet nodded.

"Right," she said. "Yes, all sorted." Cecelia arched an eyebrow before standing back to let her into the hallway.

"Clever you," she said. "We don't want anything to derail the big day, do we?" She eyed Piglet, who looked away, bending to remove her shoes.

"Oh, don't bother, darling," Cecelia said, waving at her feet. "Come."

Piglet followed Cecelia through the house: gilded frames lining the walls, red Persian rugs covering the shiny floorboards. She sucked in her stomach as it growled, pain starting to shoot across her abdomen. The halls smelled of wood polish and rosemary.

The kitchen was at the back of the house, and it was a space Piglet had envied ever since she had been introduced over lunch: a little roast at home, nothing fancy. The vaulted, beamed ceilings were high, and the windows, which spanned from floor to ceiling, flooded the room with light. Today, with the October sun at its highest point, shafts of sunlight fell across the marble countertops, the kitchen island filled with dusty bottles of red wine. Cream cupboards had been fitted around a coffee machine, a wine cooler, a double oven with a saucepan bubbling on the hot plate. A pair of glass doors that were framed by triangular panes of glass led out onto a walled kitchen garden. Their shape, a conduit for the streaming sunlight, reminded Piglet of a church.

On the other side of the AGA was the little table—an eight-seater, longer than her parents' dining room—and opposite, a pair of armchairs, their backs to the kitchen, facing towards a television.

"Hi." Kit didn't turn but lifted a hand to her from an armchair opposite Richard as she and Cecelia entered the kitchen. So, this is how it's going to be, Piglet thought. Her stomach tightened as she said hello and waited for him to look at her.

"There's my favourite future daughter-in-law," Richard said, standing to kiss Piglet on the cheek before returning to his seat. "Do excuse us boys," he said, pointing at the television. "England, South Africa."

"Oh, of course, Richard," Piglet said, pushing his shoulder. Richard laughed, his eyes on the screen. She glimpsed Kit in her periphery: glancing. She turned away from the television.

"Drink?" Cecelia asked. "White wine is open for the pork."

"It smells sublime," Piglet said, salivating, somewhere between hunger and nausea, her voice loud over the commentary of the rugby. Cecelia smiled as she poured Piglet a glass and then pulled on a pair of oven gloves. Piglet climbed onto a bar stool at the kitchen island opposite Cecelia and the AGA. She felt moisture gather between her thighs as she gulped the wine, letting the liquid sit in her mouth, savouring the alcoholic tingle on her tongue, something to swallow.

"French, in tribute to the wedding day. Although the Riesling is German," Cecelia conceded, opening a cream AGA door and pulling out a rolled loin of pork. "I bought that book you told me about—the one you gave the caterers." She inspected the burnished meat, which bulged, bound together with string. "Enchaud périgourdin," she said, nodding to the casserole dish in her hands. "Went to the butchers in town yesterday and made it myself." Piglet's mouth filled with saliva, and she swallowed.

"Wow, Cece," she said, her eyes not moving from Cecelia, trying to detect any movement from Kit. "You didn't say your mum was making a special lunch for us," Piglet called, turning her head, looking at the back of the armchair, the back of his head.

"Didn't know," he said, not turning around. Piglet smiled widely, her insides turning, as Cecelia looked from her to Kit with interest. Piglet poured herself another glass of wine, her extremities already light.

"Why don't you sit down?" Cecelia said, nodding to Kit

and Richard. Piglet slipped off the bar stool, wiping the black leather, and approached the twin armchairs. She thought about the floor: she could sit cross-legged and watch the green screen, her head tilted up like a child. She perched on Kit's armrest, balancing her body by his chest. As she sat, Kit withdrew his arm, placing his hands in his lap.

A pain grew up from her sit bones as the game continued. She sat, slowly doubling, her spine curving. When Richard and Kit jumped to their feet, cheering, Piglet was knocked from the armchair, losing her balance, wineglass sloshing. She felt vomit rise from her gut.

"Boys," Cecelia said.

"Mind the little woman, Kit Kat." Richard laughed, and Kit's lips curled as he settled himself back in his seat, eyes forward.

"I thought we'd eat at the little table," Cecelia said, her hands full with cutlery. "There's no point warming up the dining room."

Kit got to his feet, stretching.

"Is there anything I can do, Mum?" he said, walking over to his mother, his back to Piglet, who had slipped into the armchair, wiping her beading forehead on its wingback.

"Sweet boy," Cecelia said, the palm of her hand cupping Kit's face. "You're going to make someone a lovely husband one day," she said, her eyes on her son. Piglet stood, coughing a comedy splutter, and Cecelia looked at her; Kit, behind her, also finally meeting her eyes. Piglet felt her stomach turn to liquid as his face did not soften into a smile to reassure her in front of his mother. Beside Kit, Cecelia was looking at her, a hand on one hip, knives in the other. Had he told his parents? Had they understood, forgiven him, and condemned her behaviour since? Had they known? Marriage is a commitment.

"Can I help, Cece?" Piglet said, her head light, moving close behind Kit's mother. Cecelia stumbled on Piglet's foot.

"No," she said. "Just sit."

Piglet took her usual seat as Richard assumed his place at the head of the table. She had expected Kit to pull out the chair alongside her, as he always did, Cecelia opposite, but as she sat, Kit moved towards his mother, and she was across from them, alone. Kit's distance made her reach out a hand, place it on the table, and she stared as he drew back into his seat, arms crossed, eyes on his father. Cecelia watched Piglet watching her son.

"Shall I serve?" Richard said, leaning forward.

"Lovely," said Cecelia, and Kit nodded.

On her solitary side, Piglet did not feel it necessary to speak.

Richard lifted the rolled meat from its casserole of vegetables, and it dripped as he lowered it onto a platter. He picked up a thin, silver carving knife, the tip curved like a horn. He held the pork with one hand, meat bulging, juice dribbling, and with the other lifted the knife. Piglet turned away. He carved, slicing through a knot of string as he did so.

"Greens?" Cecelia asked, and Piglet, her stomach tearing, lining splitting, turned to her future mother-in-law to say no, no thank you.

"You can't resist a bit of this, though." Richard ripped off a piece of the pork rind with his fingers, crispy and bubbled with heat. He lowered it into his mouth, his lips sucking. He crunched, and his mouth remained open as he chewed. "Can't beat the crackling, can you?" Shards of fat and spit sprayed across the table.

"Just the best." Cecelia leaned forward to tear off a strip, her wet tongue coming out of her mouth as she opened it, forcing the hardened skin inside. Piglet pushed her chair back from the table.

"Oh, darling, we're being so rude," Cecelia said. "Would you like some?" She pulled a piece of the roasted loin away, offering it to Piglet. "Here," she said, proffering the pork. "Eat it."

Piglet stumbled backwards. Kit, in the chair opposite her, lifted his hand. She hurried from the table back into the hall, the first, second door along. The downstairs bathroom. She fumbled for the light, the toilet seat. It clattered back, she fell down. Her stomach, insolent, contracted like a fist, pushing her body over the bowl.

Her eyes opened, and she saw white. Her forehead was pressed against the cool porcelain of the toilet. Her throat was tight, sore with acid and lined with flecks of food that she hadn't been able to eject. She brought her hand to her mouth and felt the trails of saliva around her lips. She drew her knees to her chest, placing a hand on the floor, and tried to stand. She did not recognise herself—florid—in the bathroom mirror. She leaned forward; she widened her small, black eyes.

"Darling, you look terrible." Piglet had reentered the kitchen, Kit and his parents sitting straight-backed at the long, dark-wood table. They turned to her in concern, and Piglet stared: their plates were clean, the pork untouched. She looked away, the seeping meat and tightly bound skin making her stomach turn again.

She was sitting down, back in an armchair—Richard's this time: closer to the door, a whiff of whiskey. Kit was crouching in front of her, stroking her hair.

"Are you OK?" he asked, placing a hand to her forehead, running a finger along her nose. She looked at him, turning her head, creasing her brows. "It's OK," he soothed. "It's OK."

Richard was there, handing her a glass of water. Cecelia too: next to Kit, leaning forward, a hand on Piglet's knee.

"You haven't been yourself all afternoon, darling," she said. "Perhaps a little sieste?"

She was in the guest bedroom, a black bag lying next to her like a lover, a corpse. She had unzipped it, crawled inside, and had been cocooned by her wedding dress.

4 Days

She was tired and had not meant to burn the sausages.

She had been following a recipe, a traybake, one she had made so many times before that she did not need to look at the quantities listed, the method prescribed. But, as Piglet had been deleting Margot's voice notes, the oven had started to smoke.

"You can't ignore me forever."

"We should at least talk about what's going to happen at the wedding now."

"It would be really nice, you know, if you took a minute to ask how I am."

Now, their string of messages was clean: their last correspondence on the morning of the final dress fitting, the day Layla was born. Now, her kitchen smelled acrid, the atmosphere suffocating. The smoke alarm started to scream.

She hadn't let herself think about the little girl, the life that now was at the centre of Margot's. Before Layla had been born, Piglet had planned how she would visit, pictured it: stocking their fridge with food, taking the baby and rocking the child to sleep while Margot and Sasha took showers, had naps. The baby, when old enough, would call her Aunty, would beg to sleep over with her. Margot and Sasha, grey-haired and tired-eyed, would sigh: "Could you?" And she would. She would be a treasured, indispensable part of their family. But since Sasha's text, there had been no mention of Layla, and Piglet felt aware of her absence. There had only been texts, voice mails, and voice notes telling Piglet how she had got her life wrong, so very wrong.

She had been wrong about Margot too, about her reaction. Piglet had been shocked by Margot's indignance, by the fierceness with which her friend demanded her to want better for herself. Since Kit had confessed, she had imagined people's responses, and, in her mind, Margot had been angrily sympathetic but resigned. She would shake her head at Piglet's martyrdom, raise her shoulders, and say, "It's your life."

She had been forced to purge her text conversations with Franny too, who, after she and her mother had returned to Derby, had been sending Piglet daily updates from her life, cut with a reminder to consider her request for money, to take it to Kit. "Happy Sunday," her pixelated words read. "Normally I'd be watching Darren at the rec this morning, but we've cut Sunday league for now. Fresh air is free, we'll probs do a walk— need to get away from M&D! What are you up to? Seeing Margot? How's she doing? Still waiting for pics of baby Layla! And no pressure, but any chance you've spoken to K?"

She and Kit had not been speaking. After the smashed porridge bowl, the lunch at Cecelia and Richard's, something had broken between them, something more than before. She imagined their engagement like a bone: previously fractured, now snapped under strain, splintered in two. There hadn't been shouting—there hadn't seemed to be any point—but they had stopped looking each other in the eye. Instead, they had been taking turns to rotate the wooden blocks on their wedding calendar, waiting for the other to be in the kitchen to bear witness. Their house, when they were both there in the morning and the evening, seemed so full with their discord that Piglet felt like she had to edge around the furniture, suck her stomach in past the sofa. They had tried: one offering tea, but then the other saying no, and their feeling of resentment towards one another would swell anew.

She had been confused in the recent days, as she travelled to work, sitting alone on the train to Paddington. She was sure that she had been wronged and was unable to trace how they had arrived at a mutual displeasure. She would type out texts to Margot, trying to unpick the turns her life had taken, trying to find the words to explain. She did not send them, imagining Margot recovering from labour, grappling with far more tangible, far more legitimate problems of her own. She might roll her eyes at Sasha: "She just doesn't get it." Still, as Piglet sat at her desk, stared at her screen, she could not shake the sense of wrongdoing, a transgression against her. Toni would be talking to her and, instead of responding, Piglet would move her lips, shake her head. "Are you alright?" Toni would ask, and Piglet would glance up, roll her eyes, and remember where she was. The threads of her life were unravelling like the beaded corset from Allegra Joy's boutique: fraying, sequins scattering on the floor, boning brittle, starting to break.

Kit had found her sitting on the floor in the kitchen, the tray of charcoal sausages, plums, and red onions shoved to one side. He had started to windmill a tea towel, but the smoke alarm continued to wail, and he slid to her side until they were sitting, shoulder to shoulder, an audience to its screaming. When she had pulled the tray from the oven, the sausages had been black, smoking; the halved plums sticky husks, dehydrated hearts shrivelled by her negligence. She could cry, sitting next to him in their home. This was too hard. She had come too far, she had isolated herself from so many people, detaching herself from her support network in favour of a sense of superiority: perfect coupledom, bliss. And for what? How much of this life could be true when it had been built around a lie? But she was drained, she was done. She lay her head on his shoulder; he placed a hand in her lap. Surrender, she craved, submission. Kit stood, opened the patio door, and the alarm stopped. Her ears rang in the silence, her body rang without his.

She did not know how long she had stayed on the floor until he returned, holding food: a plate of bread and cheese, and two glasses of wine with the open bottle clutched all in one hand.

"A peace offering," he said, setting down the plate, the glasses, spreading his hands wide.

This is what it had come to: a ritual, a sacrifice. The smell of burnt pork still hung in the air, the stinging scent of charred onion.

She looked at him: hands forward, open at his side, eyes on her. She inclined her head, reached out and took a piece of bread. She swallowed, tasting nothing, feeling the bulk drop into her stomach, quelling a hunger. He poured the wine.

"So, we're doing this?" he asked.

"Yes."

She only had herself to blame: speeding towards a disaster of her own making, propelled by a momentum she had whipped up.

2 Days

"I'll see you this afternoon, then?" Kit was standing in their front door; Piglet was readying herself to turn away from him, the house. Her face was drawn, and she looked pale, even in the half dark of Thursday morning. She had not been sleeping well: waking in the night to check her messages, check her fiancé, and closing her eyes to see only the stinging blue of a screen. She looked back at Kit. He stood in the door with his shoulders rounded, his body the shape of a question mark. She smiled with her lips pressed together, she nodded. She would see him later.

It had been planned for months—since before what had happened. He would meet her, on her last day in the office before they were married, and they would walk along the river together. They would stroll, hand in hand, getting in the way of the commuters who would tut loudly at them, and she and Kit would laugh, delighted by their good fortune. She would take him along the edge of the City, over London Bridge, and down to Borough Market. In the cook shop on the high street, they would stop, kiss. "Please," she'd say, "we need to find the piping bags." She would push him away, her fingertips at his chest, and the cashier would smile, coy.

She looked at him now, dressing gown pulled tight against the chill of the late October morning, face equally pallid. Perhaps he had also been awake in the night.

"Well, see you, then," she said, without leaning in to touch him good-bye.

They had come so far now—the flowers would arrive tomorrow, and the favours—but, despite their agreement, the frost between them still struggled to thaw, both of them still stiff with a sense of offence. His parents knew, he had confirmed, and that embarrassed her. She had been hurt—absurdly, she maybe half knew—at the thought of Cecelia supporting Kit over her. Piglet imagined what her parents would have done if the roles had been reversed. She would have faced exile, and not one that had been self-imposed. But Cecelia and Richard would not denounce their sweet boy. Marriage is a commitment, but a lesser one than a mother has to her son.

Now, this day felt like a series of obstacles: work, a painful sending-off party in the office, meeting Kit in London, buying equipment for their croquembouche wedding cake, and returning home to make choux buns by the hundred. There was also a meeting with Sandra, a calendar invite dropping into her diary late last night, and Piglet's stomach turned at the thought of sitting in her manager's office, avoiding her stare. She had still not written a cover letter or opened her CV since Sandra had asked for them over a week ago. She could not bring herself to list her achievements, and when Sandra had asked her, earlier in the week, how her application was coming along, she had lied: It will be with you tomorrow, and when tomorrow had come, the day after that.

She was avoiding people, she knew, but she had started to feel irritated by the opinions of others, their needs, their insistence on sharing them all with her when it was her wedding in two days' time. Didn't they know? She had begun to feel myopic about the weekend. If people could just leave her to get through the next few days, she could get everything back under control. Then, with her husband, she would be ready, again, to help: lend an ear, a shoulder, a couple of thousand pounds. She would be herself again.

When she was inside the Fork House building, she saw Sandra already sitting in her glass-walled office. Piglet knocked before half stepping around the door.

"Sandra, sorry, I actually have quite a bit to get through before I finish today." Sandra looked up, red glasses pushed on top of her head.

"Will you come in a moment?" she asked from her leather chair.

Piglet stepped inside the office, thinking about her unwritten application letter, closing the door behind her. "Sit, please." Sandra gestured to the chair opposite her.

"I wanted to tell you," Sandra said, rolling forward, and Piglet braced herself, "that you are a very competent assistant editor"—very competent—her father would be thrilled—"and a valued member of my team."

Piglet could not look up, and she fixed her eyes on the arm of the chair.

"Thank you," she said, her skin crawling with the compliment, with Sandra's sad, sympathetic tone.

"I know it is a busy time for you," Sandra said, "and I realise you've decided to pass on the promotion this time, but I want you to know, when things are getting too much, you can always come in here and tell me that you need help."

Sandra's hands were reaching forward, opening in her lap like a book. Piglet shook her head.

"It's not too much," she said. "I don't need help."

"It's OK." Sandra nodded. "It's normal to be struggling. God knows I wouldn't be able to work up to two days before my wedding." Piglet shifted, and her face burned as she looked down, the word "struggling," said in Sandra's voice, replaying in her head.

"There're only a few things for you to do today, and one of them is attending your party," Sandra said, and Piglet could feel her inch closer. "So, take it easy, OK?" Sandra smiled.

Piglet stood, shifting her weight, unable to bear the sympathy.

"Really, Sandra, I'm fine. Everything's under control."

People started to mill at midday, moving aside as Sandra's assistant surreptitiously cut through the forming crowd with a large bouquet of flowers. There was the clink of a trolley carting dishwasher-warm wineglasses. At Piglet's desk, Toni looked up opposite her. "Sounds like wine."

It was wine, a white and a prosecco to share between the twenty women who had congregated in the breakout area. When Toni complained, talking loudly about thimbles and budget cuts,

Sandra's assistant hissed, "I didn't think it would be appropriate, with Natalie." Natalie, Fork House's copy editor, was already sat in the midst of the crowd, the gathering women standing over her. She was pregnant, her belly huge, her maternity leave imminent. She and Piglet were sharing a send-off party; it had been confirmed by the calendar invite sent around the week before.

"I don't throw a tonne of these kinds of parties," Toni whispered, the corner of her mouth drawn down, "but I'm pretty sure bridal and baby showers don't mix." She shook her head, looking at the rows of orange juice and lemonade, the already empty wine bottles. "Although"—she nodded—"they have genitalia cakes in common, I suppose."

As Toni gave Piglet the odds of Sandra's assistant ordering a cake shaped like a penis, Sandra walked over to Natalie's chair in the middle of the floor, cleared her throat, and waved to the congregation.

"Thank you all for coming over to our end of the office to celebrate two very special members of our team who both have big life events coming up." Sandra beckoned for Piglet to join her next to Natalie. "One marriage and one baby." She smiled.

"Which one's which?" someone called from the back of the crowd, and Piglet stopped breathing.

"Selfishly," Sandra continued, "I'm happy to say that we're only losing one of our team for a year." She turned to Natalie. "We wish you and your new family the very best. Come and see us, when you're ready."

On cue, Sandra's assistant produced the huge bunch of flowers: lilies blooming, roses unfurling. She handed them to Natalie, who began to cry. The women around her simpered. The hormones, one said, nodding. Sandra turned to Piglet.

"I thought you could do without another bouquet in your house," she said, as she handed over an envelope. "From your Fork House family."

Piglet's Fork House family were not looking at her; rather, they were gathered around Natalie, laying their hands on the pregnant woman.

"Help yourself to cake, everyone," Sandra said. Toni leaned over.

"Dick?"

A table in the breakout area had been cleared to accommodate a stack of paper plates, napkins, and two cakes—triple chocolate and carrot and ginger—still in their Marks & Spencer packaging. "Has anyone got a knife?" Sandra's assistant called, before starting to slice the carrot cake with the edge of a paper plate.

Piglet queued for her cake, answering questions about the date, her dress, and her diet. Somehow, once her answers were given, they were regurgitated and merged with the conversation surrounding Natalie: her due date, her maternity wear, her cravings. "The one that surprised me the most," said Natalie from her chair, "was in the first trimester. All beige food—obviously—but I couldn't eat enough pork scratchings if I tried. There was something about the little hairs on the crisps," she shrugged, jubilant in her unpleasantness. The women laughed and began to speak louder and louder, competing to tell their own anecdotes, about the time, once, when they were disgusting.

Piglet took a step back; she licked her lips clean of chocolate cake.

"Want to grab some lunch?" Toni asked, looking at her.

"This isn't a proper send-off"—she waved at the trolley of crumbed paper plates, lip balm–smudged glasses—"and I definitely can't concentrate after two glasses of wine and a slice of carrot cake."

"No," Piglet said, and Toni blinked. "Sorry," she said, looking at Toni. "I mean, I'm meeting friends for lunch. They're taking me to the Savoy." The lie had come easily as she thought about Margot—absent besides her voice notes—the weekend, the tattooed woman eating alone in the Oxford diner.

"Nice," Toni nodded. "Order the Arnold Bennett soufflé, if it's on the menu. It's one of the best things I've ever eaten and it's impossible to re-create at home."

At her desk, Piglet felt compelled to stand, to make her announcement to the office.

"I'm meeting friends for lunch," she said, pulling on her jacket. In her periphery she saw Sandra glancing up from her desk. As she walked to the stairwell, she looked at her hands: they were shaking. If she walked down, she would fall, crack her head open like an egg. She reversed her steps: she waited for the lift.

The air was cold as she left the office, and her eyes streamed as she walked into a sharp, autumnal wind. The weather was turning, leaves falling, winter starting to threaten. Her phone vibrated: Kit. "I'm leaving now, see you later." In their other life, he would have come in earlier, taken her for lunch. She imagined herself at the bar in the Savoy, a single long spoon dipping into the soufflé, him watching her, observing her eat, biting his lip as his gaze fell to her crossed legs. The thought was interrupted by another: his gaunt face this morning; the sad warm-wine party in the Fork House office; "Which one's which?" She was walking west along the Thames, and she could have gone to the Savoy Grill, ordered the Arnold Bennett, eaten alone, and returned to her desk. But her eyes were still watering, and the only way she could think to stop them was to eat until her stomach felt like it was made of stone, until she was so full, she couldn't feel anything else. She locked her phone, pushing it deep into her bag, and turned onto the Strand.

Piglet had rules, although she had never made them official by allowing them to be fully formed into thought. To have rules was to have awareness, and she didn't have any desire to inspect what she was doing. Le Bun broke her maybe-rules. She had half-consciously promised herself: no chains, no restaurants within lunchtime-walking distance of the office, nowhere someone she knew might see her and she couldn't explain away her eating as research, as essential, impressive work. But in Le Bun, the prices were London-cheap, and the service was quick. There had been Fork House birthday lunches here, Christmas parties.

Piglet pushed the door and took a seat, uninvited and unguided by waitstaff. The decor was industrial: the high ceiling crisscrossed with metal pipes and hung with black pendant lights, bulbs bright with orange filaments. Before the rows of steel tables and stools had been installed, this building could have been an abattoir: a slaughterhouse hidden in central London. She picked up a menu—laminated—and shivered. Another violation: no wipe-clean menus, no main dishes that were succeeded with the words "comes with a side of chips." But she was here now, and time was limited. Sandra would be expecting her back, Kit would arrive in a few hours, and she would be married in two days.

"Hi, I'm Kelly and I'll be your server today!" A woman had

arrived at Piglet's table: all teeth, baseball cap and pinstriped uniform. Piglet looked up. "It looks like you're a hungry little pig," Kelly said without missing a beat. "Let me guess—you want one of everything? What would your dad say about that?" She affected a Derbyshire accent. "Typical Pig."

"What?" Piglet said, eyebrows contracting.

"I said, I'll get you started with some water and give you a few minutes to take a look at the menu." Kelly produced a carafe, flipped over a tumbler on Piglet's table, and started to pour.

"I don't need a few minutes," Piglet said, watching the stream of water.

"A prepared customer." Kelly smiled. "My favourite." She clicked a pen and pulled out a pad.

"I want one of everything."

"Feeling hungry?" Kelly laughed.

"Yes."

"I can recommend the Le Bun—that's a double. The Barbecue Chicken is quite big too; the chicken is—"

"Kelly, I'd like you to bring me one of every burger you have."

"Um, are you sure?" Kelly asked. Piglet lifted the plastic menu and started to point.

"I want you to bring me a Le Bun"—Piglet's teeth were bared in a smile—"a Bourbon Blue, a Barbecue Chicken, an American Classic, an American Hot, an Avocado Smasher, and a vegan What the Cluck."

Kelly returned to her table with another waitress before Piglet had time to catalogue the other diners: the kissing couple who were compensating for something, the lunching women laughing too loudly. This was something she and Toni sometimes liked to do at book launches: Which author is a bigot? Which is known for sliding into the direct messages of teenagers on Twitter? "Problematic Bingo," Toni called it, "where all the winners are still old white dudes."

"One Le Bun, one American Hot, one Avocado Smasher." Kelly said each burger's name as she put them down. She ushered the other waitress forward to off-load her plates. She was younger, Piglet saw, with braces, acne creeping up her jawline. The younger waitress deposited two out of her four burgers but held on to the Bourbon Blue and Barbecue Chicken.

"There isn't room," she muttered to Kelly, looking from Piglet to the full table.

"Here," said Piglet, smiling up at the girl in braces. She picked up the American Hot—already on the table—and removed it from its plate, leaving a congealed blot of orange chilli cheese behind. She pushed it alongside the Le Bun before going back for the pickles, scooping them into her palms and throwing them down. Then she reached out her hands to the young waitress and the Barbecue Chicken: a towering stack of fried meat dripping in glistening, brown sauce. The girl reacted quickly: positioning herself alongside Piglet, who wrapped her hands around the burger on the young waitress's tray. She moved it through the air, feeling the solidity of the battered chicken, the crunch beneath the brioche bun, and barbecue sauce dribbled from her wrist to her elbow. She dumped the burger, with its condiments, its sides, before licking the sauce from her extended arm.

"Such an awkward spot," she said, as the young waitress stepped back. As she did, her uniformed body removing itself from Piglet's line of sight, Piglet looked up and across the restaurant. It was busy, the peak of the lunch hour, people coming in and out of the double doors, a bell ringing overhead. She looked back to her food—seven burgers, fries, nondescript deep-fried somethings—and then snapped her head back in the direction of the door.

"Can I get you anything else?" Kelly asked, watching her.

Maybe it was because she had been thinking about work. She looked back at her table. She shook her head. People from Fork House could not be here now. They could not. She looked up: a group, among them pregnant Natalie, Olivia the intern—and was that Toni? Who else could it be in those ripped black jeans, a sheer black top, leather jacket, and patent platform boots? Piglet looked down. Kelly's fingers were waving in front of her face.

"I said, can I get you anything else?"

Piglet stood to leave, pushing her chair back, standing so the table shook, the precariously balanced brioche lid of the Le Bun falling to its crowded plate. She looked around her, reaching for her jacket.

"I have to—" she started to say to Kelly, who took a step back.

People from Fork House could not be here. Toni could not be here. There was no Savoy, no friends. They could not be walking towards her table, not when she was surrounded by so much food, so many empty seats.

"Hey!"

Toni's voice. Piglet froze, her eyes darting between her table, Kelly and the young waitress, the door. She started to sink back down into her chair. Her hands were shaking again, and she shoved them beneath her thighs. She secured a smile to her face, lips wide, too many teeth to trust.

"No soufflé?" Toni asked, her lips twisted with a half laugh, as Natalie and the others loitered behind.

"A mix-up." Piglet beamed, nodding.

"I suppose this is the next best thing," Toni joked, looking around.

"The finest quality generic fried meats. Many prefer it to the Savoy, I've heard." Piglet winked back, her hands stilling. Could she laugh her way out of this? "And I see you've chosen to dine in this fine establishment this afternoon." She inclined her head, enunciating with Received Pronunciation.

"For Natalie," Toni said, nodding her head over her shoulder. "She wanted burgers."

"It's true what they say about pickles," Natalie said, leaning around Toni, beaming.

"Right, right, right." Piglet nodded, matching Natalie's grin, her lips spreading wider.

"Where are your friends?" Toni asked, peering around Piglet as if she might be hiding them.

"Oh, they'll be back," said Piglet, shaking her head, still grinning manically. Toni nodded slowly, looking down, her eyes lingering on the single glass of water on Piglet's table.

"OK," she said, taking in the burgers, their shared plates. "Will you find me when you're back in the office?" she asked, looking up, making eye contact. "I'd still like to give you a send-off myself. We can have coffee and cake. I can stop at Ladurée after this, if you want. We can have macarons." She shook her head, her eyes briefly scrunched shut. "Or not. We can just chat."

Kelly and the young waitress were still standing there,

watching Piglet, watching Toni. Piglet nodded her head and found that once she had started moving it, she couldn't stop.

"Sure, sure, sure. Sure, sure." Her head was still bobbing, and Toni was smiling, a sad little lift of the lips that didn't reach her eyes.

"I'll see you later," Toni said, and Piglet's head continued to dip, her lips still stretching across her teeth, tight, as if she were about to shed a skin.

Natalie turned to Toni as they walked away, her eyes glancing sideways, back to Piglet at her table for one.

"It's a wedding party!" Piglet called after them, and Natalie looked up, shocked, a quick smile, a quick nod. She turned back to Toni, leaned over, covered her mouth.

Piglet's hands quaked beneath her thighs. She tensed her muscles, pushing her sit bones harder onto her fingers, but her body continued to shake.

The steel legs of her chair scraped on the tiled floor, and she stumbled to her feet. She pushed her way out from behind the table and her lone glass wobbled, slopping water over the table. She pulled at the napkin dispenser, pieces of thin paper tearing in her hands before she picked it up and pulled chunks of tissue from within, disgorging its innards over her order. The restaurant was quietening around her; Kelly and the young waitress were still standing, watching. She threw the napkin dispenser down, crockery clattering, and turned to leave.

Her hand on the door, Piglet noticed that there was sludge beneath her fingernails. She saw that tiny pieces of napkin had caught on her sticky skin. She noticed her hand, which was no longer a hand. Her fingers had fused together. They were short and swollen and ended in a sharp point. She stared at it, this appendage resting on the door. It was not a hoof, but it was not a hand.

"Excuse me!" Kelly and the young waitress were behind her. She was shouting, pointing back at the table strewn with tissue, her uneaten food. "You haven't paid!"

Piglet pushed open the door and bolted onto the Strand. Kelly was still behind her, the younger waitress trailing, shouting feebly. "You haven't paid your bill!" Kelly shrieked down the street as Piglet wriggled through the ambling tourists, grunting apologies, profanities. "You're disgusting," a woman shouted as she pushed past, and Piglet knew the yell was for her, but she did not know if it was Kelly, the young waitress, or someone else who had shouted.

As she fled, she made her decision: she would not go back to the office. She could not look at Toni again, at Natalie, she could not return to receive quiet, consolatory facial expressions from Olivia. She would not meet their eyes, not now they had seen her. The woman she had been, eating alone, was no longer anonymous. Now she was someone else, someone sadder: "A woman I work with was in Le Bun today with seven burgers lined up in front of her! I'm pretty sure it's her wedding at the weekend. What's going on there?"

She ran across the road, twisting to see only strangers, late lunchers with half-interested eyes wondering what she was running from. Head lowered, she pushed her way down Villiers Street, past the Charing Cross tube, past Itsu, Five Guys—the smell of frying beef making her retch—and towards Embankment station, the Thames. On the Golden Jubilee Bridge, she turned: no Toni, no Kelly, no waitress with braces. They would not follow her across the river. She slowed to a walk, her chest heaving, and ignored the tourists who turned to look at her, phones in hand, their photos of Big Ben forgotten.

On the other side of the river, she dropped down onto the Southbank. Her breathing, which had steadied, becoming shallow again as she passed the food market, the smell of melting fat hanging in the air, huge black speakers competing with one another, making her brain vibrate. A double-decker bus serving ice creams and oil-blotted pots of churros had been parked opposite the vendors. People sat in deck chairs, the October wind whipping past as they dipped their fingers into little pots of molten chocolate. Piglet averted her eyes, keeping her head down, watching the flow of the river.

She felt her phone vibrate in her bag. It buzzed and buzzed again, and Piglet imagined emails from Toni, missed calls from Sandra, and voice notes, voice notes, voice notes from Margot. She was running again, past the Golden Monkey, past the National Theatre, onwards, onwards, and towards Observation Point.

The Thames was at low tide: rocky banks exposed. In the shadow of the OXO Tower, she slipped down onto the shore. She had seen people with metal detectors do this before, but she felt self-conscious, looking over her shoulder at the tourists leaning on the railings behind her. She made a show of looking at something and, at the lip of the river, crouched as if to investigate. She watched the water lap at her toes, her shoes soaking, their colour changing.

Through the canvas of her bag, she felt her phone buzz again: an insect trapped under a glass. She ripped the rucksack from her back, pulled it open, and upended it, the contents spilling out onto the bank. People continued to walk past above as she scrabbled in the wet sand. She felt the grit beneath her fingernails and saw grains scatter onto her phone. She thought about hurling it into the water, seeing the faces of the people behind her, watching her as if she were on a stage. She switched off the phone, and it stopped vibrating, its screen black. She let it fall from her hands. She was on her knees.

How had this happened?

She crawled towards the river to wash her hands in the water, icy cold. She could feel her bones stiffen, the blood in her veins freeze. The pebbles beneath her were silty, and she had to steady herself as she reeled. She had the urge to strip, to soak her clothes, to beat them against the shoreline rocks. She wanted to slip into the water, wash her skin, and emerge renewed. She edged forward.

"Are you alright?"

A man, above her, shaking her. He had pulled her backwards, out of the river, back onto her knees. She looked up at him and could see light dancing around his head, strands of grey hair flying, dazzling. Her father? He had come for her.

"Dad?" she croaked. The man shifted, and his body blocked out the sun. It was not her father. The man was shorter, younger, and dressed in layers of stained, fraying clothes. He wore a rucksack and held a yellow plastic bag at his side. His knuckles were dirty, the lines of his face inlaid with grime.

"No, kid," the man said. "I saw you from the bridge"—he pointed to Blackfriars, the bridge faded red in the distance. Now she was out of the river, his hands hovered in the air, reaching for her but not touching. "I thought you were in trouble, about to do something . . ." The man trailed off. "I've been there—after my own dad, actually."

Piglet shook her head.

"Are you alright?" the man asked again.

"I don't know."

———

She had told Kit to meet her in the coffee shop under the OXO Tower arches. His face looked smooth, cleanly shaven, the scent of aftershave still fresh. He was wearing one of his good jumpers: a blue Ralph Lauren with a silver quarter zip at his throat. When he had found her, sitting in a corner seat, grit beneath her fingernails and her Calvin Klein rucksack soaked with river water, he had rushed forward. She had been told to wait, and he had placed a hot chocolate in front of her, whipped cream high, wobbling as he set it down. He sat opposite her and watched her, waiting for her to drink.

"Are you in trouble?" he said when she did not lift the mug, nodding towards her dirty hands.

"Aren't you?"

"I know that things have been"—he paused—"weird." She did not say anything. She moved her toes in her shoes, still wet from the Thames.

"When I told you, I didn't think we'd be getting married this weekend," he said, his hand drifting into the air to his right, his words starting to trail. "I . . . I thought . . . Well, I didn't think we'd be here." She shook her head, a tiny movement among her hunched bones.

"I know that I lied," he said, and his shoulders started to quake. She leaned forward, touching the mug, but his eyes had closed. She shrunk back into her seat as she saw the sobs start to build.

She found that there was something embarrassing about seeing a man cry. She had only seen her father do it once, and never
in public. It had been in their back garden in Derby. She had been
in the kitchen with her mother—maybe Franny was there—and
he had been at the open window. The house had been locked,
she remembered, and her father, eyes wet, had been pleading
with her mother. "Never again, Lind," he had said, mucus on
his face, as her mother had stood, arms crossed, head shaking.

Piglet pushed a napkin towards Kit, and he took it, dabbing
at his face.

"Sorry," he muttered, and she said nothing. He sniffed,
pulling his nostrils high, and leaned back. They sat in silence.

"We have to agree," she said, embarrassed into talking by
his reddened skin, his blotched cheeks, "if we're going to do
this, or if we're not. If we're going to be in this together." Her
words felt warm in her throat, the thought of them, together,
satisfying. He leaned forward.

"We are," he said, taking her hand. "No matter what my
parents say." Piglet felt her face twitch, a fishhook pulled into
her lip. "No matter what anyone says," he corrected.

"OK." Piglet nodded, withdrawing into her seat. He was
her mirror, hands slotted between his thighs, head cast down.

Their fledgling truce, as vulnerable and exposed as the
membrane eyelid of a baby bird, held as they walked to the
Borough Market cook shop. He had been excited when she had
first suggested she make their wedding cake.

"So, you smash it?" he had asked, smiling.

"It's tradition," she had said.

They had been leaving a cake tasting, his parents behind
them. She had acted poorly in front of the white-coated pâtissier:

criticising, asking questions. "I could do better than this," she had said, and his parents had scoffed, fond. When the pâtissier had left—"I'll let you enjoy the samples"—she had puffed out her chest.

"I'm going to make our cake," she said. "In fact"—thinking of a chef she admired, a recent pâtisserie cookbook they had published—"a croquembouche would be traditional, in keeping with the catering." His mother had raised her eyebrows at her pronunciation, the rolling of the R, the rounding of the bouche.

"Aren't you a lucky boy, darling?" she had said to her son.

Now, Piglet and Kit did not kiss over the colanders, the cooling racks, as she had once imagined they would, but Kit asked questions, playing the attentive husband in front of the cashier. She picked up piping bags, stainless-steel nozzles, and leaf gold, and he paid; he carried their bags to the train. If this was what their life was to be, perhaps she could stomach it.

He reached out as they left the station in Oxford, and she met his request. They walked hand in hand over Osney Bridge, past the Waitrose, towards their house. The feel of his skin, their fingers, lightly intertwined, made her stomach light. She lifted her chest, she looked at him. He smiled, he nodded.

"Hold on," he said, reaching his free hand to his pocket, pulling out his phone. He looked down, frowned, swiped a finger across the screen.

"Sasha," he said, the phone held to his ear. Piglet turned to stare at him, her eyes wide. She shook her head. "Well, I assume if she hasn't been taking her calls, she doesn't want to talk to her right now." He paused, and Piglet heard Sasha's voice rising from the speaker. "Language, Sash." He began to splutter to her reply and then held out the phone, his hand still in hers. "She wants to talk to you."

"Yes?" Piglet held the phone to her ear, feeling the grease from Kit's face transfer to her own.

"I'll make this quick," Sasha said, her voice low. "I'm calling you on Margot's behalf—because she tells me you won't pick up her calls or respond to her messages—to tell you—in case there was some slim chance you hadn't realised—that she can't come to the wedding."

Piglet turned away from the road, from the noises of the cars, Kit's hand clinging to hers.

"What?"

"She won't be coming, she needs to recover. Nor will I, I expect it goes without saying. We need to be at home," Sasha said. She paused. "We can't watch you do this to yourself." Her voice was low. "And really, Layla is too young to be going anywhere," she continued, her words louder, faster.

"What do you mean?" Piglet asked.

"Well, Margot's looking after our child, Piglet—or had you forgotten she gave birth a few days ago?"

"No, not that," Piglet said, and Sasha snorted. "What do you mean? You can't watch me do what to myself?"

"Margot told me about Kit," Sasha said quietly. "I don't know how you can look at him."

Piglet heard a baby's cry.

"Is she there, Sasha?"

A pause.

"Yes."

"Can I talk to her?"

"She's been trying to talk to you for days, Piglet. But you've ignored her, you've shut her out."

"Sasha, please." Piglet's voice broke.

On the other end of the line, she heard the baby's crying intensify, moving nearer to the speaker and then farther away. There was a shuffling, a shut door, and then silence.

"Margot?" Piglet said.

"Hi." Margot's voice was quiet.

"Please come, darling," Piglet said, her voice tumbling over itself, a hot tear rolling down her cheek. "You're my maid of honour." She heard Margot's breath heave.

"I can't," Margot said. "Layla."

"Honestly?" Piglet asked, her eyes closing against the passing traffic, against Margot's truth.

"There is nothing I would love more," Margot started, her speech thick with emotion, "than to come to your wedding, to watch you marry someone who loves you, who is kind, who is worthy of you."

"He is, Margot," Piglet pleaded, Kit's hand tightened in hers.

"No," Margot said, the vowel sound of the word elongating. "He's not."

"You don't know us!" Piglet was suddenly competing with the noise of the cars driving past, shouting. "You don't know anything about us!" On the other end of the line, she heard Margot agreeing.

"I don't think I do, no." She cleared her throat. "But I think I know you. And the way you are about this—the secret keeping, the shutting me out—feels wrong." She paused. "And I know something's not right. Something's going on. But if you can't talk to me about it, if you won't let me help, I can't watch you do it. I can't watch you marry him for . . . for whatever reasons you are."

"You don't understand," Piglet said.

"Then explain."

"I can't."

"Then I can't come, my darling. I can't watch you do it."

"Please—" Piglet began.

"I love you," Margot said, her voice breaking, the line going dead.

On the side of Botley Road she lifted the phone away from her ear and looked at the blank screen, a dark mirror. Her hair was sticking to her cheeks, her nose was swollen, her face pink. Traffic streamed past, headlights glared, and Piglet dropped Kit's hand from hers.

In their kitchen, she asked him to leave her. He dumped the cook shop bags on their table, and she was alone, as she'd requested, to make choux pastry. Three croquembouches, she had said to him. Three hundred buns. I know, he had replied. Still so much to do.

The oven went on at 200 degrees. Three baking trays were lined. The large, heavy-bottomed Le Creuset was put on the hob, once more, over a medium heat, and she tried not to think about Margot.

To the pot she added butter, water, and sugar, turning up the heat until it liquified, bubbling yellow. She dragged the pan from the flames and metal scraped on metal, screaming. To the butter she stirred in sifted flour, a pinch of salt. She dragged the pot back. Heat, three minutes, the rawness cooking out. She didn't touch it. She watched: waiting for the wheaten paste to pull away from the pot's metal sides. When it did, she'd remove it from the heat, leave it alone, let it cool completely.

What do we know, really, about each other's private lives? she thought as she cracked one, two, three eggs into the cooled paste. Margot sometimes disclosed details of the arguments she had with Sasha and, while Piglet had always been careful to listen, to nod sympathetically, she had never responded with her own grievances. She had never told Margot everything. Surely, surely Margot also kept elements of her life—the unsavoury and pallid—private too?

She beat in one egg after another, the mixture becoming shining, smooth. Her piping bag was ready—she had ripped off the cook shop tags with her teeth. She filled the bag, and it bulged with uncooked batter. She piped three-centimetre rounds onto her first baking tray. She left space; they would spread. This, she knew how to do. This, she could talk about, if anyone asked. She put the tray into the oven, hot, heavy breathing, top shelf—it could only be the top shelf. She waited twenty minutes, watching the slicks of batter rise and bloom, becoming buns under the light of the oven. Once golden, puffed, she removed the tray and replaced it with the second. Another assembly of twenty choux buns would rise, and she would work, quickly, to pick off the cooked pastries onto a cooling rack. Pipe, space, oven, wait.

Margot didn't understand. How could she?

Soon every surface of the kitchen was lined with round choux buns, miniature pastry puffs. The sight of them, assembled, expectant, made her want to pick up the racks, take them from

the kitchen, and disperse them around the house. She knew
what she was doing. She knew herself, didn't she? Kit was asleep
when she slid a tray onto his bedside table, his eyes closed as she
picked up an empty bun and pushed it into her mouth, their
bedroom smelling like choux.

*When she asked herself what was worse—what he had done,
or what it would be like for people to know what he had done—
she was reassured by her inability to answer.*

1 Day

Once she had started to say she would make a croquembouche, she could not stop. Her ambition, her ability, had been so simply distilled by this one decision, this action, and the temptation to talk about it was always too much.

"Wow," Toni had said, when she had announced her plans to the office. "You like a challenge."

"I've made choux before," Piglet had replied, shrugging.

"Three towers of pastry on the morning of your wedding, though?" Toni shook her head. "That's another level." Piglet had not replied, quietly checking the method for making a croquembouche online again as Toni talked about the renewed vogue of craquelin. She clicked through page after page and read the warnings: the profiteroles must be eaten on the same day that they are filled; do not let the pastry stand for more than eight hours; the croquembouche should be enjoyed on the day of assembly. But no bother. She could make the pastry ahead and the crème pâtissière the day before. Then in the morning, on the day of her wedding, what was a little sugar work, a little assembly?

"Are you sure?" Kit had asked when she told him her plan.

"Don't worry—you won't be there. And anyway, I've told everyone I'll do it now."

When she had presented her practice bouche to Kit—a miniaturized version of the tower of bronzed choux cloaked in lacy sugar work—she had felt vindicated by its brilliance, its beauty.

"Look," she had said to him as she picked a bun from the stack and placed it into his mouth. "Look at what I can do."

He had been to collect the milk for her this morning—after the flowers had arrived—more than five litres, full fat, and she had enjoyed the sensation of packing him off with a list, briefly wifely, specifying the exact type of eggs that she wanted: "Burford Browns. If they haven't got them, call me." In that moment, her life had felt normal: she was contentedly wearied by its lists, exasperated by the man she shared it with.

Although he had returned with the wrong sugar, not enough butter, and she had reacted in appropriate measure.

Now, by the hob, she readied two enormous pots—empty silver bellies—and told herself there was no time to think about Margot, about her guests asking after the pregnant maid of honour. She held out her hand, a vanilla pod between her fingers, as if she were preparing to drop a coin into a wishing well. With a small knife, she slit open the pod, scraping out the paste-like black caviar seeds. They fell in, along with the husk. She did the same for the second pot and brought her hands to her face. Her fingers were speckled with sweet-smelling black. She licked them, one after the other, and tried to feel the infinitesimal seeds between her teeth. She wiped her hands, poured in the newly bought milk, and ignited the gas rings.

As the milk began to warm, she separated egg yolks from their whites with her hands. Yellow-orange orbs slipped between her fingers, slick, and she resisted the urge to test their membranes, squeeze them to bursting, as they slid from her grip.

She rinsed her hands, dried them, and measured out flour—too much—and used her fingers to return pinches to the paper bag. She added sugar to the flour, followed by the yolks, and peered into the belly pans. The milk was stuttering, edging towards a boil. Condensation fogged her face, clouded her glasses, and she pushed back her hair. She felt the dust trail of flour coat her forehead. She lifted the pans—huge—and poured their contents into the egg mix. She sucked in her stomach as she tipped the metal upwards, the bellies, hot from the hob, almost brushing her own. She whisked the egg and milk mixture, her hands moving quickly. It would be a waste for everything to curdle now.

Once the mixture was smooth, lumps of flour beaten into submission, she returned it to the twin pots. She dripped raw custard as she moved between the two: milky teardrops on the kitchen tiles. The flames beneath reignited, she began to whisk again, a utensil in each hand. Minutes passed, and her arms began to burn. She thought about Kit, overhead, limbs slack where he sat. Her arms moved faster, her grip on the whisks harder.

The custard was thickening. She tasted sweat: her tongue poking from her mouth in concentration, just as her father's did.

"You did all this, Pig?" he would say. "Your own custard too?"

"Crème pâtissière," she would correct him, a hand on his arm.

"Call it what you like, Duck." He would laugh. "It's the best thing I've ever eaten."

She readied a funnel sieve and passed the custard in batches, withdrawing the vanilla pods as they presented themselves, sucking them clean. There were not enough bowls, despite her calculations with Kit, and she looked for an appropriate vessel, landing upon a crystal vase. She would push this one to the back of the fridge. She covered each bowl—and the vase—with cling film, pressing the plastic into the warm, yielding crème.

She looked to her phone for the time and saw a missed call and a message from Margot appear: "I'm saying this in case you haven't realised—you don't have to do this if you don't want to." She remembered Kit—"I didn't think we'd be here"—and looked back at the words, the edges of the pixelated letters as fine as vanilla seeds. Delete. She wiped her face and scraped her hair back. She turned away from her phone, from the bowls, cream innards shining. She dragged the bin towards her, she opened the fridge.

She worked methodically, shelf by shelf. Jams, chutneys, and sauces shattered into the bin. Eggs, salted butter, and cheddar followed. Half a ring of chorizo, smoked salmon, chicken thighs. Broccoli, kale, spinach. Apples, oranges, grapes. Half a pint of milk was left in the door, and Piglet looked, imagining her parents—"How about a brew?" The half pint stayed.

Into the empty fridge she arranged the bowls of custard.

They fit neatly into the empty space, and Piglet decided to take this fullness, this snugness, as the good omen it surely was.

When Kit came into the kitchen, looking for lunch and finding only the crème pâtissière in the fridge, their food in the bin, he didn't say anything.

They had not been ready, really, to receive her family again. Before, they had talked about whether to put them up in a hotel—or, rather, whether Richard and Cecelia should put them up in a hotel. Piglet had decided, on behalf of her family, that this would make them uncomfortable.

But now Piglet was uncomfortable. Her issues with Kit felt unresolved, their fights unfinished, the ends of their conversations still unspooled across their kitchen floor. In addition to everything else, they had not been able to easily digest the phone call, the news that Margot and Sasha would no longer be coming to the wedding, Piglet without a maid of honour, and they chewed on the information, passing the gristle of it back and forward, unable to swallow. On the walk home from the station, when Kit had started to criticise Margot, sneering as he had sometimes done when they had first met, Piglet had not known what to do. His lips tightened, his words shortened, and he stared hard at Piglet as he listed the ways in which Margot had got him wrong, all wrong. "What does she know?" he asked, and Piglet privately thought, worried: perhaps as much as I do.

But her family were arriving: her father's battered brown Volvo pulling onto their drive, followed by Darren's blue Vauxhall Corsa on the pavement. She and Kit pasted on smiles to greet them, opening their front door as Franny called from the curb, "My brother!" She beamed at Kit, walking towards him, her hands outstretched. He laughed as if there was a sharp wedge of crackling lodged in his throat, looking down as Franny approached the house. Franny hesitated before diverting, embracing her sister instead. Piglet clutched at her body. "Ready?" Franny asked, and Piglet tried not to shake her head as she smiled.

They sat, the six of them, in their living room, as they had done nearly two weeks ago, but now, Franny was perched on the edge of the sofa bed, her mother alongside, holding a pillow to her middle. Among the buttonholes and bouquets of flowers, Darren sat with a small, wheeled suitcase on his lap, as if he were waiting for a flight.

"I'm sorry it's a bit awkward in here now," Piglet said, gesturing around the room: the monstera plant shoved up against the wall, drinks trolley pushed into the corner. Her father shook his head, leaning around the tasteful green-and-white wedding flowers: ferns, creeping ivy, cream roses, and headdresses of frothy gypsophila.

"Saves on a Travelodge," he said.

"And we can all be together," her mother added. "Although we'll miss you tonight, of course." She looked up at Kit, who was sitting on the other arm of the sofa bed. "What time are you leaving us?"

"My dad was supposed to be here an hour ago." Kit looked at his watch, a heavy Rolex that chinked as he twisted his wrist. "But—typical Dad—he's running late. I don't know why he insisted on collecting me himself." He smiled.

"It's sweet," her mother said.

"Nice to be close," nodded her father, looking sideways at Piglet.

Her parents would be sleeping in the guest bedroom, upstairs and across the hall from Piglet. Franny and Darren would be downstairs, in the living room, on the converted sofa with the third-best bedding, smelling of must, and surrounded by the green-and-white wedding foliage. That morning, Piglet had aired the guest room: opening the windows, lighting a candle, pulling fresh linen over the duvet. She plumped pillows, her body bent to avoid the bulk of her wedding dress, which was hanging on the spare wardrobe's door in its black bag, shielded from her future husband's eyes for luck. She and Kit had agreed, when they signed the mortgage papers for the house, that they would always be effortless hosts. But, as she smoothed the sheets, the thought of her parents sleeping here, rather than Piglet under their roof in Derby, on the night before her wedding left a pain in her chest.

When Margot had married Sasha—a small registry-office ceremony that had been attended by Piglet, Margot's mother, and a friend of Sasha's who read one of her own poems—they had all stayed with Margot's mother on the night before. Even the poet, who Piglet had only met once, turned up with her toothbrush and ate Margot's mother's cooked breakfast in the morning. Piglet remembered the camaraderie of it all, the frothy inevitability of returning to a parent before detaching from them.

She looked at her parents: her father, slippers on his feet, trousers too short, revealing grey socks beneath; her mother, on the sofa bed, curled around Franny—the daughter who stayed.

She had felt detached from her parents for a long time, although now, when she let herself think about it, she felt adrift, unable to inspect the details of her mooring to Kit for fear she was no longer attached, and instead, at sea, alone.

The doorbell rang.

"That must be him now," Kit said, getting to his feet.

They sat, feet shuffling, heads infinitesimally cocked, as they listened to the door being opened in the hallway, the exchange between Richard and Kit on the front step.

"Whose cars are those?" Richard was saying.

"Piglet's family are here. You're late."

There was muttering in the hallway before Richard stepped into the living room: red-nosed, red-jumpered, clad in Barbour, and wearing the mossy green, worn-at-the-knees chinos of the upper-middle classes. Piglet cringed as he took in the sofa bed, her mother and Franny half-reclined. It must have looked terrible to him, with its rumpled, greying bedding. Had he ever slept on a sofa bed? Had he ever seen one? Piglet felt embarrassed by her gathered family and by the bed in the middle of their living room: squat-like. She looked at her mother, who sat up straight.

"Lovely to see you again, Richard," she said, inclining her head. Richard nodded, starting to gesticulate.

"You too, you too."

Kit moved forward.

"Dad, you remember Piglet's parents, John and Linda?"

Piglet's father stood, reaching out a hand to Richard. In his slippers, he was shorter than Kit's father and, as he leaned over to grasp hands, Piglet noticed a gleam of skin, thinning hair, on the back of her father's head.

"Nice to see you again, Richard," he said. "Ready for tomorrow?"

"Just about," Richard said. "There's been some emergency with the page boys, one of my bloody great-nephews—that's why I'm late—but my good lady wife is across the matter."

"There's always a drama," Piglet's father said, nodding, grinning. He had thrust his hands in his pockets and was leaning towards Richard, rocking on the balls of his feet. He looked the way he did when Piglet used to watch him with his friends at the pub: ready to joke, buoyed by fellow male energy.

"Aren't you lucky to have Kit's mum?" her mother said, straight-backed, from the bed.

"She keeps us all in line." Richard nodded. "Speaking of"—he looked at Kit—"she's also keen to see you. Preparations to make. One last evening with her boy."

"I'm not going to kill him," Piglet called from the bed, a half smile on her lips. The room looked at her.

"Pig," her father said.

"No," Richard said. "Well, I'll leave you to your sleepover." He gestured at the sofa bed. "Looks like you're going to have quite the evening together." Richard turned to Kit, resting a hand on his son's shoulder. "I'll wait in the car, give you a chance to say good-bye." He looked over Kit to Piglet. "I'll see you at the church," he said, saluting. Piglet smiled, lifting her chin.

She stood with Kit in the hallway, one hand holding the buttonholes for the groomsmen. Richard was in his car, engine running, and her parents, Franny, and Darren were in view in the living room, quiet. Kit reached out his empty hand, stroked the soft flesh at the inside of her elbow, looked at her hands.

"Everything ready? With the croquembouche?" he asked.
She nodded.

"It all just has to come together now," she said. He turned.

"I'll see you tomorrow, I guess," he said, one hand on the
door. She opened her mouth, her lips parted, and waited for
words to present themselves. Then he pulled her close, crushing
her into a hug, and, pressed into his neck, her eyes stung with
tears. "I'm sorry," he whispered. For what? The wrongly purchased sugar? Margot slipping away from her? The lies? "I still
want to be in this together if you do." She felt his breathing,
uneven, and she held him tighter, aware of the buttonhole roses
crushing against her back, of her parents looking on from the
next room. She inhaled in the familiar scent of him: aftershave,
their washing detergent, the mild musk of his sweat. They broke
apart, met each other's eyes, and, before the audience of her
family, kissed.

"I'll see you tomorrow," he said again, picking up his packed
suitcase, his garment bag.

"You will." She nodded. He exhaled.

"Catch you in the church." He leaned around Piglet, waving
to her assembled family. They lifted their hands, chorused their
good-byes. She closed the door behind him and for a moment
she stood, adrift.

"How posh is his dad?" Franny hissed in a stage whisper as
the front door closed behind Kit.

"Franny!" Piglet moved away from the front door.

"Seriously loaded," Darren said. He had stood, his suitcase
deposited on the floor, and was peering out through the blinds.
"He drives a Porsche." He laughed.

"Wait until you see the mum," her mother said, her voice

lowered. "She looks like Helen Mirren's younger sister." Her father made a purring noise, and Franny pretended to vomit.

"A guest bedroom," Piglet's mother said as she ran a lint roller over a vivid green skirt and matching jacket. "When we used to have Aunty Irene and Uncle Frank, we went on the sofa, them in our room." Piglet nodded, unsure what her mother wanted her to say in response. Her father was sitting on the bed, staring at her covered wedding dress.

"That's it, then, is it?" he said, looking up at his daughter, and Piglet nodded. "That's the business to be in," he said, his hands on his knees. "A few months' wages on one dress."

"I am grateful, Dad," Piglet said. "Thank you. And thank you, Mum." Her father shook his head as if she hadn't understood.

"We wanted to buy it for you."

Piglet's father had insisted on buying a dress for her before: a tulle, floor-length gown for her high school prom. His insistence, his vocal ownership of that piece of clothing, had seemed, to Piglet, proprietary rather than proud. At that age, her body had not felt her own, and she had not wanted to wear a dress, to loom over her peers. They had shopped for the garment as a family, all opinions welcome, as Piglet pulled on gown after gown, her hair becoming static and then flat, her face red.

"Pig," Franny's voice called from the kitchen, "why don't you have any normal food?" Piglet walked downstairs and found Franny frowning, her face lit by the open fridge.

"I made that."

"I assumed." Franny leaned closer, pushing an index finger into the cling-filmed surface of one of the bowls. "What is it?"

"Crème pâtissière," she said, smiling.

"Come again?" Franny withdrew her finger, wiping it on her thigh.

"Custard, Fran. For the croquembouches."

"Ah," Franny said, her head nodding. "What happened to all of your other food?"

"Did someone say food?" Darren called from the living room. Before Piglet could answer, Franny was yelling back. Piglet winced as her sister opened her mouth wide.

"Yes! But Pig's fridge is full of custard."

"What?" Darren yelled.

"Custard!" The sound of movement came from next door, and Darren stepped into the kitchen.

"I could go for some custard," he said, looking over Franny's shoulder into the still-open fridge.

"Darren, if you so much as touch that crem pat you will not be sleeping in my house tonight." Piglet's voice was high, loud. Darren smirked and leaned forward as if to dip his finger into the nearest bowl. "Darren, I swear to God," Piglet said, her lips loose, her head shaking. Darren started to laugh, withdrawing his hand, placing it on Franny's shoulder.

"You're too easy to wind up, Crem Pat," he said, his small face creasing. "Too easy." Piglet pushed past him. Franny raised her eyebrows, and Darren made the playground noise to taunt touchiness: "Ooh." Without Kit, Piglet was jittery. She imagined him in their kitchen—"Are you alright?"—and compared the layers of him—fiancé, confidant, liar—to Darren, standing in her house, shaking with laughter. The custard bowls clinked as she closed the fridge.

"Girls," her father called from the guest bedroom. "Come up here, please."

"Now you've done it," Piglet said to Franny, and she hated herself, somehow a child again in her own home.

They assembled, the three of them, like schoolchildren in the small bedroom. Her mother was now brushing the lint roller over her father's suit while he still sat on the bed.

"Your mother and I want to take you all out for dinner tonight," he said, inclining his head like a king. "Our treat, while Piglet is still officially one of us."

Piglet couldn't decide how to feel about this meal: On the night before her wedding, she was ushered out of her house by her flat-vowelled family, who were starting to speak loudly about spiced chicken and all-you-can-eat refillable frozen yoghurt. Or, on the night before her wedding, her family gathered around her, jubilant at the chance to eat a final meal together while she was still, by name at least, theirs.

They had decided to drive, and her parents waved away the idea that they took separate cars. "There are five seats in ours," her mother had said, so Piglet, her sister, and Darren had folded themselves into the backseat of the brown Volvo, their knees knocking together. Piglet's mother had turned around from the front to look at them. "Well, this is nice," she said.

The night was cool, but the city centre was bright, alive with the energy of a Friday. Among the restaurants and the modern shop fronts loomed the older buildings of Oxford. Her parents looked up as they walked, pointing out the yellow stone, the domed roofs. They passed the front of St. Peter's College as they cut through New Inn Hall Street, and her mother gasped as if she had seen a celebrity.

As they approached the proposed restaurant—Nando's, on George Street—the group separated, began to drift. Her father and Darren pulled ahead, the energy of their conversation driving them forward. From over their shoulders, as their heads turned towards one another, Piglet heard the words "premier," "season," and "golden boot." As they turned right at the O'Neill's, where a group of men stood outside, after-work pints in hand, her father pulled Darren into a headlock, rubbing his knuckles against the finely cropped hair on his scalp. Her father was excited, she could see, by the occasion, the Oxford air, and the onlooking men. They, the women, trailed behind, quiet where the men were animated. Franny slipped her arm through Piglet's, and their mother hurried to keep step.

"I've been meaning to ask you," Piglet said, tilting her head so it stacked above her sister's, "would you be my stand-in maid of honour?" Franny pulled away, looking up.

"What about Margot?"

"The baby," Piglet said, not looking at her sister.

"Will they not come at all?" Franny asked, and Piglet stiffened, aware of her sister's searching eyes. She shook her head. "I get it," Franny ventured softly. "Layla is so small, and Margot must still be recovering. But still"—she paused—"bit naff for you."

"It's fine, Fran. Really," Piglet said, turning to her sister, fixing a smile.

"Will my dress be OK?" Franny said. "It's not in the colour scheme."

"It's fine, Fran," Piglet repeated, her smile widening as she felt her throat contract.

"Come on, you lot!" her father called from the Nando's doorway. Franny agreed as they quickened their pace, trotted along, and Darren started to chant as if he was at a stadium.

"Cheeky! Cheeky!"

She wondered what Kit would be eating tonight.

I didn't think we'd be here.

⸻

"Are we having bubbles for the occasion?" Franny asked, flipping over her menu.

"I don't think they do bubbles," Piglet said, sceptical.

"Oh," Franny said, her eyes scanning down the list of drinks, "no. Wine, then? There's an expensive Chardonnay."

"We'll get beer," her father said, looking between himself and Darren, not understanding or not caring about the convivial ritual that came with sharing a bottle of wine, the ceremony of pouring for your counterpart first and then yourself.

"Wine, Mum?" Franny asked. "We could get a bottle." Her mother shook her head.

"Not the night before the wedding. And it's not included in the voucher," she said, slipping her hand into her purse.

The food came, and Piglet's family chattered easily over their chicken, skin charred; chips, spiced and salted; and corn on the cob, slathered in butter. The men's meals were huge, served on platters rather than dinner plates: whole chickens each, burnished and bronze, flattened so the birds were splayed across the dish. Piglet rubbed her chest as she imagined a chef through the doors behind her, using his weight pressed over a cleaver to break the breastbone, spatchcock the bird. The women's meals were modest: salads and a shared side of chips. Piglet counted six consolatory olives among her rocket, her fronds of watercress, and her hand moved to her chest again, trying to rub away the pain.

As they ate, Piglet felt the conversation move around her. It was as if she were in water, her body swaying in the tide. She looked at each member of her family in turn, assembled in Oxford, here because of her. Her father: wire eyebrows jumping as he wielded his fork across the table, making a point, spilling coleslaw, then scooping it up and into his mouth. Darren: whacking the end of a ketchup bottle with his palm, peering inside the glass neck when the sauce evaded him, slapping again and deluging his chicken in red, swearing. Franny: laughing at her boyfriend between taking small sips of rosé from a tin, pushing halved cherry tomatoes around her plate, quarters of cucumber, cubed feta. Her mother, next to her, their thighs touching as they chewed, shoulders rubbing as they speared spinach leaves. She smelled like the same fragrance she wore when Piglet was a child: Davidoff Cool Water, the blue bottle pushed back on her dressing table.

"Oh." Her father looked up as he chewed through a mouthful of garlic bread. "We should have done a toast," he said, brushing his hands together over the table. On the edge of the booth, he slipped out, picking up his beer bottle as he straightened. He presided over the plates of half-eaten chicken, and Piglet's family wiped their hands on paper napkins, picked up their bottles, their glasses, their tins. A waiter looked up from the other side of the restaurant, where he was placing down another family's food. Her father cleared his throat.

"I need all the practise I can get for tomorrow," he said, and Piglet noticed the shake in his voice. "To our little Duck: While tomorrow, you will no longer officially be one of the clan, you will still always be our girl. It doesn't matter how old you are"—he smiled—"or how successful; if you ever need us, we will always be there for you." He raised his bottle higher. "Because we're your family, and you're our Piglet." He had tears in his eyes, she noticed, and the pain that had been in her chest receded, melted, as her shoulders sank, her lips trembled. "Our Piglet," her father said, raising his voice, his bottle.

"Our Piglet," the table said as one, raising their glasses, clinking, and cheering in the middle of Nando's on George Street.

The light mood that her family had created over dinner followed them back through the city centre and into Piglet's house. Franny set up a station in the kitchen among the choux to paint the women's fingernails, and the men stood next door, Friday-night television in the background, as they practised tying full Windsors on one another. They spent the rest of the evening, pyjamaed, in the living room, sitting among the flowers, Piglet and Franny on the sofa bed, her mother curling around them both. Later, on the landing, they loitered together as they cleaned their teeth, talking through toothpaste, mouths full of foam.

"Big day tomorrow," her mother said, rubbing Piglet's arm as they stood between the two upstairs bedrooms, she in a cornflower-blue housecoat, her daughter in white silk pyjamas, new initials embroidered. "Time to get our beauty sleep."

Piglet nodded.

"You go ahead. I have one more thing to prepare for the croquembouches before I go to bed."

Piglet had planned to assemble the cardboard cones that would support her pastry towers when they had returned from the restaurant, but the prospect of sitting with her parents, relaxed in her home, and curled up in soft socks with Franny, even Darren, had been too delicious. The cones would not take long. She needed to measure the card, roll it together, cover it in grease-proof paper, and run reams of Sellotape along the seams. In the morning she would cover them in choux buns filled with pastry cream.

"Dad?" Piglet said, seeing a male shadow pass the kitchen. "Daddy?" Her father leaned his head around the door.

"Sorry, Pinky, I didn't know you were still up," he said, the corners of his eyes creasing with a smile. "I was going to get some water." She indicated a cupboard behind her, and he stepped forward, retrieving a glass.

"Some final preparations," she said, gesturing to the cones.

"Ah." He nodded, moving to the sink, turning on the tap. "What is a wedding without a few cardboard traffic cones?" He took a sip of water. When Piglet didn't smile, he moved closer to her. "You OK, Duck?"

Piglet looked up at her father: his wrinkled face covered in the thick grey hair of his eyebrows, his stubble. His lips were thinning with age. He wore a matching pyjama set, chequered blue and bobbled. He followed her eyes to the buttons at his front. His crow's feet ran deep as his lips lifted. "You can tell your old dad," he said, and suddenly Piglet was next to him, had manoeuvred under his arm, her tears were on his chest, marking his flannel pyjamas. "Ah, Pig," he said, tightening his arm around her. "It's just night-before blues."

Piglet felt the heft of her father's body beside her. It was not as substantial as it had been when she was a child—her smaller, him larger, muscles thick—but it was here. He was still here. We will always be here for you. Because we're your family, and you're our Piglet.

"It's not, actually, Dad," she said, her voice cracking.

"What do you mean, Duck?" he asked, pulling her from his body to inspect her face. She averted her eyes, thinking about how he laughed with Darren, how he already did not know how to talk to Kit, how he did not know which words to use, words to make them both feel at ease.

"Kit," she said, she started.

He did not move as she told him. He stood in front of her and nodded at the information passing to him from his eldest daughter. She was in tears but restrained, unmoving. He shifted, uncomfortable with the new knowledge he had been given, sure that her mother would be a better-suited custodian, that she should be having this conversation.

Piglet had stopped talking, and he had hardly moved.

"Pig, it's the night before your wedding," he said. She nodded. "It's not really the time to be talking about this, is it? Richard and Cecelia have spent a lot of money."

"Dad," she said, "what do I do?" He shook his head, not ready for the question.

"It's not for me to say, Duck." He sighed, turning his head away. His water rippled slightly in its glass. She looked at him. He could feel her stare.

"You're my dad," she said.

"Yes." He nodded.

"So, what do you think?" she asked. She had moved closer, she had stopped crying, she looked to him for an answer.

"These things happen, Pig," he said, unable to look at her.

She was backing away from him, retreating, returning to herself. She was shaking her head.

"Silly of me," she was muttering. "Silly of me to say." He was immobile, watching her, and beneath his gaze she felt lesser than she had before.

"Relationships can be hard," he was saying. "And you have to work on things—with marriages, even more so." She was nodding, she was sitting at her kitchen table, detached from him once more. She was not making eye contact, she was attaching another ream of Sellotape to her cones, wrapping them in brown paper.

"You've got a good thing going with him. I don't think you can just throw it all away," he said. "Get some sleep. Big day tomorrow."

Piglet nodded, and her hands stilled at the table as he stepped back, stepped away, as he walked out of the door and left her sitting at the kitchen table.

How do you tell people, when the invitations have been sent, the crème pâtissière made, that the fullness of your life has been a pretence; your pleasures, you realise, posture?

0 Days

On the morning of her wedding, Piglet awoke in the dark, curtains closed, to the feeling of Christmas, to the feeling of a funeral.

Conscious, her stomach turned to liquid. As she lined her en suite toilet bowl with paper, she put her aqueousness down to nerves. As she sat, her bowels releasing themself in muffled thuds, she looked at her watch: a minute before 5:00 a.m. Two hours to assemble the croquembouches. Three hours to assemble herself.

On the unlit landing she stood for a moment, listening for her parents' breathing, heavy with sleep, her father's snoring. She tied a dressing gown around her, a gift from Margot and Sasha—white silk, to match the accompanying pyjamas, the word "Bride" embroidered above the breast pocket. They had presented the garments to Piglet over pizza, blotting their fingertips of luminous oil before handing them over, wrapped in tissue paper. That could have been an age ago—the three of them laughing about bridal showers, sequestered surnames. In the gloom she felt an aching lack: Margot's absence.

Piglet moved down the stairs, groping for the banister, her eyes wide in an attempt to refract light. In the hallway, illuminated with the orange of an outside streetlamp, she waited for her eyes to adjust, to take in the living room. It smelled like moss, the earthy scent of the wedding flowers intermingling with Franny's and Darren's stale breath, exhaled slowly through dry mouths. There was the creak and shuffle of a body turning, and she saw a black mass move—someone on the sofa bed—a shade darker than the room around her. She thought of Franny, curled up inside even Darren's short frame. She slipped past the bed, seeing the outline of Darren's face in the dark, slack with sleep. She reached out a hand for the adjoining door and turned the handle.

The kitchen was filled with plastic boxes packed with empty choux. She began to unclip the lid of each, pressing her body over the Tupperware, using her weight to suppress the sound, but the plastic cracks still sounded like gunfire. She opened the fridge, and the bowls of custard clinked. As light spilled onto her face, her early-morning eyes receded into her skull. She pulled her phone from her dressing-gown pocket, swiping to her bookmarked recipe, and it vibrated in her hand. Margot, at five past five in the morning.

"You won't be up yet, but I am, and I'm thinking of you. This is the kind of thing that ends a friendship, and that's not something I'm interested in for us. Whatever happens today, I love you, you know?"

Piglet would have to work methodically. She had 330 choux buns to fill and assemble. There was caramel to make, sugar to spin. Then there was a wedding to ready herself for, to attend. She closed Margot's message.

From the open fridge she took the first bowl of custard. She peeled back the cling film, and it hung heavy in her hands, a creamy skin. She rubbed the film between her fingers, and it was cool, firm, and resisted her pressure, like the belly of a fish yet to be gutted. She scooped crème from the bowl into a clear plastic piping bag. It wobbled, pale yellow and thick. The bag could have contained anything, and Piglet thought of liposuction, women with fat lips, and the candle scenes in *Fight Club*. She swiped back to her phone and saw the time: five fifteen. Her parents would be awake in less than two hours; Franny and Darren too. She would have to be quicker than this.

She had decided to do the croquembouches one at a time, keeping the unused, unfilled buns tucked neatly in their boxes so she had room to work. She would start with one of the two smaller towers, a practice bouche before she tackled the centrepiece: a mountain of 150 crème-filled buns and caramel. But first, ninety buns to get her eye in, to warm up. Ninety choux buns to fill generously—but not too generously—with her crème pâtissière. She began—nine sets of ten—pick, push, squeeze, fill, place. Pick, push, squeeze, fill, place.

Her practice bouche had used two bowls of custard: her calculations were off. The second and third towers would have to be scanter on crème. Although, she reasoned as she bit her lip, as she stacked empty bowls in the sink and heated sugar and water in a saucepan on the stove, the centrepiece could not be lacking. There was no time for more custard, no time for it to chill and thicken, but a half-filled croquembouche would not do. She would have to work something out. Her eyes flicked to the hob, where the sugar water had started to simmer, emanating thick, lazy, belching bubbles. Do not stir it, Pig, she told herself. Do not interfere.

The mixture had become syrupy on the stove, turning the colour of caramel. Piglet hurried, a step behind the chemical reaction, to turn off the heat, to assemble the filled buns and the first of her small cardboard cones next to the hob. She held the buns, bloated with their precious filling, as if they were baby birds, or softly poached eggs, her fingers light. One by one she dipped the choux into the caramel, coating a side in dark, sticky, shining sugar. She worked quickly, attaching the buns to the cone, and she smiled when they adhered to its surface. For a moment she stood back, awed by herself, observing the success you could have when you followed the recipe, followed the rules. Then she was dipping, sticking, smiling, and licking. Her fingers were gilded in caramel, and her tongue flashed at intervals, tasting her creation. It was sweet. Halfway up the tower, she slipped a whole bun into her mouth. It exploded with custard, and her mouth watered as she held it on her tongue. She had no need to chew, her saliva dissolving the pastry, the crème slipping down her throat. It was incredible: what her body could do.

She set the first cone aside, now covered in golden buns, wisps of caramel. Let it cool, Pig, she reminded herself. Remove the croquembouche too quickly, and the still-warm caramel would fold, the tower collapse. Follow the recipe, follow the rules. She started on the second cone, the largest, the centrepiece. This would be the tower that she and Kit, her fiancé—no, her husband—peered around as they waved to their guests from the top table.

One hundred fifty choux buns. Pick, push, squeeze, fill, place. Pick, push, squeeze, fill, place. She had not anticipated how much countertop she would need for an additional sixty cream puffs, and her workspace became smaller and smaller, until it was a sliver of laminated wood. The custard depleted quickly, but the thought of this tower being seen—being miserly—made her squeeze at the piping bag. The third bouche would have to have less.

At the sink she washed the caramel saucepan, first trying with washing-up liquid, feeling amateurish, before she boiled a kettle and poured steaming water over the set sugar. Tiny splashes of hot liquid landed on the newly filled choux, and her hands wrung in the kitchen. From the next room, she heard the creak of springs and felt panic in her throat. Her hand was at her phone: it was only 5:35. She poured the brown liquid from the saucepan and wiped her forehead with a tea towel before using it to dry the pan in her hands.

Again: water, sugar, a medium-high heat. She chewed the inside of her cheek as she watched. Come on, now, caramel, come on. The sugar bubbled, but where it had been languid before, viscous and thick, now it was brittle. Rather than burst, the bubbles cracked. She glanced at her phone, nodding, confirming that there would not be adequate time or sugar for new caramel. The bubbles continued to break.

She assembled the buns and the larger cone by the hob, as she had done before. She turned off the heat, eyeing the contents of the saucepan. The caramel had browned, but the surface was still shard-like, the traitorous white of the raw

caster sugar remaining. There was not time. She dipped the
choux, and it scraped through the sugar. She pressed it to
the cone and could have laughed—might have laughed—as it
stuck. The caramel wasn't shiny and dark, it was grainy and
flaxen, but the choux had stuck, and the spun sugar could
hide the imperfections. She imagined herself, later, in her
wedding dress, sugar spinning around the corset until she was
completely encased.

The second cone was complete with buns to spare. She
pushed them into her mouth, one after the other. The pastry
was soft, the custard slick, and she moved the contents of her
mouth down her throat like a boa constrictor, swallowing her
food whole. She turned to the final cone. It was six fifteen.
Her head ached, sugar saturating her brain. She was getting
married in five hours.

Pick, push, squeeze, fill, place. Pick, push, squeeze. She was
moving quicker, her hands heavier. The buns trembled as she
dropped them onto cooling racks. She pulled the vase of crème
pâtissière from the back of the fridge and scraped its contents
into the piping bag, now sticky and wan. She worked and the
bag deflated: the last of the thick cream pushed from the nozzle
into the base of a choux. There was only enough custard for
seventy out of the ninety buns. Why had she eaten the spares
from the cone before? She pulled in her stomach in retribu-
tion, snatched at her ribs. This tower would have to feed the
tables at the back: Aunty Irene and friends of parents, with their
insisted-upon plus-ones, eating empty choux buns covered in
hard, teeth-cracking caramel.

Soiled saucepan. Boiling water, wash, dry. Sugar, water,
medium-high heat. Bubble, bubble, bubble. Smooth, shiny: a

breath. But she hadn't done anything differently, had she? Sweat, bubble, sweat.

Dip, stick, lick. Dip, stick, lick. Dip, stick, lick.

She felt sick. Sick, sick, sick.

"Fuck," she muttered. A bun had torn as she dragged it through the caramel. A trail of custard streaked the dark sugar. Crème oozed onto her finger, and she shoved the hand into her mouth, pushing the deflating bun onto the cone with the others. She carried on. She sweated. She thought about Kit and wondered if he was awake yet.

The third cone was assembled. Next to the first two, it looked shrunken, emaciated. She had decided to disperse empty choux buns among the full on this final bouche, terrified by the prospect of an unfinished tower, an exhibition of her poor judgement. Now the empty buns sagged under the weight of their filled counterparts. She would have to entomb them in spun sugar—which she only had twenty minutes to make. But first: she had to remove the supporting cones.

In the time before, she had watched a YouTube video with Kit on how to release a croquembouche from its cone. "You can do that," he had said over her shoulder, "easy." They had been as carefree as the video's presenter, who made flipping the pastry tower over and sliding out the cone support look so, so simple. "Considering I'll have my parents in our house, this will probably be the least stressful part of my morning," she had said then, gesturing at the screen, at the smiling internet pâtissier, and they had laughed. Now, looking at the towers—the first overfilled, the second made with brittle caramel, the third peppered with empty buns—she did not feel the same sense of ease, of infallible, inevitable success.

Do it, she urged herself. Pick up a tower. Trust the process. Do it.

Whatever happens today, I love you, you know?

She picked up the first croquembouche. The buns were firm beneath her fingers. She flipped it over so the tower's point was in one hand and the base was in the other, her fingers slipping between the cardboard and caramel-covered choux. She could feel the sweat gather under her armpits as she pulled at the cone. It slid free, the glorious swooshing sound of releasing grease-proof paper making her gasp.

Overhead, she heard an alarm go off. She looked at her phone: seven. She was behind, but everything was coming together. She smiled, thinking of her parents waking up overhead, turning to one another, opening their eyes. "Today's the day, Lind." She looked at the first croquembouche—perfect, placed on its prepared cardboard base, foiled in gold—and imagined her parents with gleeful eyes, arm in arm, walking around the marquee later that day: "Our Piglet made the cake herself. Well, it's not a cake. It's a crock-em-booch."

She picked up the second tower, the biggest. Caramel flaked as she gripped the buns, and her custard-heavy stomach churned. She heard footsteps overhead, the flushing of a toilet. She braced herself. She flipped, and the caramel shifted, crumbling beneath her fingers. She pulled at the cone. She felt it move. She breathed. The footsteps descended the stairs. She pulled, the cardboard came, the footsteps landed in the hall. She righted the tower, and her face broke into a smile as the tower broke into pieces.

"It's your wedding day!" her mother trilled as she opened the kitchen door to find Piglet hunched over the broken croquembouche. Choux buns had rained to the ground and split, their innards splattered across the tiles, covering Piglet's feet with cold custard.

Her mother had been smiling, her mouth open with a singsong joy. When she saw her daughter—dishevelled; white silk pyjamas soiled in shades of brown; sweating and sprayed in custard—her lips puckered, her eyes creased. "What—" her mother started to say, a hand outstretched.

"Get out!" Piglet shouted.

"What?" her mother repeated, her expression changing, hurt.

"Get out!" Piglet screamed. Her eyes were bulging, her hair was wild. Her voice felt as if it had ripped her throat in its impatience to be heard. Her mother retreated, blue housecoat whipping around the door. Piglet thought she had seen tears in eyes. This is supposed to be my day, she thought.

She turned back to the broken tower. She could not allow herself to think about it; there was no time. It was past seven, and she needed a shower. Hair and makeup would be arriving soon, and while she had been told not to wash her hair, she knew they did not expect a bride damp with perspiration and sticky with custard.

She moved to the third tower, which gave up its cone as easily as the first. But without its cardboard support, it sagged more than ever on its golden platter, hollow buns reduced to pancakes. Her shoulders jumped high, suggesting hysterics, but what could be done now? She was committed. Everyone would be expecting her, her homemade wedding cake, her husband. She was expecting the same.

More water, more sugar, more medium-high heat. The

water and sugar bubbling, alchemising again. Perhaps she could stick the second tower back together with the spun sugar? Her eyes flicked from the darkening liquid on the stove to the broken bouche. The door opened; she registered the feeling of air moving across her skin.

"Little Pig." Franny was standing next to her, shorter and slighter, as she always was. "Are you OK?" she asked as Piglet stared at the darkening sugar. "Little Pig, it's your wedding day," Franny prompted. "Do you think it might be time to go and get ready?" Franny placed her hand on Piglet's arm: cool on clammy. Piglet continued to stare at the caramel, the colour of oak turning to mahogany. It was nearly ready. "Piglet," Franny said, her grip firmer, her voice louder. "It's your wedding day. Mum is upstairs in tears, you look like you've lost it, and the hairdresser will be here in"—Franny pulled out her phone—"less than half an hour." Franny looked up at her sister. "Maybe it's time to stop with the . . ." She peered into the saucepan. "What is that?"

"Caramel," Piglet said, watching the liquid bubble.

"Caramel," Franny repeated.

"Franny," Piglet said, not looking away from the saucepan, "if I stop making this caramel, then these croquembouches will be worse than ruined. I don't know if you've noticed," she said, waving over her shoulder, "but one of them has fallen to pieces, and another one is collapsing. If I don't make this caramel, I won't be able to piece it back together, and I won't be able to show my face today."

Franny laughed.

"Nobody cares about the cake, Pig."

"I do!" Piglet cried. "I care."

"And you've done it! You've proven to everyone that you can make three crock-em-boot-chez on the morning of your wedding and not go insane." She paused. "Well, not completely."

"Crock-um-boosh," Piglet corrected her, her eyes closing. "Crunch in the mouth."

"Crock-um-bitches," Franny said. "Whatever. They don't matter. People only care about you." Piglet opened her eyes, looked at her sister.

"That is sweet, Fran, but if I don't finish these, I don't think I can get married."

"OK," said Franny. "Then what can I do to help?"

"I need more caramel, but I'm out of sugar. This is enough for the decoration"—she gestured at the pan—"but that tower needs sticking back together." She jerked her head over her shoulder.

"Have you got any glue?" Franny asked. Piglet stared. "What?"

"PVA? I'll even take a Pritt Stick if you've got it."

"Franny, people are going to be eating this."

"Who ever eats the wedding cake?" Franny asked, smiling at Piglet with glassy eyes. "I don't." Piglet looked up, she reached out her sticky hand. Franny shook her head.

"It's fine, Pink."

"I have a glue gun," Piglet said.

"Then you spin your sugar, you get me your glue gun, and then you put your jammies in the wash and get in the shower. OK?"

"OK."

She was going to waste, she feared, she knew, the life she had made spoiling around her, turning to rot.

Part Two

Old

Her family were assembled at the kitchen table. Darren, his eye contact quick and his smile too kind. Franny, shuffling along the bench, saying something about a small one, patting the sliver of wood beside her. Her mother, watery eyed, a pot of porridge before her—"It's all I could cobble together from your cupboards." And there was her father. He could not look at her, and she wondered why. Then she remembered the previous night: how he told her that marriage takes work, how he had told her what she deserved. These things happen, Pig. She sat naked beneath her stained dressing gown, the embroidered "Bride," obstinate, over the breast pocket. Her mother began to dole out bowls, pass around the honey. When Darren offered the jar to her father, he looked up—extending a hand, smiling, shaking his head—and said, "I'm already sweet enough." He laughed,

Darren too, and Piglet wondered whether her father would have wanted more for her if she were a boy.

As they ate, conversation started to break out. They did not talk about Piglet, somehow, or the wedding; instead, they avoided looking in her direction, bending oddly around her body to look at one another, nodding between the croquembouche towers, ignoring them, encased in their spun-sugar cocoons. Piglet could see, from where she sat next to her sister, pearls of glue dotted amid the dark caramel. She wondered what it would taste like, whether the set adhesive would break her guests' teeth.

"What happened to your hands?" Darren nodded across the table at Piglet, his brow furrowed in an expression of concern that she had not seen on his face before. She looked down. Her fingertips were spotted with caramel burns, the cuticles around her lacquered nails reddened as if splattered with paint. Compared to the rest of her pale skin, her hands looked absurd. She lifted one to her face, inspecting its downy hair, its blisters. She nodded at the towers of pastry.

The doorbell rang, and her family turned their heads. When nobody moved, Franny stood—"I'll get it"—and walked out of the kitchen. She returned with Madeleine, a photographer highly recommended to Richard by the manager at the Oxfordshire after she had photographed the last two New Year's Eve gala dinners. She wore a long-sleeved Breton T-shirt and a quilted navy gilet, a camera swinging around her neck, a rucksack on her back. When her mother stood, Madeleine raised her hands.

"No, no. Continue as if I'm not here. I want to get some candids." She bent forward and started to snap. Piglet blinked, and her family sat in silence, unsure of where to look.

"Are you feeling nervous yet?" Madeleine asked, brushing past the pastry towers as she trained her lens on Piglet, her half-eaten porridge, her stained dressing gown. Piglet looked up.

"What do I have to be nervous about?" she asked as a choux bun fell from the top of the second croquembouche, landing on the floor with a dull squelch.

Madeleine continued to move around them, without saying a word, as hair and makeup arrived. Franny had squealed, leading the women through the hall, conferring with the makeup artist about laminated brows, already arm in arm. Piglet had watched on before she was steered from the kitchen table and into the living room, her dirty dressing gown complimented in too-high voices. "And you made your wedding cake this morning? Who are you, Superwoman?" The sofa bed had been folded away, Piglet noticed, the bedding piled into a corner. The hairdresser kicked at the edge of the duvet as she pulled two hooded dryers behind her, wheels snagging.

"We're still on for the messy updo that we did for your practise?" the hairdresser asked, looking in a mirror that she had propped on the coffee table, pushing Piglet's bouquet to one side. Piglet nodded, and the hairdresser sprayed the back of her neck with salt water. She flinched. The hairdresser did not ask questions while she worked, attaching strips of coarse synthetic hair to the base of Piglet's scalp, and instead the sound of Franny and her mother's chatter filled the room. She listened to them, imagining Franny's future wedding—the ease and rightness of her joy framed in Derby, their family home—as she watched her own flowers wilt as curling irons steamed. Piglet's hair had been pressed into ringlets, and now the hairdresser was piling the curls on top of her head, pinning each strand with three or four needlelike pins. When she stood back, holding up a mirror so Piglet could observe her work from the back, Piglet was not shocked to find she looked like a woman with a head full of pins and glue: falling apart, stitched together. From across the room, her mother watched, stepping forward when Piglet didn't say anything to the hairdresser's repeated, "What do you think?" In front of her, her mother was on her knees, brushing away the hair that had fallen across Piglet's eyes: the ringlets that had escaped being pinned into place.

"OK, Sister, I'm ready for you," the hairdresser was saying over Piglet's head, looking at Franny, who was sitting with the makeup artist.

"Swap?" Franny asked, resting a hand on Piglet's shoulder. Her eyelashes had been made long, her cheekbones high and rosy, and her lips had been painted a blushing pink. There was a ridge of glitter above the hollows of her eye sockets, and it shimmered as she raised her eyebrows. Piglet blinked at her sister. They changed places, Piglet standing, Franny sitting, and Madeleine scrambled to get a photograph of Franny, eyes upwards as the hairdresser started to stroke her scalp, running locks of blond through her hands.

The makeup artist wore the proof of her profession on her face. Before her were bottles of flesh-coloured liquids; compacts of pastel powder; pots of jewel-toned dust; crowns of feathery, fake eyelashes; lipsticks, stains, and glosses. She had assessed Piglet as she sat, and the corners of her heavily pencilled lips twitched as she confirmed: "We're going super natural, yeah?" The makeup artist moved closer, smelling of coconut, chewing gum, and something powdery, and Piglet listened to her breathing, the suggestion of a smoker's wheeze. As she worked, she thought of her father and Darren next door, or upstairs. Would they be washing each other's faces? Combing one another's hair?

"OK." She pulled back from Piglet, eyes darting, assessing. "Happy?" The makeup artist stepped aside, and Piglet leaned forward to look in a little mirror.

She recoiled, burned fingers at her chest. This couldn't be right: creased eyebrows and flared nostrils looking back at her. Her eyes looked too small, her ears too big. Her nose looked flat and round, and her body beneath was sack-like and soft.

"So beaut." The makeup artist beamed, lacquered lips pulling back over white, square teeth. Piglet touched her face, unsure. Her nose still felt pointed, as it should, nostrils small. She turned to Franny under the hairdresser's hooded dryer.

"Look at you!" Franny cried. Piglet looked to her mother.

"Maybe tone down the blush?" her mother said, and Piglet scrabbled at her skin, certain the makeup artist had failed to paint on the face of a bride.

Once the stain had been blotted from Piglet's cheeks and the hairdresser had pushed more pins into her head, she began to ascend the stairs to her bedroom. "Dress time," her mother had said, and Madeleine had rushed ahead, clicking with her camera as Piglet, Franny, and their mother climbed, their heads heavy with the weight of their pinned hair. Piglet was sure, as she lifted one foot after the other, that there was a drumbeat, a rolling heartbeat, and wondered if everyone else could hear it too. On the upstairs landing, the guest-bedroom door was closed. In the gap between the door and the floor, Piglet could see the lights were on, the shadows of the men inside: still.

Her mother and sister followed Piglet into the bedroom she shared with Kit. The bed had been made, and her dress, unbagged, had been hung on the wardrobe door. Her wedding lingerie—a creamy silk-and-lace set that she and Margot had snickered over—had been laid out on top of her smoothed duvet. Madeleine moved around them, squeezing past the king-sized bed, leaning to photograph the skirt of Piglet's gown, the straps of her underwear.

In the bathroom, among her shampoo, her toothpaste, Piglet eased on the lingerie, the lace feeling frail in her hot hands. She tried not to look at herself in the mirror on the back of the door as she stepped into the suspender belt, attempting to pull it over her bulk, tucking her tailbone. She heard the judgemental ripping of seams as she tugged it past her hips. The belt sat below her belly button, which peeked out above the fabric like a gouged eye. She pulled it higher, until the smooth strip of skin that covered her ribs was all that could be seen over the silk. She sat on the toilet, pointing her toes, rolling up gossamer stockings. She eased them over her ankles, the denier cool on her skin, and felt delicate as she extended her legs, covering herself in sheer fabric. She began to hoist at the stockings as they unfurled up her thighs, stopping short of the trailing belt, and she felt the sense of femininity evaporating. She bent over, and her manicured nails chipped as she struggled to extend the hanging straps, inching them farther toward the stockings, now shrivelling, rolling down her legs like the uncasing of a sausage. As she twisted, a pin fell from her head, tinkling on the tiled floor, and a strand of hair came loose. It hung before her, bouncing like a spring. She was muttering, swearing, and someone knocked at the door.

"Is everything OK in there?"

She straightened, pulling her dressing gown over her underweared body, stockings half strapped to the silk garter belt, which had started to ride up and fold in response to her bending body. She opened the door, the mirror behind her reflecting the room, and her mother cocked her head, smiled at her daughter. "Come here," she said. Piglet's body moved involuntarily as her mother pulled, straightening her, and there was a comfort in being clipped into place by a parent, as if she were six, her coat being zipped up around her. Franny was asked to step aside so Madeleine could get a better shot, and Piglet sucked in her stomach.

"Ready for the dress?" Franny asked from behind them. Her mother nodded, slipping the robe from her eldest daughter's shoulders. Piglet felt aware of her nakedness beneath the thin layers of lace and watched her mother and sister not looking at her body, their eyes fixed on her face, smiling. Madeleine clambered onto the bed, sheets creasing, her camera pointed at Piglet.

"Madeleine," her mother said, and the photographer looked up from behind her lens, nodded, and climbed back onto the floor.

Franny was unbuttoning the body of the dress, starting to spread the sides of the corset, a black hole for Piglet to lower herself into. "Here you go," she said, guiding in her sister's stockinged ankle.

Piglet stepped into the dress, organza rising around her. This much fabric, outside of Allegra Joy's boutique, looked unnatural, out of place next to their IKEA wardrobe, their bedframe. Her mother and sister stepped forward, climbing over the white netting. They moved around her, working together, wrapping her in fabric, embalming her, covering her in lace and beads.

She shook her body, trying to help the gown fall into place, and the material lifted and dropped, as if it were breathing, as if it were a living thing.

Her mother moved the body of the gown over Piglet's hips in one swift heave. Madeleine clicked her camera, and Piglet could not imagine a time when she would want to look at a photograph of her mother, hands white with tension, trying to push her into a dress that her parents had bought rather than taking their annual trip to the Algarve.

"Did you do the fast?" Her mother panted behind her, the unbuttoned corset in her hands. Piglet could feel the sweat on her mother's fingers, the dampness of it on her back.

"Yes," Piglet lied. The pressure of her mother's hands at her back started to strain.

"Would you open the window, Banana?" her mother said, her voice low, her eyes direct. "Get some air circulating in here." Franny dipped her head, her face expressionless, and Piglet felt a tapeworm of jealousy settle in her stomach at their easy teamwork, their unproblematic bodies, the blankness of their features: unsurprised, as if rehearsed. A gust of wind pushed across the bedroom as Piglet's mother began to pull. Piglet's skin pimpled, and her body shook involuntarily. Her mother huffed, dropping the dress. "OK," she said, "Franny"—summoning her youngest daughter as the dress fell around Piglet, the corset, undone, resting on her hips. Piglet looked down as her sister picked her way across the room, slipping past Madeleine, and noticed how her stomach jutted under the garter belt, how her belly button sagged beneath the silk that she had tried to cover it with.

"Now, I'm going to need you to—" her mother started,

and Franny moved alongside her, their hands on Piglet. "That's right," her mother said. "On my count."

They heaved, and Piglet felt herself lift. They moved around her, folding her body away, grappling with handfuls of netting.

"Buttons," her mother said, her eyes on the bodice. Piglet wondered why they were not looking at her, why they were discussing the dress, moving around it, as if a stranger were inside. She stared at them both, but they only had eyes for each other, for the fabric in front of them. She felt Franny's fingers, low on her back, scrabbling with the pearls that ran up the centre of the corset. Her mother was leaning over, pulling the bodice together as her sister tried to seal the fabric shut. Franny faltered at the base of Piglet's rib cage. "The hook," her mother said, casting her eyes around. Madeleine stooped, passing it over, silver handle catching the light. Piglet felt it scrape and twist against her spine, the dress closing around her. Her mother muttered as her sister readjusted, regaining her purchase. "If you just—" her mother said. "That's it." She bit her lip. "Try that one again, with me pulling in." She exhaled as she tightened her grip around Piglet's waist. "Oh, Christ." Piglet felt the sharpness of her mother's words puncture her chest as she dropped the corset, still unbuttoned.

Beside her, she felt her sister quickly look up, glancing at her face. Piglet turned to inspect the expression, but one of her mother's hands flew to her shoulder, stilling her.

"Just leave them for now, Franny," her mother said. "Let's come back after we've done the sleeves."

The sleeves, Piglet thought, smiling, feeling the heat of the room swelling her arms, the sweat in the crevices of her skin. Madeleine lifted her camera. "Such a special day."

Franny took one of her sister's arms and guided it through the sheer lace sleeves sewn onto the corset. Their fingers entwined, and they could have been children again: Franny leading Piglet forward. Her mother held the other arm, gently directing it through the fabric and into place. Their hands had been so soft on her skin, the resulting strain of the meshed material did not feel right, her reflection in the mirror opposite a deception. With both arms sleeved, her body looked apish. She was hunched forward, forced into a half bow. She let her limbs hang, afraid the material would tear if she was herself, if she stood up straight. Madeleine let her camera fall to one side, confirming what Piglet already knew.

"OK, come here, Franny." Her mother gestured. "Gently, now: one, two, three." They pulled, their strength combined on the seams, and the dress moved, her shoulders covered. Madeleine made a noise from beside the bed, picking up her camera. Piglet looked at herself in the mirror and she was a woman again, she was a bride.

"That's the shoulders, at least," Franny said, turning to her mother.

"But look at the buttons." Her mother pointed, shaking her head.

They were talking as if Piglet was not there, and for a moment she wondered if she was. She moved her stockinged feet, hot, on the carpeted floor.

"I don't know if I can do this," Piglet said.

"Just keep still, love," her mother said.

Strands of her mother's blow-dried hair had started to come loose, thickening with moisture, curling, unruly, into the air.

Franny's cheeks were flushed, and Piglet could see her mother sweating beneath her foundation, a sheen on her top lip.

"We're going to need your dad," her mother said, her eyes on Franny. Franny nodded once, climbing over Piglet's train, and lifted it out of the way as she opened the door. She returned, guiding their father by the arm, his hands covering his eyes, cheeks bulging with the smile below. While Piglet had been half-packed into her lace casing, her father had shaved and changed into his suit. The trousers gathered around his ankles, too long, and Piglet saw, in the mirror on the back of the en suite door, a little wad of white paper pressed to his neck, red-brown with dried blood.

"Ready for the big reveal?" he asked from beneath his interlaced fingers. Her mother reached up, pulling gently at his hands.

"John," she said, and he opened his eyes. Piglet could see his expression in the mirror: smile fading, the shape of it staying on his face, now filled with disappointment.

"What's happened here, Pig?" her father said, lifting his head in the mirror, not meeting her eyes. Piglet thought she could feel Madeleine flinch. Her mother placed a hand on his, looking up into his face. In the mirror, Piglet watched her: nodding at him, her fingers clasped tight.

"We just need your help to close the buttons. An extra pair of hands."

"What's the problem?" Her father leaned forward, her mother's carefully placed hand slipping away from him. He inspected his daughter's back. She imagined it there, half-dressed, spilling out of the wedding gown like overproved dough, and wondered what it would be like to knock herself back, fold her flesh over, and tuck herself in. "Oh, Pig," he said. "What have you done?" She did not know how to answer, but he did not need her input. He continued: "This is three thousand pounds of dress, Duck."

"Not now," her mother said. "She knows. If you could just pull the corset together."

So, her father was there too, with her mother and sister, at her back, trying to hold her together. She could smell him now: male, shower gel fresh, a whiff of black coffee on his breath.

"Pig, breathe in," he said. She did as she was asked but only seemed to swell in size. She heard the lace strain.

"Stop. Stop, stop." She stopped. Her inflated body slumped.

"Pull your shoulders back," her mother said, and she did: arching her back, contorting her body, making herself as small as possible. Around her, she felt her family force her body into a dress too tight, the buttonhook at her back, the metal implement connecting the four of them, their energy moving between them as if it were electricity. In the en suite mirror opposite, she could only see their bent backs, their bodies shuffling to accommodate her.

"Just a few more now." Piglet felt her father's hand push against her flank, his knuckles hard and swollen with effort, and she thought she heard a huff of laughter, or some pressure, some worry, releasing.

"Don't move," her mother said, tapping fingers lightly on her shoulder. "We're nearly there," she puffed, and Piglet turned to look, tempted by the sight of her smiling parents.

"No!"

She felt the popping release of a button—buttons—coming undone.

"Did you not hear your mother? She said don't move!" Her father had shouted. In the mirror, she could see a vein popping in his forehead. With his eyes bulging, he reminded her of Kit on that night. She stared at him, this man, who would later hand her over, entrust her to someone else, and she saw his frustration with her, she saw his disgust.

"You couldn't have waited, could you?" he said, closing his eyes. "You couldn't just control yourself, for once?" He shook his head. "You—this dress—greed," he said, his words failing him in his displeasure. She wondered, as he spluttered, whether his anger had been prompted by the gown's price or her overspilling body. "You've already got so much: Kit, your new job."

She met his eyes in the mirror and had the urge to fall, prostrate, before him.

"I didn't get the job, Dad," Piglet said, and her father took a whole step back.

"What? Kit said that you did. A couple of weeks ago."

"He lied," Piglet said, the words coming out as a sigh.

"Lied?" Her father's face contorted. "Why would he lie about something like that?"

"He wanted me to get it." She shrugged. "I didn't. Sorry, Dad."

"People your age," he said, rolling his eyes. "You think you deserve everything. Well—people your age who haven't got their heads screwed on." She thought she saw his head jerk backwards to the hallway, to where Darren stood. "Here's a life lesson for you, Pig," he said, his voice louder. "You don't get everything you want just because you want it. You have to work hard for things. You have to behave like a grown-up. If you're offered a promotion, you do everything you can to get it. If your partner gets himself into trouble, you do everything you can to fix it. And if you've been bought a dress worth more money than my car, you do whatever it takes to fit into it." Piglet felt the force of his words land with spit on the back of her neck. Madeleine had slipped from the bedside and secreted herself in the en suite, closing the mirrored door behind her. "It's just greed," he said, his eyes averted to the ceiling. "What is it about you and more, more, more?"

"Who will walk me down the aisle?" Piglet asked her mother from the backseat of a ribboned Rolls Royce, a croquembouche next to her where her father should have been.

He had left, slamming the front door behind him, and it had been Darren, his neck turned, eyes averted from her uncovered flesh, who had sealed her into her dress, who had helped her down the stairs, his touch unfamiliar, his hands surprisingly soft.

"I will," her mother said, lifting her chin, passing Piglet her bouquet of flowers through the car's window. She was wearing green: a matching skirt and jacket over an avocado blouse, her curled hair beneath a fascinator, strips of ribbon streaming from her head like cress. Piglet's stomach crumpled at the thought of the congregation watching her short mother stride to keep up with her down the long aisle of the church.

"Love it," said Madeleine, who was there too, her camera clicking, tone-deaf. "So empowering."

"OK?" her mother asked, a hand lingering on Piglet's

cheek. Piglet looked past her to Darren, who was running back and forth from the house, shrugging in discomfort beneath the jacket of his three-piece suit. The ankles of his trousers flapped as he ferried one of the smaller croquembouches from the front door to Franny's lap in the passenger seat of his blue Vauxhall Corsa.

Piglet nodded. Her mother's hand withdrew.

"Are we ready?" the driver asked, looking at her from beneath a hat in the rearview mirror. She nodded as her mother waved with both hands. "OK, then," he said. "Next stop: University Church."

Piglet had suggested to Kit the Holy Trinity Church in Ardington. "Guests could walk to the reception," she had said. But Cecelia had turned to her. "It's the University Church, darling. Not just anyone can get married there. And no one expects to be asked to walk through a village in October." When Piglet and Kit had accompanied Cecelia and Richard to carols—a twinkling tree in the Baroque-style porch, evergreens in the aisles—the vicar had indulged Cecelia in a lengthy conversation at the arched church doors, laughing, touching her arm, leaving hatted ladies queuing behind them, exhaling loudly, tutting under their breaths.

Cecelia had also extolled the beauty of the photos they would be able to get if they were married in Oxford. "It's such an important place," Cecelia had said, extending a hand, "for all of us." Piglet, who had felt the irresistible pull of a new family, had felt persuaded to agree.

The chauffeur was looking at her in the mirror. They were driving in silence, the only sound the rushing of the road passing beneath them. His fingers inched towards a radio, reaching for a volume dial, as she counted the petals of her bouquet, the tendrils of each fern, and kept one hand on the gold base of the croquembouche. As they passed over Osney Bridge, she twisted in her seat and saw Darren's small blue car behind them. Franny's face was obscured by the second croquembouche. Darren lifted his fingers from the steering wheel and gave Piglet a closed-lipped smile.

She turned back, closing her eyes, and still saw Darren's sympathetic smile, Margot's text—"Whatever happens today, I love you, you know?"—and her father's vein-popped face in her mind. These things happen, Pig. How could this have happened to her? She had been so careful to follow the rules, to build her life with Kit so meticulously. She felt the water gather beneath her eyelids and she tipped her head back, swayed by the motion of the car. She had traced this journey with Kit, wandering in the shadow of the Bodleian Library, and they had told each other how wonderful their wedding would be, their life: how beautiful, how much more magnificent it would be than any of their friends'.

She opened her eyes, swivelling her head to look at the tower of pastry beside her. It was not magnificent. It was not beautiful, and she felt the shame fill her like soup, scalding, skin prickling with heat. Then her fingers were upon it, a sense of impatient urgency surging. She tugged at the tower, but a bun did not yield. She tightened her grip, but still the choux remained in place, attached to the tower by caramel, by glue. Her fingers bore down on the pastry, and it burst, leaking cream across her fingers and onto the buns below. What was she doing? She withdrew, glancing at the rearview mirror. The chauffeur's eyes flicked away; he said nothing.

The car slowed, turning right, pulling onto the High Street, and Piglet felt fear hatch between her hips.

The University Church of St. Mary the Virgin loomed on their left, its spire reaching high. Piglet's breathing became irregular, the hatchling of dread climbing into her stomach, clawing its way up to her throat. Cecelia would be in there, standing in the first pew on the right, looking behind her, waving with her fingers, hair blow-dried beneath a hat. Kit would be in front of her, Seb by his side, wearing matching suits, identical buttonholes, as if they were schoolboys. They would be turned together, heads bowed, thumbs brushing lips, cheeks, chins, as they smiled, glanced at the open doors at the back of the church. Their expressions would change when she walked in with her mother, every body turned towards her, a collective anticipation, a hunger.

The ribbons on the bonnet of the Rolls Royce billowed as the car slowed to a halt. Piglet was looking down, shaking fingers in her mouth, her tongue fluttering, cleaning herself of custard.

"Here we are, then," the driver was saying, looking at Piglet in the rearview mirror, his seat belt still fastened. There was a knock on the window of the car. "You know him?" the driver asked, looking at the man in a too-big suit bending at the back window.

"Yes," Piglet said, voice muffled, her fingers still in her mouth. "That's my dad."

Her father bent to open the door. The chauffeur stayed in his seat, looking from Piglet to her father to the leaking croquembouche in the back of his car.

"Dad," she said, as he pulled her from the car, taking her

saliva-dampened hand in his, lifting her train as any other father might have done. Her limbs were light with relief: he was here. She swayed where she stood, and he lifted a hand to steady her. Her father looked up from beneath his grey eyebrows, lips pressed together.

"Alright?" he asked, and she felt herself smile. He had come for her. "The dress looks . . ." he said, trailing off. "Where's Mum? Franny?"

Piglet turned, pointing down the High Street. "Darren's car," she said. "The croquembouches."

"Those cakes, Pig," he said, shaking his head, and she felt tears again. "Don't be silly, now," he said.

"There's one in your seat," she said, gesturing to the open door. Her father stepped forward, peering into the car. She could hear him greeting the driver, confirming that he was the father of the bride. He withdrew with the croquembouche, lopsided, held out in front of him.

"At least you weren't alone," he tried, smiling. "Are they coming with us?"

"They were supposed to be in your car," Piglet said, and her father looked down at the buns, one burst, cream innards dissolving the surrounding caramel. "Now, I don't know. I don't know, Dad. I don't know." Her head had started to shake, and her father leaned back, leaned away.

"We've got them." Franny: next to her, in a backless floor-length gown embellished with miniature flowers, moons, and stars, lifting the tower from her father's hands. "Darren will take care of it." She was nodding at her sister, inspecting her glassy eyes. "You OK?" She looked from Piglet to her father. Piglet's head was still shaking as she looked at Franny. Next to her, she saw her father avert his eyes. "You're OK," Franny affirmed. "We're all here, now, so you're OK."

"You're here," her mother said, beside Piglet in green, looking at her father as Franny ferried the croquembouche back to Darren, orange hazard lights flashing behind the Rolls Royce, his arm out of the Corsa's window, waving traffic past.

"I am," her father said simply, and her mother opened and closed her handbag.

Darren's car passed in a blur of blue, Darren with a hand at his neck, loosening his tie, and Piglet imagined the towers flying in the Corsa, custard ingrained into the floor mats.

"It's nearly time," her mother said. "We should take our seats." She held out a hand to Franny. As they moved towards the church, Madeleine manifested, stepping forward.

"Can we just get a quick shot of the family?" she asked, her hand on Piglet's father's forearm, as if he might run. As they shuffled together, arms around one another, smiling, Piglet tapped her forefinger and thumb together, feeling the tacky stick of remaining custard, sugar on her skin. The shutter clicked, and clicked again, and Piglet winced.

Her mother kissed her as she left, telling her that they had never been prouder, and Piglet, in her dress and caked makeup, holding flowers she had not selected herself, felt a lump harden in her throat. She and her father watched her mother and sister leave from the arched doorway of the church. They saw her mother and Cecelia cross paths on the aisle. Cecelia had been striding, walking with purpose, towards Piglet, her hand lifted in a wave, a gaggle of cream-puff children following in her wake. Piglet's mother had held out a hand as Cecelia passed, and for a moment Piglet saw Cecelia struggle to place her. She had looked from her mother to Franny before leaning back, her mouth open in a smile, her eyes wide. "So lovely," Piglet had heard from where she stood with her father, "so exciting." Cecelia turned to the children behind her, and Piglet's mother nodded. Cecelia ushered the children forward, and Piglet's mother slipped into her seat.

"You're here," Cecelia said, her effervescent energy corrosive as she kissed Piglet's cheek. "And looking wonderful"—she leaned back, appraising—"and fashionably late!" She turned to Piglet's father, her vivacity evidence of the different morning they would have had in the Summertown house: hugs, champagne, tearful toasts. "Here's to our best boy."

"And don't you look dapper, John?" Cecelia smiled, and Piglet watched her father blush.

"As do you," he said, nodding, eyes fixed on Cecelia's shoulder. She was wearing pale gold, satin shoes just visible beneath a sleek floor-length dress, an embroidered coat skimming the pavement. Her blond-white hair had been blown back into voluminous waves around her face, and a crown of golden leaves glinted from among her curls.

"Look at me!" one of the cream-puff children shouted— Lilly, Piglet knew, the loudest of Cecelia's great-nieces.

"Look at you, indeed." Her father smiled, and Piglet felt as if she might choke as Cecelia turned to the troop of cream puffs, heads and tiny buttonholes adorned with gypsophila and ribbons.

"Now, everyone," Cecelia bent down and whispered, "are we all ready?"

"Yes, yes, yes!" the children cheered.

"OK, then." Cecelia nodded. "What are we to do?"

"Steal the show!" the children chanted in unison.

"Exactly." Cecelia looked up at Piglet's father and winked. "Now, girls, you're at the front with your petals, as we practised. And what do we do?"

"Sprinkle, not throw!" Lilly and her two small doppelgängers squealed.

"And gentlemen?" Cecelia turned on her heel to the page boys. "As in the rehearsal, you'll be behind our beautiful bride and doing what?"

"Holding the train," said the smaller boy, nodding his head.

"Making sure she doesn't go arse over tit," the older boy muttered, plucking at his knickerbockers.

"Do we need to have another little chat, Jeremiah?" Cecelia said. "I hope not." Jeremiah rolled his eyes. "OK, I'm going to take my seat." She smiled, her eyes not meeting Piglet's. "Be brilliant!"

The children shuffled, jostling for position. The three little girls stood in front of Piglet and craned around to look at her, eyes wide, smiles gap-toothed. She had met these children only once before it was decided they would be in her wedding: at a garden party, last summer, where the idea of flower girls had been floated by Cecelia in front of the girls' parents. It had been decided on the spot that Lilly, Amelia, and little Chloé would be just adorable. She blinked at them, her vision blurring, her heart thundering. Her father looped his arm through hers. "Would you look at that?" he said, inclining his head. "Might not be long until you have one of those."

Piglet tried to swallow, tried not to picture Margot: You deserve more than this. Her head swivelled, a knee buckled, and her father's arm became tighter on hers. "Steady now; you're fine," he was saying as her mouth watered, her lips tingling. The boys took up their position behind her, and Piglet heard Jeremiah exhale as he bent to pick up a handful of lace train.

"Wedding dresses are stupid," he muttered, and Piglet turned to look at him, blinking as her vision failed, spots of black appearing on the boy's face. He blushed. She tried to clear her throat.

"Jeremiah, do you have anything to eat on you?" she asked. Her voice cracked.

"What?" he asked, his nose wrinkled, as Piglet's father chattered with the flower girls: "How old are you? And you? Wow, that's a big number." Her stomach contracted; she tried to cough the hard lump in her oesophagus clear.

"Anything," Piglet gasped. "A snack or something?" Jeremiah shook his head.

"No pockets in these things." He waved at his silk knicker-bockers. Piglet shook her head.

"Me neither," she said, gulping, pointing at her dress.

A piano sounded, and her father straightened, his arm a right angle in hers. At the music she started to laugh—she couldn't help herself—and she grinned at Jeremiah, who smiled back, uncertain. Her father turned to her, lifting her veil over her face, obscuring her smile, making her ready. Madeleine darted ahead.

"OK," her father whispered. "Let's go, girls." The children moved forward, and Piglet thought about tripping one over. A grazed knee and tears stringy with saliva would delay things, start things over. But they were capering forward already, sprinkling their petals with deliberate care.

She was moving, she was wiping her eyes beneath the veil, stumbling, half a step behind her father, who had started a slow walk, stepping from the wooden doorway and into the church. He was pulling her forward, and she had to fight the urge to yank back, twist her arm out of his, a child refusing, the beginnings of a tantrum. The floor beneath her turned from flagstones to smooth, black-and-white tiles, and, as they entered the church, she felt the urge to submit—let it happen, let herself be guided forward; behave nicely, as expected, like the flower girls: sugar, spice, subordination.

They processed. A cello played: mournful minims relieved by hopeful quavers. The girls were ahead of them, bobbing, sprinkling, as the melody of "Le Cygne" drifted across the church, climbing over the congregation. The sound filled the space, and Piglet looked up at the arches that reached to the ceiling, directing music, words, and worship towards the sky. She was not religious—why was she here? Who were all these people? With her face turned up, her head pounded, and she noticed the sensation of lace pulling against her skin as she inhaled. Beneath the beams and either side of her were rows of dark pews, mahogany ends trailing her wedding flowers: tendrils of ferns, ivy, and Queen Anne's lace. Smiling faces were turned towards her, nodding as she moved forward, and she found she could not look at their bared teeth, their hungry eyes; she could not witness their appetite for the bride. Where she had been hysterical, laughing, she was now fearful, feeling small next to the statue bones of her father, his straight back and his surety driving him forward, pulling her in his wake. Did he know, more so than she, what was best for her, what she wanted? They had never walked like this before: so slowly, side by side, as if sewn along the seams of their clothing. His pride was hot as it radiated from his skin. What purpose he must feel as he led her onwards, downwards.

She could no longer feel her body, only the dress around her, the bodice tight on what she thought was her flesh. The organza floated as it moved, stirring in the air. She saw her mother, she saw her sister. Their tears fell freely, racing down their cheeks, beading on their lips. They smiled as they drew near, and the salt water dripped onto their teeth. How it hurt—a needle slid into her side—to make them so proud, now, when really, the woman they looked upon, who walked down the aisle, was not her. She turned: Cecelia in gold, Richard in wedding-party navy, Seb beside him, Sophie waving, a fascinator flying on her head. And finally, there was Kit: her fiancé, her husband-to-be. She could see his chest heaving, the wetness on his face, and his expression, the crease of his lips, looked something like relief: the antithesis to her dread, her unwilling lips pulled down in her reluctance, her resistance. I didn't think we'd be here. He waited, as she walked, slowly, for her father to deliver her to him.

The cello sighed its final notes, and her father stopped. There they were: the aisle had run out. Her father turned to her, lifting her veil. He looked her in the eye. "There," he said, taking her hand, placing it into Kit's. Her father nodded to Richard and Cecelia. He retreated to the front pew on the left. Her mother shuffled to make room.

The cellist laid down their bow. Kit took both of her hands in his. The vicar stepped forward.

"Are we ready to get married?" the vicar whispered, the clerical collar neat at his throat, kind eyes blind. Piglet felt tears fall, the powder dissolution of her makeup, the slip of her mask as Kit took her hands in his and nodded, consenting for them both. She looked down—his nails neatly clipped, hers shining with her sister's manicure—and knew she would not say a thing, she would not protest, and this realisation gripped her: a hand at her throat.

As the congregation stood for their first hymn—fascinators quivering, song sheets rustling—Piglet found she could not shake the vice at her windpipe, the strangling fear that held her. It was happening, she realised, as if in slow motion: their decision to preserve the veneer of their public selves, their immaculate lives, was being confirmed, becoming their union. She heard her father's voice rise from behind her—"Amazing Grace"—his proud and even tenor clear: how sweet the sound. She could hear Cecelia's reedy alto with Richard's bass, and the voices of her sister, her mother, and her cousins, who had travelled from Derby. She could hear it all: the sound of people she knew, people who loved her, people she'd never met, and, in front of her, Kit, his lips parting shyly.

She tried: opening her mouth, moving her jaw, but her voice snagged, and she was a rip across the fabric of their lives, a loosening thread that had begun to pull. Her throat contracted, and she choked.

When they reached the vows, the vicar leaning closer, his golden stole swinging from his shoulders, she could not look at the congregation. All these people here to witness her, this life she had built, this lie. She did not want to see the creased-eyebrow expressions of their assembled guests, her parents' nodding heads, her sister's tears of joy. When the time came, she whispered her promises, hoping that if there was a divine witness, they would fail to hear.

When they kissed, her mouth on Kit's for the millionth time, his lips felt cold, and the applause, the roiling cheers, made gooseflesh ripple beneath her dress. When they broke apart, she observed her body. Beneath the meshed lace, her skin was puckered, hair follicles swollen by cold and by the realisation that she was married, that she had made a mistake. Because shouldn't she be full now? Shouldn't she be satisfied? Despite everything, she was hollow.

She was hungry.

The vicar, for his own entertainment, liked to speculate on the wedding menu, his estimations based on the congregation: their footwear, their fascinators.

He looked from left to right—department-store dresses and Velcroed shoes; inherited jewels and tailoring—and pondered.

What compromised fare would this union produce?

New

They had left the altar to the melody of "Be Our Guest," and, as it played across the church, Piglet looked down, her arm in Kit's, and saw their wedding bands: glinting, new. The guests clapped, clicked their fingers, and Kit pulled her closer, his new wife, his mouth at her cheek, murmuring something she could not hear, his lips smothered by her veil.

In the doorway of the church, they watched as his mother assembled the congregation, passing out little paper bags of rice, swatting at Madeleine when she tried to intervene. She felt him, beside her, laughing, tipping his head back in ecstasy— "OK, who put my mum in charge of the rice?"—and knew he hadn't realized that everything was wrong.

As they left the church to the snap, snap, snap of Madeleine's camera, the whoops of their guests, and the patter of rice on the pavement, Piglet kept her head down, watching her feet, treading carefully, grains of rice lodging themselves in her tightly curled hair.

"Look up!" Madeleine called. "Look at me!" Piglet had been continuing to walk towards the High Street, on through their guests squinting in the October sun—hands lifted to shield their faces, empty paper bags doubling as visors—when Madeleine flung out an arm.

"We can't do the photos without the bride!" Madeleine teased, and the guests around them roared with laughter. For a moment, Piglet stood prey-like, frozen.

Madeleine moved around her, positioning her body, and told her to smile and smile and smile! You just got married. Kit stood next to her, beaming. When Piglet looked up at him, trying to intuit how he could be so at ease, so thrilled, when she was not, Madeleine called from behind her camera.

"Yes! That's perfect. Hold that look right there."

Piglet did as she was told, her eyes drifting from Kit's face. His throat bobbed with laughter as Madeleine continued to call to them. Piglet watched her husband swallow, neck expanding and contracting beneath his white shirt, his pale-pink tie in a full Windsor.

Between photos, he would look at her. "We did it," he would say, smiling. "We did it." When she did not reply, did not squeeze his arm to reassure him that she shared the same sense of achievement, he pulled her closer.

"Would you mind if we got some family shots?" Cecelia said, one hand on Madeleine's shoulder as Piglet was photographed among the groomsmen. She had been hoisted onto their shoulders, her body swaying as they steadied themselves, Seb grinning below, Kit looking on. Madeleine looked up from

her viewfinder and nodded. Piglet was lowered to the ground,
the navy suits straightening, dispersing, and Cecelia ushered
Richard forward. "You don't mind, do you?" Cecelia said, and
when Piglet shook her head, Kit's mother indicated the space
behind Madeleine. "Then, could you . . . ? We just so rarely
get the chance to have one of the three of us." Piglet stood
behind Madeleine and watched Cecelia stand behind her son,
snake her arms around his torso. Richard stood on Kit's other
side, tiptoed, a hand on his son's shoulder, and Piglet understood
how it was, how it would always be: they, the family; her, the
imposter—still, always.

Kit tried to apologise for his mother as he held the door
for her at the Rolls Royce, now trailing a rattling of tin cans, a
wooden sign hitched on the bumper. Piglet did not look at him
as she lowered herself onto the padded cream seat, swinging
her legs, picking up fistfuls of her train, muddied by the High
Street pavement. He helped her, pushing in handfuls of dress,
and smoothed the gown around her waist and into her lap before
he closed the door and hurried around to the other side of the
car. He was starting to panic, she realised.

In the backseat, he tried to align himself to her body, coax
her to nestle in the crook of his arm. "I love you, you know,"
he tried, in a whisper, his eyes flicking to Madeleine. As they
pulled away from the church, Kit leaned forward, waving to the
guests left on the pavement. From the backseat she could see
her parents gripping one another; Franny, smiling; and Darren,
nodding, a smear of custard across the front of his jacket.

"How are you feeling?" Madeleine asked, and Kit sighed,
eyelids fluttering. Madeleine smiled, looking at Piglet, inclining
her head, questioning.

"It's a big day," Kit said in a rush, compensating for Piglet's silence. "All the adrenaline, all the people. It feels weird now, actually, it feels—"

"I'm hungry," Piglet said, cutting across him, and Madeleine laughed.

"We've got a while until the wedding breakfast, haven't we? Enjoy this, though," she said, holding the camera to her face. "This is always one of the best bits of the day: just the two of you."

As the car pulled away, tourists waving, Kit began to chatter, excited or embarrassed by Madeleine's attention. He kept lifting his hand, showing it to Piglet. "We're married," he would marvel. "No backing out now," he would say, his voice rising. Madeleine would laugh and look at Piglet, waiting for her to smile. When she did not, she turned her lens on their hands, Piglet's in Kit's, their new rings gleaming, and the shutter snapped. Kit shifted beside her, and Piglet felt the blossoming of his trepidation, his reaction to her mood. He nuzzled into her neck, asking her if she was OK, telling her that he loved her, and when she did not reply, he pulled away, he looked up at Madeleine. "Such a crazy day," he said, too loudly, his smile broad.

Ardington House was in technicolour when the car pulled up on the gravel drive, tin cans scraping behind them. The lawns, a green so verdant that she could almost taste them, stretched to their left. To their right stood the house, red and grey bricked, many-windowed, in the shade of a towering cedar tree, evergreen among blush-leaved cherries, orange horse chestnuts, browning oaks. A few shining conkers and a scattering of acorns missed by the grounds team shone on the driveway as the chauffeur opened the bride-side door.

They were shown to the bridal suite by a tall woman in an elegant grey suit with thick gold jewellery at her wrist, her throat. "If you need anything," she said, "just say." Piglet asked if the caterers had arrived and was told that they had, that they had been working all morning. When she had asked for directions to the kitchen, Kit had placed his hand over hers, squeezing. The suited woman had bowed when she left the suite, calling Piglet by a name she recognised only as Cecelia's.

"I'm going to see how they're getting on," Piglet said, and Kit's grip on her hand tightened.

"Photos first, no?" he said, his words a question only for Madeleine.

"Someone should check on the food."

"They've been paid enough to check on themselves," he said, coughing a laugh, glancing at Madeleine, his lips starting to curl into something that wasn't a smile. She could feel the air between them begin to curdle, and the photographer stepped forward.

"How about," Madeleine said, as if she were coaxing a toddler, "we get our photos around the house, and then we'll finish up in the kitchen? We could get some really fun ones of you doing the cooking." Piglet drew her shoulders back before releasing them, letting herself slump as much as her dress would allow.

In each room of the house, Madeleine asked Piglet to tell her about another dish on the menu, list the ingredients, describe the textures. Piglet felt she was being placated, but she answered as Kit draped himself on sofas, hung himself over banisters, propped himself by fireplaces. Madeleine asked her to join him, and when she refused, or only shuffled alongside him, the photographer's eyes started to dart. Kit had begun to shake his head, to roll his eyes, standing, waiting for her, comforted by his own dedication to doing as he was told. She knew if she stayed, their life would be one of arguments, taking score over who had embarrassed who, who had made who a fool. She could see it now:

"I did everything I could," he would say. "You're the one that decided to make a mockery of our wedding. Do you have any idea how embarrassing that was for me?"

"How embarrassing it was for you?" she would scoff, a hard laugh that would force her head back, expose her throat. "Don't you think I was embarrassed? Marrying you like a fool after what you'd done."

"Then you made a fool of yourself," he would say. "No one forced you to do anything."

"Now, I'm not going to force you"—Madeleine was smiling, her chin dipping down in a question—"but it would be lovely to have you both by the front door, between these two pillars."

They were outside the house. Guests had started to assemble on the lawn, milling around an oyster bar, listening to the options for aperitifs recited by white-gloved waiting staff, and their presence, their attention, was somehow worse now, more real than it had been at the church. The sun had started to turn in the sky, beginning its descent. Piglet's stomach gurgled. She flicked her wrist and found it bare.

"What's the time?" she said, turning to Kit. He tucked the wrist wearing his watch into the crook of his arm. He beckoned with his other hand, inviting her up the marble stairs outside the house.

"Have this photo and I'll tell you," he said, his eyebrows raised. Piglet closed her eyes and sighed. When she opened them, she knew Kit had sensed her shortness. He changed tack. "We have to get at least one good photo." She shifted, aware of Madeleine, aware of the guests, but did not move. "Come on," he said. She had decided that she would, that she was here, and a photo in front of the white doors of Ardington House might be something nice to give to her parents. She imagined it in their living room, propped next to their own grainy wedding photo, on the opposite side of the television.

"Why are you making this so hard?" Kit said before she began to move.

She looked at him, and he dropped his eyes. She walked towards him and felt ugly when he leaned his body away from hers, as if she might strike. She strode past him, on and through the doors, into the entrance hall, and under the chandelier. She felt the hurry of him in her wake.

"Where are you going?" he asked.

Her movement, decisive, felt purposeful, right. She knew where she needed to be.

"I told you: I'm hungry."

"I can get you an oyster," he offered, half jogging to keep up with her, Madeleine rushing along behind them.

"I don't want an oyster. I want something to eat."

She was savouring the motion of her body, the air stirring between her legs, the folds of her dress.

"Our guests are waiting for us." He grabbed at her wrist, and she was shocked by the physical contact of him, hard on her skin, his hand wrapped around her bones. She stopped, her breath shallow, her eyes on the floor.

The carpets of Ardington House were like Richard and Cecelia's, she noticed: a deep Malbec red, with sweeping, angular patterns in shades of orange, yellow, and brown. There was also, she saw, a small, round hole, charred and blackened—a cigarette burn among the fibres.

"Then go," she said, turning round to Kit, whose head jerked back, his eyebrows contracted. His grip softened.

"I can't go back without you," he said. "You're the bride. Wives aren't supposed to behave like this."

"No," she confirmed, feeling a warmth in her cheeks. "Neither are husbands."

"What do you mean?" he asked, moving closer, his voice lowered so Madeleine could not hear them.

"You lied to me, Kit," she said, and there was a power in those words, spoken aloud, finally, as piquant as sherbet, fizzing on her tongue. His forehead creased.

"I thought we were getting over that together."

She swallowed.

"I'm not sure if I am."

"Well, perhaps you should have told me that before our wedding day," he said.

Madeleine moved closer, lifting her camera. Kit turned.

"Could you give us a moment?" He looked back at Piglet. She could see worry on his face. "We discussed this, didn't we?" He leaned closer, his eyes searching. "I thought we agreed that we were in this together?"

Piglet considered: one corner of her lips lifted, her head tilted to the side.

Being in it together, she thought, being over it, was like

eating a birthday cake that wasn't yours. You began with good, manageable intentions, but when things started to go wrong, spin out of control, you couldn't stop yourself. Instead of taking a step back, putting the fork down, wiping your hands, you kept going. Eating away until there was nothing left. The consequences you would have to deal with later, but at least it was all gone for now. At least you had worried at the problem until you had eviscerated it into nothing.

Married to Kit, the new ring tight on her finger, she had that urge again: to continue wheedling at the problem of their relationship, their union, and the lies it had been built upon. She had that urge to eviscerate the problem—their marriage—into nothing.

"I don't think I want to be in it together," she said. "I thought when we got married, it would feel different. But"—she paused, confirming, nodding—"it doesn't."

Kit held up his finger, his golden ring, and pointed, his eyes starting to bulge.

"It's a little late for that now," he said. "There's more than a hundred people out there." Piglet shrugged. He gripped her shoulders, started to shake. "How can you shrug?"

"Maybe it's a good thing. Maybe if people knew, it would be part of the healing. Maybe it would feel better." It has to feel better, she thought.

Kit's eyes widened. He took a step back.

"This isn't what we agreed," he said, and she was silent. "I'm not telling anyone."

"OK."

"Please don't tell anyone," he said, stepping forward again, taking up her hands. He sank down, his forehead on her torso, strands of hair snagging on the embroidered bodice of her dress. "It'll ruin everything," he said. "I'm not ready."

"OK," she said again, pulling her body away from his, leaving him in the hallway, on his knees, swaying in her absence.

The movement of the kitchen did not stop when Piglet stepped inside, pulling her train behind her. Porters and suited waitstaff walked past and only looked up, sparing a glance, when they noticed her gown, her trailing veil. The windows were steamed, the small room warmed by glowing ovens, flames alight on an island of gas rings. The place was small, barely enough space to move, and Piglet exhaled, at home, feeling coddled by the kitchen.

"Behind!" A short woman in black clothes was moving towards her, arms full with a tray of empty oyster shells. The woman's eyes widened, her head jerking. "Behind!" she shouted when Piglet did not move out of her way.

"I'm the bride," Piglet said, gesturing at her dress.

"I can see that," the woman said, stopping. "We should be starting service on time; don't worry." She looked over her shoulder.

"I wondered if I could get something to eat." She knew the request was unusual, made her look strange, but she forced herself to sit with the feeling, to stand by her desire.

"Um," the woman said, adjusting her tray, empty shells shifting, "I'm not sure it's ready."

"Please," Piglet said, her voice lowered. The woman inclined her head.

"Let me ask the chef," she said, retreating into the kitchen.

She returned with a platter that Piglet recognised as her wedding menu, reconstituted. The woman apologised, saying something about a crucial point in the preparations, how the bourguignon needed another thirty minutes, pay no attention to the texture yet. She directed Piglet to a high table at the back of the kitchen where she set down the food, the dishes sliding slightly as she did.

Piglet and Cecelia had chosen the menu together: French, they had agreed almost immediately, and they had nodded at their likeness, their shared taste. Cecelia had wanted to import foie gras from Gascony, as they had been doing since the millennium.

"It's not cruel, my darling," she had told Piglet. "It's traditional." But Piglet had insisted, and they had compromised: if it were to be pâté, it would at least be goose liver.

"Table service?" Cecelia had asked and Piglet had shaken her head.

"I was thinking family style. A cassoulet for every table."

"Peasant food, rather than fine dining," Cecelia had said.

"It's very chic." Piglet had nodded. "And I think everyone would be more comfortable that way." Cecelia had inclined her head, deferent to Piglet's knowledge of food, of what would make family feel most at ease.

"And I suppose," Cecelia had said, "we could always do oysters and aperitifs before—perhaps on the lawn, weather permitting, for those who want to partake."

"Sure." Piglet had nodded. "We could."

On the platter before her there was a bowl of beef bourguignon, the sauce dark with merlot; the corner of dauphinoise potatoes, gruyère-crusted top browned, bubbled with heat; there was a small plate of girolles, black kale, and white beans, scattered with breadcrumbs, mushrooms like trumpets; a sliver of a golden tarte tatin, confit garlic pressed onto the pastry like tear drops; a ramekin of pink-grey pâté, finished with a flurry of chives; there was a slice of fresh baguette that felt steamy to the touch, and a curl of butter imported from Isigny-sur-Mer at Cecelia's instruction, accompanied by a wooden bowl of fleur de sel.

"Obviously the breakfast will be served on the tableware you selected," the woman said, straightening her dark jacket.

Piglet shook her head.

"Thank you." The jacketed woman looked her up and down as she started to dip her fingers into the bowls of food.

"Can I get you a fork or something?" the woman asked. "A napkin?" she said lamely as Piglet looked up, already tearing into the bread, dunking it into the bourguignon. Piglet shook her head. "I'm gonna . . ." the woman said as she backed away, slipping back into the movement of the kitchen.

Piglet let herself sink into the food. Bourguignon would not let you down like a lover. Confit garlic would not abandon you like a friend. Her legs began to swing at the high table as porters rushed past, their eyes sliding sideways as they took in her dirtied hands, her white dress. She did not care. She was careless. This feast was hers. Let them stare. She was picking up a girolle, splitting its meaty body down the middle, when Franny walked in. Her sister looked small among the rushing kitchen staff, and she enjoyed watching her search from the table at the back: her eyes childlike, worried. When Franny saw her, Piglet could not help but wave.

"What are you doing?" Franny asked.

"I was hungry."

"Kit sent me to get you."

"Did he?" Piglet said, dropping half a girolle into her mouth. She chewed the mushroom, her lips parted—what did it matter? Everything was on show now.

"Why are you being weird?" Franny asked, watching Piglet chew. "It's your wedding day. People are waiting out there."

"Never seen a woman eat before, Fran?" Piglet asked and felt herself wink before immediate regret shrouded her like a cloak, her neck prickling with shame. She had not meant to hurt her sister, to lash out at Franny when she had done nothing wrong, but Piglet felt so dangerously close to the destruction of herself, of her marriage, it seemed that anyone who came too close to her would also suffer the flying shrapnel of her discontent. Franny recoiled, looking down, her hands clasped together at the front of her dress, miniature moons flashing as they caught the light. "I didn't mean that," Piglet said, the mushroom in her mouth turned to rubber.

"OK," Franny said, not lifting her head.

Piglet tried to hug her sister as they walked back through the house, throw her arms around her, but Franny pulled away.

"Please, Piglet, let's just get back."

Piglet groaned, dragging on her sister's wrists, and when she did not look at her, Piglet cried out.

"Give me my phone!" she said. Franny stopped.

"What?"

"My phone. You've got it, haven't you? Give it to me." Franny exhaled, opening a small bag that had been swinging from her shoulder.

"Here." She offered Piglet the phone, and it lit up as she brought it to her face. Six messages from Margot. Another from Sasha. One from Kit, dated from this morning: "I can't wait for you to be my wife." Piglet swiped past them all, navigating to her banking app. She selected their joint account. She tapped in a number. She chose a recent payee. She pressed transfer.

"There," Piglet said. "Two thousand pounds is in your account." Franny looked at her, shaking her head. "Happy?"

"That doesn't count as a sorry," Franny said, continuing to walk.

"Sorry, then!" Piglet called after her, tripping on the hem of her dress as she followed.

"Thank you," Franny said. "Now, will you tell me what's wrong? Why wouldn't Kit come and get you himself?" Piglet looked at her sister and could not will herself to speak. She knew that his failure was hers, and still, there was a part of her that needed to feel better than her sister, standing before her, collarbones at angles beneath her dress.

"Nothing's wrong." Piglet smiled, contained, and Franny rolled her eyes.

"You can tell me anything, you know? I'm not judging you."

Outside the house, at the oyster bar on the lawn, the air was cool. The sky had become overcast, greyed, and guests shivered, pulling their shrugs, their pashminas, more closely around their bodies. Congregants from the church had been joined by reception-only guests, and they mingled, holding empty shells and empty glasses. Friends from work did not quite catch her eye, Toni among them, dressed in defiant black, a highball in her hands. Her Derby relatives were laughing, daring each other to neck oysters, poking one another in the ribs. The Oxfords looked on, eyebrows raised discreetly beneath wide-brimmed hats as they tipped their glasses skywards. Piglet did not recognise some of their faces: red-cheeked men throwing their heads back, gargling shellfish, their gullets swollen, straining at their shirt collars; silver-haired women in wide-legged trouser suits and jacquard coats, oversized hats askew, coaxing Tabasco from tiny bottles. Piglet saw Madeleine in conversation with Cecelia and Kit by a silver bathtub filled with ice, sliced lemons, and half shells, ears of creamy oyster glistening. The two women were bent necked—Madeleine shaking her head, Cecelia drawing back in surprise—and Kit was nodding. They looked up as the people around them started to clap, noticing Piglet emerging from the house, walking towards the guests guzzling their molluscs. Piglet felt Cecelia's eyes on her as Madeleine darted forward. Piglet had been walking towards her family, following Franny to her mother with her half-raised hand, when Kit intercepted her, gripping her upper arm.

"People have been asking where you've been," he said through a smile. "What have you been doing? Why have you been transferring money out of the joint account?" he asked as he raised a hand to guests on the lawn. Piglet looked up at him.

"How did you know?"

"I got a notification on my phone."

"It's for Franny," she said, looking at Sophie and Seb, who were lifting glasses in their direction, Sophie miming parallel skiing so her champagne slopped.

"Whatever you're planning, whatever you want to do, please just wait until after today. My parents . . ." he pleaded. Her eyes wandered to Toni, who stood turned to her in the crowd, her eyebrows raised in a question.

"Are you OK?" Toni mouthed. "Do you want me to . . . ?" Toni gestured towards her. Piglet shook her head and watched as Toni nodded, raising a clenched fist to her chest.

What did she want to do?

"Here they are!" Cecelia cried, spreading her arms wide to the assembled guests, beaming. "My daughter-in-law takes her food very seriously. Expect this to be the best wedding break-fast you've ever eaten." One of the red-cheeked men rubbed his hands together before sucking back another oyster. Cecelia turned from the crowd, and the smile dropped from her face. Without it, she was slack-jawed, and looked like Kit had done on that night, when he had leaned over her in bed.

"Darling." Cecelia's hand was on Piglet's shoulder. "Kitty and Madeleine told me what happened with the photos. Is everything alright?" When Piglet did not answer, Cecelia shook her shoulder a little. "This is a very special day, isn't it? We wouldn't want to spoil it with your feeling a little over-whelmed." Piglet looked at her mother-in-law, who was glanc-ing from her to Kit.

"A very special day," Piglet said, rolling syllables, weighing the words on her tongue. Kit laughed, cleared his throat, and swallowed.

"Remember, all of our friends are here," Cecelia said, smiling widely, and Piglet spied a glint of gold at the corner of her lips: a false tooth that she hadn't noticed before. Piglet looked around.

"I'm not sure if they are my friends," Piglet said, and Cecelia's smile became smaller, tighter, until only her front teeth showed. She looked up, over Piglet's shoulder, and waved as Piglet felt a hand on her arm: her father.

"I just wanted to say, Cecelia, thank you for putting on such a lovely day," he said. "Linda and I are very grateful for your generosity, and so is Pig." Her mother was standing next to her father, slightly behind him, half of her green-jacketed body obscured. She was looking at Cecelia, her eyes darting from the fine golden embroidery of her coat to the crown of leaves in her hair.

Cecelia relaxed, her lips loose with laughter.

"I was just saying to darling Pig," she said, emphasising the last word, "what a special day this is for all of us." Cecelia moved closer to Piglet, wrapping an arm around her, embroidery thread catching on the beads of the wedding gown. Cecelia squeezed, and Piglet felt a fracture in her chest as she watched her parents glow. Her mother-in-law extended an arm to catch Richard, who had been passing them, an empty glass in his hand, eyes on the bar. Cecelia pulled her husband in, and the air was spiked with the scent of mouth-soured champagne.

"Darling," Cecelia said, "John and Linda are just very sweetly saying thank you."

"Oh, no need," Richard said, smiling, eyes unfocused. He placed a hand on her father's shoulder, swaying slightly. "Only the best for our kids, right?" he slurred, and her father shuffled.

Cecelia pulled Piglet closer. "And sweet of you," she addressed Piglet's parents, "to have bought the dress."

"We wanted to make a contribution," her father nodded,

not looking at his daughter. Piglet stood up straighter, pulling her shoulders down, shrugging off her mother-in-law. Cecelia nodded, her nose wrinkled with a smile.

"Sweet of you," Cecelia said again. "Have you tried the oysters?"

How long do you give it, then? the waiter asked as they uncorked a red burgundy at the back of the marquee, a double bassist slapping out the final notes of a Nina Simone song.

Well, the waitress replied in a low voice, twisting the screw, Judging by the bride's expression, maybe about a quarter of an hour?

Borrowed

Who was Mrs. Edwards?

She was aware of clapping, a hollering on her right by someone who sounded like a person she knew. She found herself jerking backwards, shying away from the noise, as if she were a horse spooked by the sound. As she recoiled, she noticed the grip of her husband tightening. Around her, beneath the canopy of fairy lights and garlanded eucalyptus, figures lifted phones, and she was bleached to the colour of her gown beneath a scattered flashing. They walked forward, through the marquee of round, white tables, guests standing in front of place settings, spindly ribbon-adorned chairs pushed back. She found herself looking at them as she passed, assessing the calligraphy and the miniature boxes of pastel-coloured sugared almonds, and recognized them for what they were: a farce.

A jazz trio was playing, a breathy alto sighing her way

through "My Baby Just Cares for Me," clicking, hips slinking. She had chosen this band with her mother-in-law, the other Mrs. Edwards—a woman who, she comprehended now, had also been someone else before she was a wife, a mother—and she remembered that afternoon: the thrill of being treated as an equal, a grown-up, when they had sat, feet curled beneath them, listening to music in the Summertown house, deciding how they would spend their money. It had been mouth-watering to be legitimate, discerning, to be a woman to which all worldly pleasures were available and her indulgence encouraged. Now the recollection was bittered, the experience poisoned. The singer extended her arms towards them, indicating that they, the newlyweds, were the reason for the song, that they gave meaning to the lyrics. More pretence, she thought as she looked ahead to a table at the back of the tent bearing her croquembouches, now hidden beneath a draping of wedding flowers, crème pâtissière oozing thickly onto the tablecloth below.

This walk with her husband, through their marriage's audience, was excruciating. She could not look at the guests assembled there, cheering, their teeth shining, their eyes dark. She had been picturing this day: this moment. Adulation for her efforts; heaping glory; witness after witness to her success. Her skin crawled with the reality, her breath catching in her throat, and she felt herself, then, slipping away.

"Mrs. Edwards," her husband said, pulling out her throne at the top table.

Mrs. Edwards took her place, pulling at her dress, squashing at the netting, trying to make it fit under the table. Piglet had thought that these thrones, ornate and golden, would make a nice picture, something enviable to share on the internet. Mrs.

Edwards saw them plainly: the metallic paint chipped to reveal a black plastic beneath, the red velvet cushion synthetic, suspiciously smooth.

She leaned back, assessing the marquee from this new angle, and realized she could see everything.

A table of grandparents, heads craned in their seats, chicken-skin necks wobbling, were appraising the centrepieces. A waitress behind them, a napkin over her forearm, held a black bottle of wine in her hand. A man with a torso wasted by age, a spine curved with rheumatism, was shaking his head—"Gout"—as the woman next to him pushed her glass forward. "Just a small one." Mrs. Edwards watched as the waitress leaned over, liquid like deoxygenated blood filling the glass.

The waitress moved between tables, exchanging smiles with a white-shirted waiter. Mrs. Edwards knew, of course, what they were grinning about.

"Where's the food?" Mrs. Edwards called, to a smattering of laughter. She cleared her throat: she had not been joking. She saw Darren nodding, looking down, a stilted chuckle dying on his lips, and the thought of him laughing on her behalf, attempting to make light of her behaviour, was almost as terrible as the memory of him helping her into her wedding dress, pulling her together when her father could not. She noticed the custard again, now dried on his jacket, and remembered the croquembouches, how he had taken care of them before, she knew, handing them over to Cecelia.

"And what's this?" her mother-in-law would have asked, outraged, inspecting the choux. "Glue?"

Cecelia was staring at her as she pulled in a platter of pâté, baguettes sliced and arranged around bowls of butter, wooden ramekins of seasoning. She piled bread onto her plate, scooping out pâté with her fingers, before going back for butter, pinches of salt, leaving flecks of ground goose liver in the fleur de sel. Cecelia's lips tightened, a hand on her son's thigh.

"It's no wonder, my darling," she would be thinking, Mrs. Edwards knew, "her family call her Piglet."

Her family: Mrs. Edwards marvelled with a tinging curiosity, as she wiped her mouth with the back of her hand. Were they still her mother, her father, Franny? Or did she already belong to her in-laws? Did they still want her? She trembled as she took one bite after another, as she met her mother-in-law's hard stare and smiled, her teeth browned by macerated liver.

"More."

The dishes kept coming.

"I don't know what to do," her mother would be saying to Franny, her hands shaking above the bourguignon. "What's wrong with her, Franny? What's wrong? Why couldn't she be like you? Why couldn't she be like the rest of us?"

Children, impatient and unimpressed by the oysters, the girolles, had started to run across the marquee, miniature tailoring bunching at their shoulders, flower arrangements toppling in their wake. They had found her croquembouche and sunk their tiny fingers into the choux. Mrs. Edwards watched as custard oozed along their arms, onto the tablecloth, dripping onto the floor below, and her heart was a profiterole, crushed.

She told herself she was not thinking about Margot.

She told herself she was not thinking about the family she had failed to make.

"More!"

Her sister glanced at her, her own plate untouched.

Mrs. Edwards's husband leaned over.

"Please," he said.

She wondered as to the end of his request. Forgive me? Stop eating? Return to the remit of my control, to the image that people believe our lives to be? No, Mrs. Edwards repeated to herself as her hands reached, her fingers grabbed. No, no, no.

Her bites quickened, her jaw mashing, her lips no longer closing as she ate. She could feel a soup of chuck steak, béchamel, and breadcrumbs on her tongue, burgeoning in her gullet.

Next to her, her father had withdrawn notecards from his jacket pocket and was murmuring an audible rehearsal over her chewing.

"This is typical Pig," he would say, his glass raised. "With her, it's always about more, more, more."

"The speeches," her husband said as he leaned over her, his body shielding her own. "You have to stop for the speeches."

Mrs. Edwards pulled platters towards her, smeared with leftovers. She scooped up pieces of mushroom, uneaten crusts of tart, and crushed soft garlic between her forefinger and thumb. She licked her fingers. She wasn't finished.

Mrs. Edwards had not meant to interrupt her husband.

But she was standing, her body rising, arms extended, asking for the microphone.

"Can I borrow it for a moment?"

He had been playing to the crowd—telling an edited version of how they had met, pausing for laughs, nodding to their guests, winking—and she had been jealous, for a moment, that the nourishment of their approval was still available to him. When he realised, he stopped midsentence, lips in a half smile, head to one side. He might have looked charmed, she thought, and was amused in spite of herself. She imagined a great-aunt whispering, whistling through her plastic teeth, "They are thoroughly modern."

He did not offer her the microphone, and in the end she had to take it from him, the thunk and shuffle of changing hands echoing over the speakers. The guests had stopped laughing, their jaws now loose with discomfort, disbelief, and she felt the happily soused mood in the room shift.

Next to her, her husband sank into his chair, his head bowing. She had drunk her champagne, but she picked up the empty flute—she felt she should—and her in-laws looked towards her; her family, away. She sensed her father's body shift as he distanced himself from her and found she was not sorry enough to stop. As she lifted the microphone to her mouth, speakers whining, the guests farthest from the top table leaned forward, and the ones closest leaned back.

She tried to listen for their reaction as she told them what he had done, her voice echoing, but blood was pounding in her ears, and the bones of her dress creaked and groaned across the speakers, as if in reproach.

She was raising a toast—"To us"—lifting her glass higher and higher, when she felt her dress give, a sick ripping snagging through the speakers. It was the seams, not even the buttons, she thought, and in a moment of wild hilarity she laughed out loud at the thought of herself. What must this look like? What would Margot say? Briefly, she imagined the story, how Margot would laugh, wave her hands—"Stop." Mrs. Edwards peered beneath her armpit, appraising the rip of her dress, the bulge of her body, and the microphone, held away in her inspection, amplified the edges of her exhilaration, the sound echoing unevenly across the tent. She did not see the wide eyes of the guests as she dropped the microphone, their covered mouths as they eyed the fringe of her lingerie, cream silk cutting into white flesh. Mrs. Edwards's eyes were cast down, her right hand twisting at the ring on her left.

This is the best wedding I've ever been to, a guest said as the bride's ring slipped free, tinkling to the table. What a mess, the guest continued as a murmuring started to break out, followed by a shout. What a beautiful, fucking mess.

Blue

Piglet pushed herself away from the table, and her throne clattered to the floor. Kit, next to her, was immobile, his flute still full of champagne. She tried not to run. She stopped at the table bearing the croquembouches and picked up the largest tower. Behind her, the band had started to play, and she looked over her shoulder to see Cecelia gesturing at the pianist, nodding, her eyes wide. The husky alto began to sing, "L is for the way you look at me," as she pushed the other two smaller croquembouches off the table. They landed on the floor with a wet smack. Guests gasped. Garlands of ivy fell from the choux as she strode through the marquee, weaving through tables, mouths still open, eyes following her, a frenetic hi-hat tsk-tsk-tsking. At the back of the tent, as she struggled with the plastic folds of the door, she heard one waiter call to another: "Laura! You were right. I owe you a tenner."

Outside, the air was cold, and she felt the chill of late October on her exposed ribs. Beyond the soft glow of the fairy-lit tent, the sky was already darkening to navy; the lawn stretched out before her almost black. The house glowed in the distance, windows illuminated. She adjusted the croquembouche, shifting it into one hand, and looked at her wrist, hoping to find the time.

"It's nearly five," her mother said from behind her, out of breath.

Piglet turned.

There were her mother and her sister, panting, watching her, their chests rising and falling. Franny was closing the little bag at her side.

"Poor Kit," her mother said. "Poor you."

"What the actual"—Franny screwed up her eyes—"and I can't stress this enough—fuck?"

Piglet turned away from them both, striding across the lawn, early evening dew soaking through her shoes, dragging at the hem of her dress.

They hurried across the grass behind her, heels sinking into the soft earth, clods of mud flying into the air as they asked her if it was true, for how long, and why, why hadn't she said anything until today? She didn't have any answers for them, and when her mother said that this must have been very hard for Kit, Piglet told them that she was leaving. On the gravel drive outside Ardington House, her mother said, "Oh"—as if it were a shame, as if she should have stayed for the first dance.

"Darren said you could take his car," Franny said, opening her bag, passing Piglet a bunch of keys. "It's round the side of the house."

"Are you well enough to drive?" her mother asked.

"I've only had one glass of champagne," Piglet said.

"Are you sure?"

Piglet lowered the croquembouche into the passenger seat of Darren's blue Corsa, throwing a grey hoodie onto the backseat, and her mother shifted beside her.

"I can tell Aunty Irene not to come to your house tonight," she said. "But she is eighty-seven."

"It's fine, Mum. I won't go home." She withdrew from the car, and Franny wrapped her small body around her. The night was drawing in, and her sister was warm against her, covering the rip in her dress.

"It's OK," Franny whispered into her neck. "You're strong. You're going to be alright."

"It's a shame about the dress, Duck," her mother said from behind them, running a finger along the split seam, her fingernail grazing Piglet's rib cage.

"I don't think she's going to be using it again, Mum," Franny said, pulling away from her sister. Her mother shook her head, opening a mossy clutch bag, and withdrew three folded notes.

"Here," she said. "In case it helps."

Franny did the same, opening her bag, offering Piglet her phone back. She took it, seeing Margot's name.

Piglet dismissed the string of messages, opening her banking app once more. She considered their joint account, her finger hovering, before she navigated to her own.

"I haven't got enough to pay you back completely," Piglet said to her mother, "but I've just transferred two hundred fifty pounds to your account. If I can pay in instalments, you'll have your money back for my dress in a year's time."

Piglet's mother opened and closed her mouth.

"We wanted to buy it," she said. "We wanted to buy both of your wedding dresses." Her mother turned between Piglet and Franny.

"I know," Piglet said. "Thank you. I'm sorry."

"Will you text me tonight?" her mother said. "Let me know you're safe."

Piglet turned the keys in the ignition of the Corsa, and the engine started to hum. She beat back her dress to grasp the gearstick and kicked it aside as her feet found the pedals. Franny held up a hand as Piglet reversed, the croquembouche shifting beside her. The wheels of the car crunched as she crossed the driveway of Ardington House. As she leaned forward to turn on the headlights, she saw Cecelia standing on the edge of the lawn. Her mother-in-law was illuminated in gold as the headlights flared, the crown of leaves still glinting among her blow-dried curls. She watched as Piglet drove past, and Piglet looked straight ahead, feeling the pound of her heart, the slip of adrenaline into her veins. She had been speeding, she realised, down the track that led away from the house, stones flying from beneath her wheels. As she passed through the gates, she slowed, pressing the brake, and the car came to a stop at a junction on the edge of the grounds. She looked in the wing mirror. There was nothing behind her, only the exhaust fumes that rose, red, illuminated by her brake lights, across the gravel road. She fumbled for her phone, scrolling for Margot's name.

"I just left my wedding and I'm on my way to yours. I hope that's OK because I'm about to turn off my phone."

She pressed send and waited for the message to be deliv-

ered before she held a button on the phone's side, the screen
turning to black, and shut it into the glove compartment. Piglet
looked out at the junction: pretty, red-bricked village houses
before her. She turned from side to side, guessing, before dragging the steering wheel down, pressing the clutch, and turning
right. The petrol-tank light was shining red, she noticed, and
she thought of Darren, earlier, volunteering to drive; ferrying
her family, her croquembouches. She imagined him watching
the fuel dial tick lower as he made the journey from Derby to
Oxford, calculating the mileage, the pennies to the gallon. The
dial's hand sank lower as she watched, and she knew she would
have to stop. She bent over the steering wheel, urging the car
on, through the village of Ardington, following the signs for
Oxford. On an A road outside Abingdon she saw the glowing
yellow shell of a garage loom out of the night on her right. She
guided the Corsa into a bay and considered what it would be
like to get out of the car.

Darren's grey hoodie smelled like deodorant and chewing
gum as she slung it over her shoulders, stuffing her mother's cash
into the pocket. Outside, she had to shove her organza skirt
beneath the Corsa in order to make space to navigate the pump.
As the scent of petrol filled the air, flowing through the rubber
hose in her hand, she watched as her skirt shifted, coming away
from the car's underside covered in grime. There was a small
boy in the back of a neighbouring Toyota. He watched her,
wide-eyed, as she held the pump. At the till, the cashier made
no attempt to hide his surprise as she handed over her mother's
folded notes. He looked at her lace-covered body, at the crisp
packets in her wake that had fallen off their shelves as her train
had swept through the station's shop. She turned to leave, and

a man behind her holding a fistful of chocolate bars in brightly coloured wrappers said, smiling, "Runaway bride."

And Piglet was running, speeding, from one life to another. She was in the margins of her decisions, inhabiting the space in between. It felt oddly lonely, she noticed—or spacious, maybe—when there was enough room to spread out. As she drove towards Margot's, she felt tears prick at the corners of her eyes, and she did not know if it was relief or grief that made them fall.

She exhaled when she turned onto a familiar road outside of Oxford. Margot was waiting in her painted blue doorway when Piglet stepped out of the Corsa, organza catching on the gearstick, a choux bun falling from the croquembouche as she pulled it from the car. As Piglet crossed the garden, maple leaves beneath her feet trodden to brown, she noticed her friend's belly had deflated a little since she saw her last. She held the collapsing pastry tower out in front of her, and Margot stood back. Under the overgrown ivy, Piglet was ushered inside—"It's OK, darling, just come in"—and Margot closed the door behind them, chips of cobalt paint flaking to the floor.

Piglet sat in Margot's kitchen, her dress squashed beneath the wooden table, netting snagging on closely packed chairs. She watched her friend open cupboards, reaching for a mug, not quite looking at her. Margot's body was different: no longer taut with a baby but soft, folds of skin visible through her clothes. She was moving slowly, hesitant between her hips, as she boiled the kettle, poured steaming water into the selected mug. The oven was on, Piglet could see, the yellow light glowing. "Here," Margot said, sliding the mug towards her, a tea bag filled with mint leaves floating, the water around it turning green. "Sasha put one of your pies in." She nodded her head back to the oven. "I didn't know you were bringing dessert," she said, her lips curling in a smile. The disintegrating croquembouche had been placed on the kitchen counter: moisture-bored holes in the caramel, buns flabbily pale with leaked custard, integrity gone.

"Where is Sasha?" Piglet asked, pulling the mint tea towards her, wrapping her fingers around the mug.

"Upstairs." Margot flicked her eyes towards the ceiling. "Layla's threatening to sleep."

"Sorry," Piglet said. "I know I'm intruding."

"You know you're always welcome here."

Piglet bowed her head, knowing that while Margot meant what she said, it had been Piglet's pride that had kept her from her friend. Even now, a part of her wished she were dancing the Macarena with Kit, Cecelia, Richard, and her parents on the dance floor of the marquee. That life, though, she knew, was over for her now. She had failed to become the person she had craved to be. She could not look at Margot, or stand her sympathy, and so instead took a sip of tea, her lips scalded.

"What happened?" Margot said, pulling a chair from underneath the kitchen table, bending slowly to pick up a foam cushion shaped like a doughnut. Piglet closed her eyes. How to say that she had built a life that relied on the mirrors of others? How to tell Margot that she had carefully crafted her personhood on a lie— and not Kit's, even, but the fallacy of their bliss, the superficiality and shallowness of it all. She pressed her lips together. These were the things she knew: she had married Kit; she had told her father; her family were not the people she wanted them to be; she was not the daughter that her in-laws desired. Images from the day flashed through her mind: the croquembouche collapsing this morning; the dress; her father leaving; the church; the vicar; Kit; the creeping realisation that really, really, they had made their vows in the pursuit of living a life that looked good rather than felt good.

She took a breath and told Margot everything.

Margot nodded, shifting in her seat as Piglet spoke, popping two powdery ibuprofen tablets from their blister pack. Piglet tried to finish speaking, to ask how she was, if she was in pain, but she could not stop. She sounded like a child, her breath coming in jagged gasps, tears falling down her face, cutting tracks through thick wedding makeup, and it was not lost on her that, in this moment, she was asking Margot to mother her too. Her friend reached a hand across the table, and Piglet's breathing steadied, her tears slowed. She looked up at Margot, this woman who was someone between friend and family.

"And why did you bring the edible Eye of Sauron?" Margot asked, nodding towards the croquembouche.

"I stole it," Piglet said, wiping her eyes so mascara smeared the back of her hand.

"Can you steal your own wedding cake?"

"I pushed the other two on the floor," Piglet said.

"You went full Terminator." Margot laughed, nodding.

"The bride and groom are supposed to smash it," she said, breaking off a piece of caramel, crushing it between her fingers.

"I assume we're not inviting Kit over to do the smashing?" Margot asked.

"No, but I couldn't leave it. Before I made them this morning, I was so proud of it all. I couldn't wait to smash them. I could imagine the photos."

"You can still smash it, you know?"

"What?"

"Yeah." Margot smiled. "Go and smash it. Do it in the garden. Why not?"

"Traditionally—" Piglet started.

"Traditionally, you're supposed to hang around for your reception and not just do one after the lunch," Margot said. Piglet laughed, and then she cried.

"Have you got a rolling pin?" she asked, sniffing. "It's normally done with a rolling pin."

Margot eased herself from her chair, the cushion beneath her slipping to the floor.

"I can do you one better," she said, walking wide-legged from the room. She returned with a baseball bat. "Here," she said.

"Why are you keeping a baseball bat in your house?"

"For armed burglars, murderers, rapists, and spontaneous games of rounders." Margot held out the bat. "Go on."

Margot secured herself in the living room, closing the bifold doors behind Piglet as she stepped out into the garden, the croquembouche tucked into the nook of her elbow, the baseball bat in her other hand. Margot smiled from behind the glass, lifting a thumb in encouragement, but Piglet did not see her. Her eyes were fixed on the mound of choux, looking small, somehow, on Margot's unevenly cut lawn. She drew the bat over her shoulder. She felt the night air stir the ripped fabric at her side—cold, on the penultimate day of October, the season beginning to change—and she noticed her body, responding, with a surge of pimpled flesh. She felt the hair on her scalp stand. She shifted the bat between her palms. She held it higher.

She hadn't planned to take the microphone. She hadn't planned, really, to do any of this. When he had told her, two weeks ago, she had seen no other route forward than the one they had already laid. Marriage, still, to him, had been the best thing for her. It was absurd to think that she could tell people, share how he had failed, how she had. She could not disclose how her fiancé, her house, her life, were not so delicious after all.

But her wants, her desires, she had come to realise, were untrustworthy allies. Since he had told her, revealed how he had indulged his pleasures, she had decided to follow her own. She did not entertain the idea of hurting him back, and instead she permitted herself the kind of revenge that she could stomach. A revenge on him, a revenge on herself. With every mouthful, she let herself believe that everything, still, was fine. It would be fine because she could make it so, imbibe it, consume it until it was true.

She had eaten her heart out.

It had not changed a thing.

And then, listening to her new husband's speech about how they were meant to be, how he had known from the start, she had found herself, despite her gorging, hollow. The attention from their guests, their wedding-day admiration, had not filled her up. Her father's pride, wrested from him, had been bitter; her in-laws' approval soured. She had plumbed the depths of this shallow life they had constructed and found there was nothing left to do but leave it.

She had felt guilty. She was killing them, she knew, as she drew the bat down. But he would survive. People like him always did.

What did she want, she wondered afresh, and did it matter, as long as she could choose?

Part Three

1

Light was streaming onto Piglet's face when she woke on Margot's sofa. She was hot under the skylight, the sun beaming onto her body. When she opened her eyes, it took her a moment to place the leather sofa, the bifold doors, and work out why she was here, wearing pyjamas that were not hers. She remembered the shower, the night before, after they had eaten her shepherd's pie with oven chips and ketchup. Margot had sent her to the bathroom, borrowed pyjamas in hand, and told her to take as long as she liked. The ripped wedding gown had been easy to remove, even on her own. She had arched her back, flexed her spine, and the buttons had burst open. She had shaken herself free and watched the ruined corset, ripped along the right-hand side, fall from her body. She had picked up the gown, draped it over the toilet, and, next to the porcelain white, it had looked dirty, deflated. She had tried not to think of her parents. It was in Margot and Sasha's black bin now, organza bursting from the lid.

On Margot's sofa, Piglet's eyes drifted to the garden, and she saw the remnants of the croquembouche: swollen choux pastry smashed on the grass, custard spattered on the patio. For a moment she was shocked, scared at the sight of her creation destroyed, desecrated on the lawn, before she remembered that she had chosen this ruin over the one she had been living. It would take her a while, she knew, for this choice to settle into her brain as fact, her decision like the death of a loved one: easy to forget, terrible to realize over again. She thought of Margot, last night, trailing a hand over her shower-wet hair on the sofa as she walked the baby through the house in the middle of the night. She thought of Kit, picturing him in the bridal suite, waking up, his body in the middle of the vast, white-sheeted bed. She thought of her family: the breakfast buffet they could share with Cecelia and Richard; the conversation, dead, over the sausages; the congealing scrambled egg. The images of them all made her stomach ache as if she were hungover. But it was done now, for better, for worse. She pushed herself up, a blanket falling from her body, and felt her bones ache. She rolled her neck, her shoulders, she twisted until her spine cracked. She squinted at the sun overhead, warm on her face, and wondered what the time was. She could hear movement coming from the kitchen and could smell coffee, burning toast.

"The kettle's just boiled," Sasha said as Piglet entered the room. Sasha sat at the kitchen table, which was strewn with plates, knives slicked with butter, and a crumby pot of marmalade. Margot was on Sasha's other side, her foam pillow beneath her, Layla curled onto her chest in an orange top, sleeves rolled up around her wrinkled hands, which clung to her mother. Margot smiled over Layla's head, which was covered in a shock of black curls.

"Sleep well?" she asked as Layla stirred, burrowing her forehead into the hollow of Margot's breastbone. Piglet lifted her hands, palms to the ceiling.

"Fine," she said, trying to swallow the feeling of rawness. She turned to the baby. "Look at that hair, though." She smiled at Layla and found she could not look away. She felt behind her for a mug, fingers fumbling at ceramic handles.

"We're a family of early risers now," Sasha said, nodding at Layla, lifting a mug to her lips. "Coffee's just there, by the way." She pointed.

"That's a misrepresentation, Sash. It implies we actually go to sleep," Margot said, as Piglet spooned brown granules into her mug, her eyes on Layla's cheeks, the curve of her ears.

"She's getting better," Sasha insisted. Piglet poured boiling water, stirred through milk, and could not help but smile at the baby as she shifted on Margot's chest.

"She's just over a week old." Margot rolled her eyes and turned to Piglet. "Sasha is ready to get Layla and I into a routine." Piglet took a seat at the table and shuffled where she sat.

"How is it going?" she said, aware that it was the first time that she had asked. Margot inclined her head, looking at the baby below. Piglet followed her gaze.

"You know," Margot said, and Piglet knew that she did not. "I think we're doing OK."

"Margot's been amazing," Sasha said, leaning forward to stroke Layla's back, Margot's arm. Piglet watched them, quiet, and felt embarrassed by her presence.

"Do you want to hold her?" Margot said, looking up. Before Piglet could say anything, Margot was repositioning Layla, placing a hand under her domed skull, extending her arms across the table. "It would be nice if her godmother held her, don't you think, Sash?"

"Oh, yes," Sasha said. "I think it would be nice."

Piglet looked between them both as she received the little girl, Layla's limbs stretching into the air.

"Really?" she said, and her heart broke at the size of Margot's.

Margot nodded as Piglet brought Layla closer to her body. The baby's eyes were still closed, her eyelids smooth. Her cheeks were full, spilling over her mouth, her lips slack with sleep. Piglet watched her breathe, felt Layla's body move beside her chest, and noticed how her tiny, curved nostrils flared, shining, a little dry skin flaking as she inhaled, as she exhaled. The baby moved against her, and Piglet was shocked by the realness of her, the solidity of the fists pushing against her chest, grasping at the strap of her pyjamas.

"I can't believe you made her," Piglet said, looking at them both across the table. Sasha nodded, sipping coffee, and Margot beamed, her eyes filling with tears. Sasha put an arm around her, and Margot shook her head.

"Ignore me. I cried at a yoghurt advert this morning."

When Piglet handed her goddaughter back, she noticed that Layla had been dressed as a pumpkin, a jack-o'-lantern grin emblazoned across her round belly. When Piglet smiled at the orange outfit, Sasha held up her hands.

"I know, I know. I've become one of those people. But how could I not? I've already thrifted her a Christmas-pudding one too." Piglet laughed, and Margot deadpanned over the marmalade.

"She has to be stopped."

<hr />

Piglet had stripped in the half dark of Layla's nursery. Margot or Sasha had laid out clothes that would fit on their easy chair: grey jogging bottoms, a bobbled green jumper, and a red T-shirt that read, "For the many not the few." Piglet dressed beside the wooden crib, the changing table, her hair catching in a mobile hanging overhead. How her friend's life had changed. How different it was to hers—whatever her life was now. She straightened, looking down at herself, and saw the jogging bottoms were too short, the jumper too tight. In the pocket of the trousers, she felt the curl of paper and reached in to withdraw five twenty-pound notes.

Sasha whistled when she entered the living room. They had moved from the kitchen table to the sofa, Piglet's blanket thrown to one side, Margot's cushion beneath her again.

"Suits you," Sasha said. "I especially like the joggers with the wedding shoes."

Piglet had slid her silk slippers back on in the hallway. Her pale ankles showed beneath the too-short grey jersey.

"Are you going?" Margot said, lifting her chin but not moving, Layla still stationed on her breastbone.

"I can't stay here forever," Piglet said. "And you've got enough going on without me hanging around."

"You're no trouble," Sasha said, and Piglet smiled in spite of the lie.

"Still," Piglet said, "I have to face it all at some point. My husband"—she gestured, rolling her eyes, trying to make light of her life. "My family." She tugged at the cuffs of the green jumper, trying to pull the fabric to cover her wrists. She wanted to leave. Although she was safe here, and she was loved, this was not her home, this was not her life.

"I would get up," Margot said, "but it's a physical effort on many fronts." She dipped her chin to the baby below. Piglet crossed the room to hug her friend, moving her body around Layla, stooping to kiss her goddaughter on the head, her skin surprisingly warm, her hair soft. She extended her arm to Sasha, and they grasped hands. Piglet straightened.

"You can come back any time you like, you know?" Margot said.

"I know."

"Will you go home?" Margot asked from the sofa.

"No." Piglet shook her head. "I'm going to Waitrose." Margot inclined her head, nodding sagely.

"Of course." She smiled. "Silly of me to ask."

Piglet pulled at the cuffs of Margot's jumper as she stooped to lock Darren's car in the Waitrose car park. It was busy: Sunday morning shoppers with canvas bags bulging with joints of beef, trusses of pork, whole sides of Scottish salmon, sustainably sourced. She slipped among them, her feet cold and pale in her silk wedding shoes.

Inside, she picked up a basket and stood by the flowers at the front of the shop, thinking about her empty fridge, and waited for desire to guide her. Previously, her trips here had been about

Kit, about whoever they were hosting for dinner, and she had picked up ingredients she knew they would like, had made dishes that would make their eyes round, their mouths water. But what did she want? She watched a man ten years older than her bend down to pick up a bouquet of orange lilies and red roses, turning the flowers to read the cellophane on the side, eyes glancing over the price. He looked up as Piglet stood, watching. He rolled his eyes, placing the flowers in his basket, and grinned at her. She watched him walk towards the other end of the shop and imagined him checking out with chocolate, later presenting the lot to a woman—his mother, his wife—and turning to whoever was closest by and rolling his eyes at them too.

Piglet dropped a bulb of garlic into her basket and a bundle of flat-leaf parsley. Tinned plum tomatoes—the good ones—and dried whole wheat spaghetti. She had walked to the next aisle before she turned back, replacing the spaghetti with a pale-yellow linguine, imagining its starchy flatness on her tongue. She picked up capers, anchovies, and the expensive Kalamata olives with the stones in.

She passed the tills, the man with the flowers laughing with one of the cashiers, and onwards towards the self-service checkouts. She scanned her own groceries, packing them into a green Waitrose bag for life, and paid, feeding Margot's money into the machine before her.

In Darren's car, she placed the shopping on the passenger seat and reached into the glove box for her phone. She turned it on, and the screen shone white. She was hurt to see Kit had only tried to call her twice. What had she expected from her jilted husband? She scanned her messages, looking for him, but saw only the names of Franny, her mother, Darren, Toni, Cecelia.

She tapped on Kit's name and saw his last message, from yesterday morning. "I can't wait for you to be my wife." This was harder than she had expected. She inhaled, the car smelling of parsley, and started to type.

"I'll be at home in ten minutes, if you want to talk."

She deleted the message, pressing backspace, the cursor flashing.

"I'll be at the house in ten minutes, if you want to talk," she typed. She pressed send.

The house was empty. Piglet called for her aunty Irene, but she was gone, leaving only the smell of talcum powder in her wake. In the kitchen, the scent of caramel still hung in the air, and Piglet saw, as she set down her bag of groceries, a smear of dried custard on the countertop. Upstairs, the bedsheets were smooth, the black bag for her wedding dress still hanging, empty, on the back of her wardrobe door. There was a pool of drying water in the tray of her en suite shower. The house was still around her, as if the people living there had died.

She was lying on the bed, her silk wedding shoes fallen to the floor, when she heard the front door open. She thought of Kit but heard her sister's voice.

"Piglet?"

"I'm up here," she called from the bed. She heard her sister climb the stairs, a quick jog towards her.

"When did you get home?" Franny asked as she entered the bedroom. From the bed, Piglet shrugged. Franny climbed onto the mattress and lay down next to her. "You look weird," she said, picking at the green jumper, the red T-shirt beneath. She placed her hand in Piglet's and shuffled over to her, draping her body over her sister's. "Mum and Dad are downstairs," she said. "So's Darren." Piglet nodded on the bed.

"Kit's going to be here soon," she said.

"Do you want us to stay?" Franny asked, speaking into her sister's neck. Piglet shook her head. "Come down with me, then. I can get them to go." Piglet turned to her sister, burying her face in Franny's collarbone.

"I don't know if I've done the right thing," she whispered.

Franny stroked her hair, a finger snagging on a forgotten pin, which she pulled away and held in her hand.

"If you felt like you had to do it, it was right," she said, holding her sister closer. "But probably no backsies now, I bet."

Her parents stood in their coats in her living room. Her father was wearing his orthopaedic shoes, round and brown, and her mother was in navy clogs. Her mother's hair was still pinned to her head, the echo of eyeliner smudged around her lashes.

"We've just come to get our bits and pieces," her mother said as her father thrust his hands in his pockets, looking at the curtains. "Our suitcases, Darren's car keys." Piglet nodded; she gestured upstairs. Her mother started to bend to remove her shoes.

"Don't worry, Mum."

Piglet retrieved Darren's keys from the kitchen, where she had left them next to her bag of shopping. She passed them to Darren in the living room, and he nodded his head.

"Thank you," they said in unison, not looking at each other.

"Will you come home now, then?" her father asked the curtains as her mother climbed down the stairs one at a time, suitcases bumping behind her.

"I live here, Dad," Piglet said.

"This is Kit's house," her father said, still looking towards the window.

"It's both of ours."

"He'll feel differently now, I expect."

"He'll be here soon," Franny interjected. "We should get out of their way."

Her mother had opened the front door, a suitcase in one hand.

"He's here now," she said, and Piglet felt her stomach contract.

"On his own?" Piglet asked.

"On his own," her mother confirmed, before saying, "Hi, love."

"Well, then," her father said, moving towards the front door.

Piglet watched her father lay his hand on Kit's arm as they passed in the doorway. In another life, her father might have boasted to his friends about his well-to-do son-in-law. Still, Piglet reasoned with herself, he would not have been boasting about her. Kit held his hand over her father's, and the two men looked at each other, exchanging the closed-lipped smiles of funeral mourners. Her father stooped to pick up a suitcase and ducked out of the door as Kit stepped inside.

Piglet watched her husband nod at her mother. She watched him seek out Franny, who did not smile. His eyes travelled to Darren, who was stony-faced. Kit looked at her, his shoulders lifting in a tiny shrug. Darren crossed the room to where Piglet stood.

"Take care of yourself," Darren said, standing on tiptoe, placing one arm around Piglet's neck before quickly removing himself. "If you need anything," he said, before following her father.

Her mother shuffled in the door, and Piglet could see her deciding whether or not she should hug Kit. She settled for a hand on his back as she passed him to her daughter. In front of Piglet, her mother raised her face.

"You'll stay in touch with us, won't you?" she asked.

"As much as you want to hear from me," Piglet said, and her mother shook her head.

"He defended you, you know. After you left," her mother said, lowering her voice. Piglet raised her eyebrows in question. "Your dad—at the wedding, after I got back, said you were gone, told him you were paying us back for the dress. He defended you." Her mother nodded. "Some horsey-faced girl—Sophie, I think her name was—started spouting off her theories about you, about us, and he told her, he told her to—" Her mother drew her fingers across sealed lips.

"Well," Piglet said. Her mother nodded again, her lips still pressed together.

"So, stay in touch," her mother said. She hugged her daughter, held her at arm's length for confirmation, and then followed Piglet's father and Darren out of the door.

Franny, the only one of her family left, stepped forward as Kit hung back.

"We love you, Pink," Franny said, and Piglet watched Franny look from her to Kit, her gaze changing, soft to hard. "Call, won't you?" she asked. "Call tonight."

Piglet nodded.

"Of course, Banana."

"OK, then," Franny said, as she threw her arms around her sister, both of them stumbling backwards. Franny looked up, still wrapped around Piglet. "OK?" she whispered.

"OK," Piglet said.

"I didn't know there would be a welcome party," Kit said as Franny closed the door behind her.

"Neither did I," Piglet said. "You're lucky my aunty Irene wasn't here."

From the hallway, Kit bent his head, trying to shield his smile from her, and for a moment she wondered if they could reverse it all: her leaving, the wedding, what he had done.

"You wanted to talk?" he asked, and she remembered that they couldn't reverse anything: she had already tried.

"I thought we should," Piglet said, and she sat on the end of their pink velvet sofa. He moved into the room, resting on the sofa arm farthest from her. He looked at her, lifting his hands, palms facing upwards.

"I don't know," Piglet said. "I don't know what to say."

Kit opened his mouth, his hands dropping into his lap.

"I thought I could do it," she said. "I couldn't."

"I realised," he said, "when you started telling all the people we know what had happened." He nodded, his voice coarse.

"You started this," she said, and his shoulders sank. They were silent.

"I don't think I've ever seen my mum so angry," he said, smiling beneath his slouch.

"Cece," Piglet sighed. She would miss her.

"She's not happy with you."

"No," Piglet said. "I don't think anyone is happy with me."

Kit slipped onto the sofa, the velvet creasing beneath him.

"Are you?" he asked. "Are you happy?"

Piglet looked across to him, her eyes on the hands in his lap. She shrugged, her shoulders jerking. Was this happiness: this rawness, this uncertainty, this promise of something new, something without him, something for herself?

"I'm sorry," she said, her voice a whisper. He extended a hand to hers, and she let him hold her for a moment, savouring the feeling of being with someone.

"Why didn't you tell me before?" he asked.

"Why didn't you?"

He was quiet.

"What are you wearing, by the way?" he asked, looking at her too-short jogging bottoms, her tight green jumper.

"They're Margot's."

"Margot's," he repeated, his voice low. "How's the baby?"

"Small," Piglet said. He nodded.

"What do you want to do now?" he asked, rubbing his thumb across her knuckles.

Piglet considered, her hand in his. With the velvet soft beneath her, she felt her body, still aching from Margot's sofa. She flexed her limbs and felt the blood tingle in her extremities. She swallowed and found her mouth dry from talking. She noticed her stomach gurgle, rumbling at her core. She could only tell him what she knew. These infant desires were all she had.

"I want to make some food," she said, and she pulled her hand from his.

"For both of us?" he asked, and she could feel him turn towards her. She shook her head.

"No, just for me," she said. He paused. He nodded.

"Is this it?" he asked, his hand still open on the sofa next to her.

"This is it," she confirmed. He drew his hand back, palm down on his knee, and they sat, at either end of the sofa, breathing steadily. He stood.

"OK," he said. "Well, I guess I'll be in touch in the next couple of days. We'll need to talk about the house, work out if we need an annulment. I'll text, I suppose, I don't know." He shook his head as he walked across the room, past the drinks trolley they had chosen together, the top-shelf spirits they had bought in Waitrose. He turned to look at her, still on the sofa. His hand was on the front door, the handle starting to pull down under his weight.

"Yeah," she said. "Text." She splayed her fingers, not knowing what to do with her hands.

The door opened, and for a moment he stood. She could feel his eyes on her, the breeze of the last day of October on her face. She looked up and saw him in their doorway, her doorway, a doorway. There were tears in his eyes, she noticed, his chin dimpled, his lips pressed together.

"See you, Pippa," he said, his voice low.

He nodded, he walked out, he closed the door behind him.

She sat, for a moment, breathless.

In the kitchen, she turned on the radio and pressed the volume dial until sound filled the room, the house, her head. She started to sing, started to shout, and continued to push at the volume until she could not hear herself over the music, until it thundered between her ears.

On the floor, her face wet, she asked the speaker to stop.

What do you want to do now?

In the quiet of the kitchen, she stood, and she turned to the stove, the bag of groceries on the countertop where she had left them. She laid out each item: dried linguine, the papery bulb of garlic, tinned tomatoes, jarred anchovies, Kalamata olives, capers, the bundle of parsley. From her spice cupboard she pulled chilli flakes and pepper. She slid her pig of good salt towards her. She pulled a tall bottle of olive oil from another cupboard. She set a saucepan and a skillet on the stove. She was ready.

She filled the kettle. As she waited for it to boil, for steam to fill the room, she looked out the window. She watched a neighbour go back and forward as they pushed a lawnmower—perhaps the last cut of the year before the ground was too wet—a reddened forehead visible over the short garden fence. As she watched, a magpie, brazen and unconcerned by the noise, landed on a fencepost, ruffling its iridescent wings, dipping its tail feather. The kettle clicked, and she turned back to the kitchen.

She turned on two hobs, flames bursting into life after one, two, three clicks of the gas. She poured boiling water into the saucepan before dipping her fingers into the salt pig, scattering crystals into the steaming liquid below. She held her hand over the surface of the skillet and felt the heat of the gas ring permeate the black cast iron.

She unscrewed the cap of the good olive oil and slicked the skillet. She dipped her finger into the swirl of the yellow-green liquid—her manicured fingernail, chipped, sensing the heat beneath—and lifted it to her mouth. The oil was peppery, slippery on her lips. As the oil warmed, becoming loose with heat, she dug her fingers into the garlic, two fat cloves falling to a chopping board below. She removed their dry skins before wielding a chef's knife, slicing the cloves until they splayed out like sycamore seeds. She could smell and feel the stick of allium on her fingertips. She dropped the sliced garlic into the pan, and the oil sizzled, a sweet-savoury scent perfuming the air. With a pop, she unscrewed the lid on the anchovies and pinched at the preserved fish, dropping a shoal into the skillet with the garlic. She watched the oil spit as the hot fat bubbled at the edges of the fish until they began to erode, their bones dissolving to nothing. She sprinkled over the chilli flakes; the white garlic freckled red.

She turned back to the water, the surface unsettled by bubbles. She lowered the heat as she pulled open the packet of linguine, strands of dried pasta spilling towards her, fingerprints on the torn packaging. She felt her way, guessing at one hundred grams, and twisted the linguine in her hands, holding it over the saucepan, condensation on her knuckles. The pasta fell as she had intended it, spreading out like a sunflower. As the linguine began to soften, sink into the water, she opened the tinned tomatoes. She held out her left hand over the skillet, feeling the fleck of oil on her skin, and with her right, she tipped up the tin. Cold, peeled tomatoes fell into her outstretched hand, and she crushed each of them as they slipped into her palm. Seeds squirted up her arm, and Margot's borrowed clothes were spattered. She rinsed her hands, drying them on a tea towel, and left a streak of red in her wake.

She opened the capers, green and freckled as amphibians, and with a teaspoon eased them from their brine. The olives were next, and she pushed pits from the aubergine-dark fruits, dropping their flesh into the tomato sauce. She ate as many as she added, and, as she stirred, she spat out the stones.

The sauce bubbled, and the hob became flecked with red.

Heat had started to rise in the kitchen, and she turned to the parsley, cool as morning grass. She chopped the herb to a finely mown darkness, her fingertips stained lawn-green when she pulled back, when she wiped the blade of her knife.

She waited, watching the linguine languish in the water below, her kitchen window turning opaque. She took a fork, dipping it into the saucepan, retrieving a strand of pasta, catching it between her teeth, assessing: seconds from al dente. She dipped a mug into the pan and withdrew a gulp of water, fogged by starch. She tasted the sauce. Half a pinch of salt; four, five, six grinds of pepper. She stirred with one hand and opened a cupboard with the other.

She turned off the gas rings, holding a pair of silver tongs. She dragged tendrils of linguine from one pan to the other, salted, clouded water dripping onto the hob, sizzling on the cast iron. She poured a little milky cooking water over the pasta, the tomatoes. She stirred. There was too much sauce, but what did it matter? She poured the pasta water away, steam clouding the window, fogging her glasses, leaving a wet sheen on her face. Her vision obscured, she tipped the linguine into a deep, wide bowl, sensing her way, leaving a little sauce in the pan. She could eat it later, if she liked. This was enough for now. She felt for the chopped parsley, pinched at it, and scattered it over the dish: vivid green on the red and white. She picked up the fork she had used to test the pasta, tines gilded with starch, and moved to sit.

At the table, in front of her, the linguine steamed, each strand covered in sauce. She could see flecks of chilli, the edges of garlic, the echo of an anchovy. She lifted her fork.

The linguine was salty on her tongue, gratifyingly hot, and pleasurable in its heft as she swallowed.

Her lips turned red as she looked out of her kitchen window, the fog starting to clear. A second magpie had joined the first, the pair on the garden fence, and she watched the birds, their tails dipping, and ate until she was satisfied.

Acknowledgments

This book and I have been shaped and championed by many talented individuals whom I would like to thank here.

I am indebted to my agent, Harriet Moore, and her sharp eye, warm heart, and unfailing rigour. It is an immense and humbling pleasure to collaborate with someone you so admire. Thank you, H. My gratitude also to Sophia Rahim, David Evans, Georgie Smith, and everyone at David Higham.

The hugest thanks to my publishing teams here and across the pond. To my editors and advocates, Bobby Mostyn-Owen and Caroline Zancan, I knew I had found my people in both of you—a hunch confirmed by our lengthy conversations about Viennetta. Bobby, thanks especially for your scarily accurate knowledge of London public transport systems, and Caroline for your commitment to momentum.

Thank you also to the teams at Doubleday and Henry Holt: it takes a vastly skilled and passionate village and I feel beyond fortunate to be part of two. Particular thanks to my publicists, Izzie Ghaffari-Parker and Catryn Silbersack; to Vicky Palmer, Eloise Austin, Sonja Flancher, and Alyssa Weinberg for your marketing genius; to Beci Kelly and Jenni Oughton for the eye-catching covers; to Tamsin Shelton, Holly McElroy, and Molly Pisani for the incisive copyediting; to Cat Hillerton and Molly Bloom for production; and to Tom Chicken, Emily Harvey, Phoebe Llanwarne and the entire sales team for your advocacy and enthusiasm. Thanks also to Georgie Bewes, Lori Kusatzky, and everyone at Doubleday and Henry Holt who had a hand in making this book and connecting it with readers.

Piglet started life as the creative component of a PhD and I am grateful to Loughborough University for giving me the opportunity to research and write. The beginnings of this novel would still be lurking on a hard drive if it were not for my supervisors, Kerry Featherstone and Jennifer Cooke. Thank you both, I can't think of two people with whom I'd rather discuss good food and bad weddings. Thank you also to Deidre O'Byrne and Claire O'Callaghan for your early reading and encouragement, and to Barbara Cooke and Naomi Booth for perhaps the most enjoyable viva ever had.

I am grateful to every cookery writer that has kept me company and kept me fed. Laurie Colwin was right when she said that a cook is never alone in the kitchen. Nor is a writer, I've found, when among books.

Thank you to my family for instilling in me a singular and unwavering dedication to serve a minimum of three desserts at any gathering. And to my acquired family—the Hazells, the Heaths, the Lingards—for your encouragement and group-chat cheerleading.

And finally, to my boys at home, to my tiny but mighty team: thank you for everything.

About the Author

Lottie Hazell is a writer, contemporary literature scholar, and board game designer living in Warwickshire, England. She holds a PhD in creative writing from Loughborough University, where she studied food writing in twenty-first-century fiction. *Piglet* is her first novel.